HOLLOW POINT

LAST CHANCE DOWNRANGE - BOOK 3

LISA PHILLIPS

TWO DOGS PUBLISHING, LLC.

Copyright © 2022 by Lisa Phillips

All rights reserved.

No part of this book may be reproduced in any form or by any electronic or mechanical means, including information storage and retrieval systems, without written permission from the author, except for the use of brief quotations in a book review.

eBook ISBN: 979-8-88552-130-7

Paperback ISBN: 979-8-88552-131-4

Large Print Hardback ISBN: 979-8-88552-134-5

Published by: Two Dogs Publishing, LLC. Idaho, USA

Edited by: Christy Callahan, Professional Publishing Services

Cover Design by: Ryan Schwarz

1

Washington State

FBI Special Agent Stella Davis needed a massage. Or two weeks at a health and fitness retreat in Mexico. That sounded pretty good right now. Instead, she was at the spa. But not for any personal reasons, no. This was purely work.

Stella adjusted the plush robe and wandered on her fluffy guest slippers to the pedicure stations. She'd specifically requested the end foot bath next to her target. That was exactly where she headed now, thanks to two twenty-dollar bills in the hand of the nail tech who she'd promised would not tickle her with another twenty.

As she eased her feet into the steaming bubbles, Stella wondered if this might not be an awful idea for an undercover operation. It felt pretty good.

She glanced at the woman beside her. "Hey."

The woman had dark hair and a fashion model physique.

She sized Stella up with one glance and a lift of her perfect eyebrows and returned to her magazine.

Beyond the woman was an older lady Stella recognized even though they'd never met. Edith Hummet had the same pixie cut as her, though it was a completely white crown of wisdom. And something else Stella had never quite been able to put her finger on. Honestly, the woman scared her. Though, if pushed she'd have admitted she wanted to be just like Edith when she was older.

Bubbles tickled her toes, massaging the soles of her feet.

"Okay, that feels good." Stella eased out a chuckle.

She worked out Tuesday to Saturday every week simply to maintain her muscle mass and keep herself straight mentally. Lately it hadn't been as effective to work out her problems while pounding the trails around the town of Benson, Washington.

Maybe she needed a hot tub so she could feel these effects on her whole body, not just her feet and lower legs.

"You can turn on the massage chair, too." The target waved at the remote on the little table attached to the arm of Stella's chair with a manicured finger she'd probably just had painted.

"Thanks..." *Take the bait.*

"It's Bridget."

"Hi, I'm Stella." She included Edith in it, just so it wasn't obvious she was targeting the girlfriend of the man who'd killed Stella's partner.

"I'm Edith, dear."

Stella nodded. "Nice to meet you."

Edith knew exactly who she was. After all, her grandson was Eric Hummet. Benson PD officer. Good guy. *Fine, hot guy.* Stella looked at her feet. The last thing she needed was to be thinking about him—or the kiss that had come out of nowhere in the gym hallway a couple of months ago.

This was about Kyle.

The nail tech got to work on her feet. Stella knew exactly their state after she'd spent the weekend camping. She'd needed those two days alone, going over her case notes. Thinking through everything she'd come up so far. It had brought her to this lead, but wearing flip flops walking around on the grass and dirt and then going for a ten mile run up a mountain also meant being here was probably needed.

If she had any hope of drawing out Bridget, she'd have to mention Kyle. Build a bond with the woman.

Stella felt the prick of tears in her eyes even though it had been six weeks. As though time made any difference.

She leaned back in the chair, succumbing to the steady rumble of massage beads. Maybe this wouldn't be *completely* about work. "I went camping this weekend, so my feet are extra tough and dirty." She spoke to no one in particular, hoping Bridget would respond. "My friend died a few weeks ago, and it was something we did together. Pitching tents and spending the night out where you can see the stars."

She smiled, absently. "We're both city folk at heart, but we decided to embrace the wild being out here."

Bridget glanced over.

"I went out there to honor him." She wiped under her eye. "Now I don't think I'll camp much. It isn't the same without him."

Kyle had liked to show off his outdoorsman skills—that he'd learned from watching videos on the internet. Stella liked to sit in a chair and read her book, before she headed to her tent to read more while he watched more videos for half the night. Making coffee over a fire had been a learning curve, but eventually he figured it out.

Stella didn't drink coffee except occasionally, but she'd

made it for her absent partner last weekend. The smell of it had brought a fresh round of tears.

They'd been close after working together for six years, but too close to get in a relationship with each other. Plus, neither of them was attracted to the other so it made a nice buffer when they were too busy with work to date.

This time when she wiped under her eye it wasn't to swipe away an imaginary tear. This one was real.

"My boyfriend died a few weeks ago." Bridget laid the magazine down in her lap. "Isn't it funny how we can find commonalities with a stranger?"

Stella nodded. "I'm sorry for your loss." She waited a beat before she said, "How long were you together?"

"A couple of years." Bridget leaned back in her chair and turned her head toward Stella. "And now he's just gone. Suddenly I've got no anchor."

Beyond Bridget, Edith studied Stella with one brow lifted. Yeah, she knew why Stella was here.

Stella held Bridget's gaze. "It's hard, isn't it? They're always there and then one moment they're just…gone."

Bridget nodded.

"Was he good to you?"

Bridget's expression shifted. "Sometimes. He worked a lot, so I had to go to his club if I wanted to see him. I always thought it was so he could show me off."

"He wanted you on his arm."

Bridget said, "I was getting tired of it, so I started to pull away. A few days later he was killed by the cops." She practically spat the words. "It was wrong. They had no business shooting him on the street like that."

Except Stella knew exactly what'd happened. "I'm sorry."

There wasn't much more she could, or would, say. Not without the anger rising. Bridget's boyfriend, Orlando Salvatore, and his friends had fired an RPG at a car Stella had been in with Kyle.

She'd stayed in the hospital for a week after being pulled out of the car by Isaac and Lyric. Kyle had been killed on impact, as had the two men in their custody in the back. The whole time she'd heard Eric was, "holding vigil in the lobby." Like that was so gracious of him.

Did he come to see her? Not once.

A woman in white pants and a pressed white shirt appeared. "Ladies, can I get you anything?"

Bridget said, "Acai berry smoothie."

Stella smiled wide. "I love those. I'll take one as well."

They shared the smile, and Stella submitted to picking a color to be shellacked onto her toes. That she would then stuff into a pair of shoes as soon as she got out of here.

"You mentioned a club," Stella said. "Your boyfriend worked at one?"

Bridget waved a hand. "His dad owns a bunch of businesses around town. Orlando ran one of them, but I never got into it much. Too boring."

So she had no idea about his business dealings. That was a disappointment.

Stella had no way to sneak into the club office, and they'd found nothing on the cell phones Orlando or any of his guys had on them when they were taken down. Despite Bridget's opinion, it had been self-defense when Orlando was killed, but maybe she simply chose to believe what she wanted to.

Maybe Bridget was the kind of girlfriend oblivious to what was right in front of her face. One who simply wanted the trappings of the high life, but with no awareness of what it took to get it.

Edith waved a hand. "I've always thought men had the wrong idea about what's important. Like knowing when to quit work and relax." She leaned forward to look at Stella with a gleam in her eyes. "It's good your friend went camping with you."

"Only to show off how he could build a fire, and all those survivalist things." Stella chuckled. "Why do men think one of those multi-tool things is essential to life?"

Bridget made a face. "I don't think Orlando knew what that is. He never had anything like that."

But he'd had plenty of guns. Drugs. Men he commanded, contacts who could get him illegal weapons.

"And camping?" Bridget shook her head. "I'm sorry you lost your…friend. But Orlando took me to the Bahamas. He still worked, but I got to relax at least."

Stella made a mental note to look up their travel history. She had to figure out who Orlando's associates were, and whether he flew private, or commercial. That could lead her to everyone he did business with. Where he'd gotten that RPG from. How he made money.

All of it.

It wasn't enough that Orlando had been taken out. Stella was after his father, Francisco, who held the strings on all the business. *And* she wanted everyone he was connected to. She wanted their whole business and everyone connected to it taken down for what they did to Kyle.

"Did your man Orlando do that a lot?" Edith said. "Traveling for work, schmoozing?"

Stella bit the inside of her lip to keep from frowning. The nail tech massaged her calves, which actually felt pretty nice. But right now she needed to worry about Edith.

Officer Hummet must have told her Stella was FBI. She wanted to think of him like that, and not like the guy who kissed her at the gym.

Did Edith think Stella needed help questioning her person of interest?

Bridget shrugged, shifting her magazine like she would open it again. Stella would lose her if they did that.

"Do you ladies want to hit the sauna after this?" Stella asked.

"Sorry, I can't," Bridget said. "I've got a massage booked and then I have a lunch date." She made a face. "With my boyfriend's father."

"You're having lunch with him?" Stella tried to keep her question neutral, just curious.

"He probably wants to offer me money again, so I'll move out of Orlando's apartment."

Edith said, "Men always think they know what's best for us."

Bridget's nail tech finished up. The woman waved and trailed out of the room, headed for her massage.

"I'm done, too." Edith swung her legs to the side and slid them into fluffy flip flops, a whole lot more spry than a woman her age could accomplish without working consistently on mobility. "How about we go to lunch?"

Stella bet the woman could keep pace with her on a hike. "My treat."

"Why does that sound like a dangerous proposition?"

Edith laughed. "Because you're of sound mind. But of course I have no idea what you're talking about. After all, I'm a perfectly harmless old woman."

Stella narrowed her eyes. "Sure you are."

If Edith wanted her to believe that she wouldn't have let anything slip. Instead, Edith had given her a glimpse into the truth beneath her silver sneaker exterior.

"I'll see you in the café in thirty minutes." The older woman hopped up, then headed off before Stella could say anything.

Back in the locker room, Stella got dressed and then took a second and checked her phone. She replied to the text from

Addie Franklin, her supervisor at the Benson FBI satellite office. Without Kyle it was only the two of them working there.

The two of them had rejected every personnel file Addie received for a replacement. Still, one of these days they'd have to accept another transfer.

Stella hadn't even decided for sure if she would stay in Benson. The long-term motel worked fine, but that wouldn't last forever. If she was going to stay, she would need a townhouse or condo. But none of that mattered when she hadn't brought down everyone who had a hand in her partner's death.

Kyle wouldn't have done any less for her.

Her phone rang in her hand, jolting her from her thoughts. *Campton Correctional.* Stella answered it and accepted the charges because it could only be one person.

She kept her gaze on the locker room bench seat when the line connected. "Hey."

"They're letting me out, baby. I'll be a free man!"

Stella sank onto the bench and winced. "Uh, that's great, Dad."

2

Officer Eric Hummet tossed his phone in the cupholder. Not that he'd have answered it anyway, but there was definitely no chance with his captain in the patrol car. His youngest cousin could wait.

Downtown traffic wasn't rush-hour heavy, but it still took twenty minutes to get to the west side of town.

Captain McCauley spent the entire time on the phone, intermittently saying, "Yes, sir" and "I understand, Mr. Mayor."

There were a lot of sighs and shifting in his chair, and zero chance for Eric to ask about taking the detective's exam.

The captain pointed a finger, indicating Eric take a left.

He indicated and switched lanes. It irritated him that everyone around him drove under the speed limit the second they saw his black and white police vehicle. They should drive like normal and follow the rules of the road rather than be overly cautious in a way that made him wish he was a plain clothes officer in a standard vehicle.

"Thank you." McCauley hung up.

Eric took the left turn. "Everything okay, Captain?"

The guy had been on the fast track to being Benson's first African American chief of police when one of their detectives had been exposed as a serial murderer. Eric couldn't even believe Hank Maxwell had been so evil, not that he'd been friends with the detective. Rather, he hurt for the department and what that meant for all of them.

Hence the reason McCauley was in his car, giving him another sigh. "The mayor's got it in his head that we need an interim police commissioner since he let Philburn go."

The chief had resigned as well, and the deputy chief had been given the position. The mayor still insisted on cleaning house, getting rid of everyone who'd had a hand in Maxwell never being found out.

Eric gripped the wheel. "Does he have someone in mind for the position of police commissioner?"

McCauley said, "It won't be someone from the rank and file, we can be sure of that."

The implication the mayor's office believed what much of the public did was there in his tone—that the police department carried a poison within it. Or a virus. One that led to a decorated detective being a serial murderer for years before the town's first FBI agent discovered the truth.

The fact none of them saw what had been right under their noses wasn't good.

Eric didn't like the fact they'd all been duped, but it was true that those closest to a murderer like Maxwell often didn't see the truth.

"As far as I can tell he's leaning toward Russ Franklin of all people." McCauley sighed again. "I know he was a US Marshal at one point, but his niece is the one who figured out about Detective Maxwell, so how is that not a slap in the face?"

"It's not a permanent post, though. Right?" Appointing Russ as interim commissioner didn't mean he'd get the job for the long term. "He's just filling the spot for now, while things settle down."

McCauley was about to respond when Eric's radio went. The dispatcher called out regarding an altercation at the mall.

"We're about two minutes away."

"Go ahead." McCauley nodded.

Eric grabbed his radio and called in that they were responding, then flipped on his lights and siren.

In the end, he had to balance wanting to make detective so he could be a solid cop doing the job, and the accompanying need to stick with the uniform and patrol. People needed to see good policing. Community trust in them was at an all-time low.

They headed inside, and Eric took the lead. The captain was riding along to see how he was doing, not so Eric could follow the guy's direction. That meant showing the captain how he walked this beat and kept the people of Benson safe.

Besides, it'd been a while since McCauley was a beat cop. Who knew what life as a cop was like decades ago?

The security guard met them at the door and took them up the escalator to the food court. "Two guys," he said. "Both fighting over the same woman it looks like."

"Weapons?"

"Just a plastic knife, as far as I saw." The guard waved at the crowd gathered around the center tables, then stopped to let Eric and the captain proceed.

Eric headed for the group, one hand close to his stun gun. "Make some space. Benson PD, let us through."

A woman closest to him spun around, her phone up in her hand. Recording.

Eric bit back what he wanted to say and held his hand up instead. "Excuse me, Benson PD."

The crowd parted enough he could get through to where two men wrestled on the floor.

Eric waded in. "Break it up, guys. That's enough." He grabbed an elbow and braced to make sure he was ready in case one of them turned and decided to attack him instead of each other. "Time to break it up."

The one on top had his hands around the other's throat. Eric tugged gently but firmly on his arm. "That's enough."

He let go of the guy's neck and slumped.

The guy under shoved him off, and the attacker rolled to the side.

Eric took one look at the man's stomach and clocked several things at once. He glanced at McCauley. "We need an ambulance."

The chief pulled a handheld radio from his belt and called it in.

"Neither of you move." Eric grabbed napkins from the nearest table. He put pressure on the victim's stomach with both of his hands. Blood coated the shirt, and Eric was pretty sure the broken top half of the spork on the floor had a missing handle, currently under the napkins. Inside the man's abdomen. To the other guy he said, "You stab him with that thing?"

"He attacked me!" the guy shot back.

The victim yelled, as though suddenly realizing what had happened to him—and that it hurt.

"You're hurting him!" someone cried out.

Eric turned and saw it was the phone lady, who was still recording everything on her cell. "Did you see him get stabbed?" he asked.

McCauley rolled the attacker to his stomach and cuffed him.

"Well…?"

The woman shook her head. "You're hurting him!"

"He was stabbed." Eric didn't need to get into it with her and her accusations. As much as he wanted to go toe to toe with the whole town, that would be pointless. People would believe what they wanted to in situations like this. Video could be spun. Edited. Changed.

The truth was that the guy under his hands would go to the hospital and get treated, and the man who'd attacked him would be arrested. Charges might be filed against both of them if it came to that.

"Ladies and gentlemen, if you could take a step back the EMTs will be able to get to this man with their gear. Thank you." McCauley's voice remained steady.

Eric looked at the guy on the ground. "You with me?"

He flashed gritted teeth and moaned.

"Your brain is catching up to what happened. Just breathe. The EMTs will be here in a second, okay? We'll get you to the hospital." Eric figured they'd give the guy a shot of pain medicine as well. That would help.

He glanced around and saw the two EMTs heading over. Eric motioned with his head to the guy with him.

"Hummet." Trey dumped his bag on the guy's right side on the ground.

"Banning." Eric let go of the napkins and Trey took over.

"Hummet." Freya had the backboard.

"Olson." He took it from her and shifted out of the way so they could load the guy. "You guys know Captain McCauley."

The captain assisted the second man to stand, holding onto his elbow since the guy's hands were secured behind his back.

Trey packed the wound with gauze and taped it down for transport. Eric helped load the guy onto the backboard.

"Need help carrying him out?" Eric reached for one end as the three of them stood, the two EMTs with different ends of the backboard. "I can come back and take statements."

"We're good, but thanks, Eric." Freya nodded.

The chief walked the cuffed guy to sit in a chair. Eric got out his notepad and approached the woman who'd been videoing them. She was probably posting it already, calling out the PD for something she'd decided they did or didn't do.

He shoved down the resentment he didn't need to carry and said, "Can I ask you a few questions about what happened?"

"I didn't see nothin'."

"Did you get it on video?"

She looked up from her phone, eyes narrowed like he'd caught her doing something she shouldn't have been.

"Were you recording when it kicked off?"

She made a face. "None of your business if I was. It's a free country last I checked, or it's supposed to be one." She huffed out a breath. "But tell that to my boss."

Eric decided which way he was going to play this. "See that guy behind me?" When she'd looked he said, "That's *my* boss. That means I need to ask you what you saw. Sorry, but I'll get written up if I don't."

She glanced again at McCauley. "He tell you how long you can pee for, like it's any of his business?"

Um, no. "Seems like there's a rule for everything these days, right?"

She nodded. "I'll bet they dock your pay when you lose equipment."

"Don't get me started about the paperwork." Eric waited a second for her to lose some of her animosity. "Do you know why they were fighting?"

The woman shrugged. "Something about the parking lot. Like one of them cut the other off or stole a space. Who knows?"

"Did you get it on video?"

"Some of it."

"Can you send me what you have?"

"I won't have to, like, testify, right?" She frowned.

"Might be a good way to get a day off work." Eric smiled. "But I can't be certain if you'll need to, or not. Depends what happens with the two of them next."

"What if he dies? Will it be murder?"

He said, "That's a bit above my pay grade, you know? I don't get to decide that stuff."

She nodded, commiserating. "Figures."

She emailed him the video, and he got her information for the report. When they were done, McCauley walked the cuffed man to their patrol car and loaded him in the back seat. After he shut the door, he turned to Eric. "That was nicely done."

"Thank you, Captain."

He nodded. "Let's get this guy to holding. That food court made me hungry and it's about lunchtime."

Eric got in the driver's seat and checked his phone still in the cupholder. There was nothing new, just the same texts from his youngest cousin asking him to call because it was important.

If he wanted to make detective, he couldn't be close to his cousins. Not when they'd always been bad news. Who knew what they were up to these days? Maybe his grandma did. Or Edith had given up and didn't want to know. Who would blame her?

Eric got going. Heading back to the police department meant they'd have to walk past the FBI office located in their building. It might just be two agents now, but both women were the kind no one could miss.

He only had eyes for one.

Eric shut that thought down before he was back in the

hallway at the gym, days before her partner was killed. He'd finally gotten her to admit there was nothing but friendship between her and Kyle. Then he had been killed.

Since she'd been released from the hospital, she'd refused to talk to him.

He'd screwed up not going to see her. But now she didn't even want to know him? As if he was supposed to accept that when he'd finally admitted to himself how he felt about her.

3

Stella gripped the phone. "Thanks, I appreciate it."

She hung up as fast as she could, her stomach churning. In the end she'd blown off Edith's offer of having lunch, opting instead to focus on work. It had nothing to do with her dad's call to tell her he was getting out after his twenty-year stint in Oregon State Prison in two days.

Maybe she should've eaten something, but she would probably be throwing it up right now if she had.

"Uh...you don't look well."

Addie had come in the office, and Stella hadn't even noticed. *Not good.* "Hey, how was your meeting?"

Addie made a face. "Uh-uh. You first." She crossed the room to stand close to Kyle's empty desk. "What's going on?"

She'd never told Addie the story of her father. "How much do you know about me beyond my file? Like, family stuff."

"Why don't you just tell me what you think I need to know?"

That didn't mean that Addie hadn't ever gone digging. It

simply meant that she wanted Stella to talk it out. "When I was nine my father was arrested. He was a police sergeant, and the charges included bribery, extortion, and attempted murder."

Addie winced.

"Yeah. We lived in Portland. After he was given twenty-five years with the option of early release for good behavior, my mom moved us to Seattle." That turned out to be so that her mom could move them into a commune outside Olympia. Stella had lived there for four years before her grandma came and got her. After that, she'd gone back to public school and then college in Boise.

Stella felt the tightening in her stomach and said, "He's getting out in two days. He served twenty, and the prison warden confirmed it. They had a hearing. They're letting him out."

Addie said, "How do you feel about it?"

"Much like everything concerning my parents, how I feel isn't relevant. I have to deal with it all anyway." She picked up a pencil, but quickly put it down because she didn't want to snap another one in two. "He listed me as his contact, and he's allowed to come live in Benson."

Addie lifted a brow. "And you agreed?"

As if she'd had any choice. Kind of like she hadn't had a choice when he was arrested, a dirty cop in a town where they barely tolerated the good ones. They'd all been brandished. It forced her mom to escape into free love, open relationships, and communal living as an "artist." Until her health declined and her family asked her to leave.

Evidently suffering didn't fit their narrative.

Stella had buried her nearly ten years ago, three years after her grandma passed in her sleep. She'd buried her partner six weeks ago, and she knew that there was no way she'd feel about his death this same ambivalence she had for her mother's end in ten years.

Stella made her own, and that had been law enforcement.

"You can say no to this."

She cringed. "I really can't."

Her dad had tied her hands.

"Are you going to pick him up then?" Addie said carefully. Probably trying to figure out how to change Stella's mind.

"I guess so."

"And if I don't give you the time off work?"

Stella pressed her lips together.

"Fine, you can have it. But we're about to get hit with something that could be big, so get him settled fast and let him make his own choices. He doesn't get to drag you into his new life."

"He's going to live at a halfway house close to the motel."

"Good. He gets a job, stays out of trouble, and figures himself out on his own."

Stella said, "Maybe you should pick him up."

"I would. Are you going to let me?"

"Not sure that's allowed." Stella didn't want her friend and supervising agent to take the responsibility from her, though. She didn't want to put it on Addie when she had no idea how her father was going to be.

She hadn't seen him in over twenty years between the sentencing and how long it took to get him to trial to hand that ruling down.

"It'll be fine." Stella was trying to convince herself that was true, at least. "What's new with you?"

Addie had gotten engaged to her high school sweetheart recently, and there had been a seriously crazy story in the intervening years. The woman was an amazing profiler, a great agent, a great boss—except when Kyle hadn't made the coffee right and ended up with grounds in the java—and was becoming a friend. She was also on this kick of learning about being a Christian.

Stella had watched her change, becoming more peaceful. Content. Even happy.

It was great to see, and Stella had even been thinking about asking some questions. Then Kyle died. Now she had no enthusiasm for anything but holding herself together and finding everyone who had a hand in his death.

Addie got a cup of coffee. Something else that'd changed since Kyle's death as Addie had to get accustomed to being the only one drinking it and make less than a whole pot.

She dragged over her chair and sat in the aisle between desks with the mug in both hands.

"Wow, this is serious."

Addie shrugged. "Just exhausting. I honestly didn't know this job would come with so much politics, but here we are."

"You." Stella pointed. "Not me." She made a face like there was a bad taste in her mouth.

"Figures you'd abandon me to the brass."

"You're the more experienced agent, that's all."

"Mmm." Addie grinned around her mug. "So I was at a meeting this morning with the deputy mayor, the police chief and two district chiefs—fire and ambulance."

"They still didn't pick a new commissioner to replace Philburn?"

"Well, that's the thing. According to the deputy mayor, they're going to appoint my uncle Russ of all people. Apparently the mayor's mind is made up." Addie shook her head. "Russ is the interim commissioner, liaising between the police department and the mayor's office."

"To smooth things out."

Addie nodded. "He's not short of things to do, even retired. Why he agreed to this is beyond me."

"Maybe for the sake of smoothing out things with the public," Stella suggested. "The mayor shows everyone things are going to change. People love Russ. They're fans of yours, given all you've been through and how you solved the case."

Addie winced. "I don't think I earned any favors with the police department when I exposed the fact it was their best detective who had murdered so many people."

"Best detective, *or so they thought*." Stella had talked about it with Eric. In the *before*, when they'd regularly chatted at the gym. "I don't think the bulk of the department has a problem with you. Good cops want the bad ones rooted out. It's the establishment, the good ole boys that don't like having egg on their faces."

Addie tipped her head to the side.

"Or whatever." Stella had tried to reword what Eric told her into generalities and ended up sounding like an imbecile. "It's not like they're trying to run us out of town."

Addie nodded. "I just wish our presence here meant positive things, not federal checks and balances on their ability to do their jobs."

"We're not IAB." And that wasn't the job of the FBI in Benson, Washington.

"True, but people think we're here to clean them up in a way."

Stella didn't plan on doing that. She had her own cases to work, and federal jurisdiction didn't cover the antics of a few bad seeds in the Benson police department. "Anything to do with an actual case, or just politics?"

"I'll send you my notes." Addie's expression shifted to guarded. "There's a case coming down the pipeline. Might be connected to Kyle's death in a way."

Stella pretended she was only curious. As if Addie would be fooled. "Oh, yeah?"

Addie's lips thinned. "It has to do with a batch of stolen weapons. PD picked up a guy a couple of weeks ago, connected to an armed robbery. Ballistics on the weapon he used came back as being from a batch of military weapons commissioned for destruction. The RPG used to shoot the car you were in came from the same batch."

Stella leaned forward in her chair. "Did he know anything?"

"He wants a deal before he tells the cops where he got the gun."

Stella nearly burst out of her chair. She could badge her way into an interview room and get it out of the guy, no problem. But was that the right thing? Going off suddenly would only lead her into a minefield of having to explain, among other things.

"They'll get him to talk." Addie said, "And in the meantime the PD is floating the idea of a taskforce. They want the source of those weapons, and they're convinced it's a bigger issue than just this one batch."

Stella held herself still. "An interagency taskforce?"

"If you want in."

She carefully nodded. "I do."

"Okay."

Stella let out a breath. That was a much better outcome than either her conversation with Bridget, or the impending arrival of her dad. Her love life didn't factor since it'd been an arid desert for years. Not just because she blew off Eric's attempts to talk to her.

When he'd walked that suspect in earlier, he hadn't even looked in the windows at her.

He used to wave.

But next to the loss of her partner, it wasn't like she could call the feeling grief. It was nothing like the gaping hole inside her where Kyle's friendship had resided.

Addie left in time to have dinner with her fiancé.

Stella looked up a while later and realized it was dark, and she should probably head home. She'd been reading the file sent over from the prison, writing her report on the conversation she'd had with Bridget and a million other things, and fielding a couple of calls from the big Seattle FBI office.

She stretched as she stood, realizing how tense she was. And hungry.

Opting for the grocery store, she grabbed all the fixings for a huge chicken salad to eat at home and a few other things she'd run out of or was about to. Her motel room had a kitchenette. The nomad nature of it did appeal to her. She could leave whenever she wanted.

After she did what she had to.

With no Kyle in her life, what good would going back to Seattle be? He'd been her best friend there and her best friend here. She would only be exchanging empty grief for more of the same. At least in Benson she could get a fresh start. The town was admittedly growing on her and the traffic was crazy better since this was a glorified small town.

Still, the idea of being here forever wasn't one that brought peace. She should commit to either staying in Benson at some point or going home to Seattle and kicking out her subtenant.

Thoughts of doing that swelled in her mind as she parked in the motel lot and climbed out to grab her things.

A heavy weight slammed her against the rear door of her car.

Stella cried out. She drew her weapon, but he grabbed her wrist and slammed it on the roof. The pistol clattered to the ground.

She tried to twist around but couldn't with no room between her and the car.

Hot breath wafted over her cheek. "Whatever you think you know? Leave it alone."

His weight ground her hip bones against the car. Stella cried out.

He grabbed the back of her head. With her short hair he couldn't grip strands, so she was able to turn her head to the side. He slammed it down on the roof of her car.

She felt her body hit the ground and watched him race away, unable to get up.

4

The radio on Eric's dash erupted to life. Halfway home at the end of his shift, and a call came over the police frequency. His foot slipped off the gas as he listened. Female victim of assault at the motel where Stella lived.

She'd be responding, her commanding nature taking charge of the situation. Making sure the woman got the help she needed.

The dispatcher continued, clarifying it was an officer down. A federal agent.

Eric hit his turn signal, checked his mirrors, and swerved across two lanes. He turned left in front of a delivery truck that honked at him. Since he wasn't on duty there wasn't much he could do about it.

Assault.

A million things went through his mind, every one of them worse than the last. Stella was hurt.

It took far too long to get to the motel, even just a few miles.

He fumbled with the keys getting the engine shut off, and they fell to the floor beside the pedals. Eric was halfway so he just left them there and jogged to where the black and white had parked in the middle of the parking lot, blocking the aisle.

Two floors of motel rooms, one long row with the office on the left and an empty pool with cracked concrete on the right. Dog run behind the building. Parking lot in front.

Two officers. One helped Stella to her feet. The other shifted as Eric approached.

He held up his hands. "Hey." Eric recognized the two men. "Miller, right? And Sanchez?"

Both cops' body language lost some of its tension.

Eric made a beeline for Stella. "Hey." He kept his voice soft and took in how she looked. Goose egg on her forehead. Flushed and flustered. She wasn't going to deal well with this. The woman wasn't stubborn necessarily—she was just all about control. She needed things to be ordered the way she'd arranged them. Getting hurt wouldn't fit in her plan.

Especially when he was pretty sure she was on a one-woman mission to get justice for her friend.

Eric pushed aside all his approaching thoughts about Kyle. No need to go there when the guy was dead, and how Stella dealt with it was her business.

She'd certainly made a point to tell him it wasn't *his*.

He closed in and she switched her grip from the cop to Eric's arm. That was progress, at least. She was willing to admit he existed—but only because she needed help.

He braced and held her weight. "Where are we headed?"

"My room."

He had no idea which one it was.

"Someone get my groceries put away, and bring my things."

"Good idea," Eric said. "That way when the ambulance takes you to the hospital it'll be all squared away."

She stopped and looked up at him. "I just need to sit down, that's all."

Eric glanced at one of the cops and mouthed, *Ambulance?* The guy nodded and held up three fingers. Good, it would be here soon.

"I'm not going to the hospital."

At least she didn't tell him she was fine. Eric said, "Which room is yours?"

"Twelve." She pointed with her free hand, then touched it to the side of her face and hissed out a breath.

"You have ice in there?"

"Mm-hmm."

They walked together to her room and one of the cops brought her purse. Stella said, "Side pocket."

Eric found her keys, and let them both in. She flipped the light switch, and he got a look at her face. He must've made a noise because she turned.

"That bad?" she said.

His hands curled into fists by his sides. "Did you see who it was?"

She eased down onto the sofa.

Eric found the tiny refrigerator and got an ice pack from the freezer compartment at the top. He crouched in front of her and she pressed it against her face. She cringed for a split second before the two police officers headed in with her things.

"Thanks, guys." Eric appreciated them going above and beyond.

"You can cancel the ambulance."

Eric frowned at her. "Is that a good idea?"

He wanted to make a crack about her having some sense knocked into her. Considering the fact she'd been attacked, he figured that wasn't a good idea any more than her not getting looked at by a medical professional.

"I'm good," Stella said. "I'll make my statement for the report, but I don't need to see a doctor. I just got knocked around." She let a tiny reaction slip.

He saw it.

Before he could argue, she said, "And I don't need anyone to stay with me."

Eric pressed his lips together. Maybe she should contact Addie and have her friend watch out for her tonight.

"I'm good."

Eric reached for the ice pack. He tugged her fingers gently away and looked beneath it. "Why'd you have this in your freezer?"

"For special occasions."

He frowned.

"Sometimes my knee hurts after spin class. If I push myself too hard it aggravates an old injury. I've had that ice pack for years."

"You've got a serious goose egg but the skin isn't broken."

"Hardheaded. My dad used to—" She caught herself and swallowed. "He's getting out. Early release for good behavior."

Eric held himself very still. She'd told him little about her history. A bit about the grandma she'd lived with, and the barest hint about her hippie mom and her dad—the dirty cop.

She closed her eyes. "I'm fine."

"Sure you are." The words slipped out before he could hold them back.

He got a look at those brown eyes, seriously not happy with him. "I'll go see if they have security cameras."

He was out the door before anyone could say anything. The cops would do their jobs, and she would deny there was anything wrong. Eric would end up just as frustrated by her, and this whole situation, as he'd been for weeks.

Sure, it wasn't Kyle's fault that he'd been killed. In the same incident, Stella had nearly been killed when local club owner Orlando Salvatore had one of his guys shoot an RPG at the car they were riding in. Transporting cuffed suspects to jail.

He didn't like being mad that she was grieving.

He should be more understanding.

Eric walked off the frustration and headed for the motel office. Since he didn't have his badge, he pulled a business card from his wallet and slid it across the desk.

"Security footage?" The woman behind the desk sucked on a vape pen for a second.

"Yes. You have it?"

She made a face and pointed with the pen. "Through there."

He entered the white door marked Employees Only and found an office between the lobby and the reception desk. "It's on the computer?"

"Password is p-a-s-s-w-o-r-d. No caps."

Frowning, Eric logged in and found the program running that showed several blurry cameras around the property. He figured out how to toggle the slider back on the parking lot camera and watched himself arrive in reverse. He kept going, the cops left, and a truck backed into the lot. The footage of her attack played in reverse, then let go before it happened.

Stella pulled into the parking lot. The truck followed her, but she hadn't noticed it for some reason.

The occupant wore generic jeans, a jacket, and boots. The image was too blurry to see a face, but he had no hat on. Dark hair. It was the truck that snagged his attention.

Not the way she was shoved against the car, and almost knocked out.

He let go of the clench of his jaw and focused on the

vehicle. There was no way to get a license plate, but he had to admit it was familiar. Same kind of truck a lot of guys in town drove. Still, the lines weren't nearly as generic as his clothes.

Eric called out, "You want me to turn this off?"

"Do whatever, darlin'."

He headed back to the motel room, where Stella talked to the cops. He stuck his head in. "You good?"

She didn't answer.

One of the cops said, "Anything on the cameras?"

Eric shook his head. To Stella he said, "Let me know if you need anything."

She gave him a slight nod of her head.

Eric got in his car and drove to a bar his cousins frequented. The same truck wasn't in the parking lot. He might be able to get some intel, or he might just be checking on Nigel. Hopefully his uncle Aaron wasn't in, just the cousins. Nigel, and his older brother Ian.

His family was exhausting. Edith didn't see Ian or her son Aaron. Nigel came around once in a while but usually just left frustrated.

Eric ordered a beer he would barely start, let alone finish. Not that he objected in a moral sense to alcohol—just to its damage when it was misused and people suffered. Particularly kids. His own dad had been a mean drunk.

He appreciated Stella's need to exercise command over her life and everything around her. She needed order. It might look like control, but it also meant she knew how to survive and even excel. He wanted to use the same tactic to pass the detective exam and get promoted.

He knew he could do good in this town.

The drink had an inch of liquid gone. He set it down, disliking how easily he drank it. Which was why he never bought any for his house. He knew his limits, and his weaknesses.

Thoughts of Stella filled his head again. He hadn't managed to dig beneath that thick shell of hers before Kyle died, but he'd been making progress.

Now there was nothing.

Maybe a grudging respect, but that wasn't even close to what he wanted from her.

A heavy hand slammed on his shoulder, jolting him from thoughts of Stella. He glanced at the man beside him. "Ian."

Eric glanced at the guy's knuckles. Considering he always had abrasions like he'd just been in a fight, there was nothing new today. He might've hurt Stella. The clothes fit, but basically every guy in this bar wore the same uniform of denim and construction dust.

He fit better here than he did with an FBI agent who didn't want more from him than professional respect.

"Where you been, kid?" He squeezed the back of Eric's neck.

Even though Ian was just a handful of years older, he'd always called Eric that. "Seen Nigel? He called me a couple of times. I thought he might be here."

Ian shrugged. "Pool tables, I think."

Eric took the drink, even though he was going to set it down and forget about it the first chance he got. He circled the bar looking for Nigel. Turned down a couple of interesting offers from women who evidently didn't know he was a cop.

They'd get wise pretty soon.

He headed for the back hall, just in case Nigel was down there. A conversation drifted to his awareness. Eric kept going, keeping it casual. Just looking for Nigel.

"…said he'd better not be late paying."

"They really asked for an extension. That's crazy. Apollo will kill them."

"They're lucky he didn't do it right then."

Eric shoved the door open to the back hall. He checked the bathrooms, but didn't see Nigel, so he hit the back exit, then began thinking through that conversation.

Apollo had been deemed nothing but a myth before Eric became a cop. Now he was the boogey man for kids who thought they could double cross anyone they did business with. A way for criminals to keep other criminals in line.

An engine revved.

Eric found the source of the sound and spotted a red truck with the same trim lines exit the parking lot. The driver bumped the curb and nearly leaned on two wheels as the driver turned onto the street.

Gone.

The same truck.

And he had no way to find the driver.

5

Technically, she had the day off, but Stella still got up early even with a throbbing head. She just didn't go to the gym. Anything would be better than lying in bed staring at the ceiling, freaking out about every little noise.

She'd told the cops most of what happened, just not the words that guy had whispered in her ear with his hot breath.

It made her shiver as she walked into the downtown apartment building where Eric's grandmother lived. She managed to smile for the security guard at the front desk. For a residential building this place had some strict regulations about who could enter and exit.

The guy made a call upstairs and asked Edith if Stella had permission to visit. She was given a proprietary key card, which she was to return upon her departure.

"Thank you." Stella strode to the elevator with the card in her hand.

Addie's fiancé, Jake, lived in the penthouse and reportedly owned the whole building. Maybe his local celebrity status as a photographer, and the fact Addie and Jake had survived a run-in with two killers, meant he needed to feel safe.

Stella might have to see if they had any openings here. She could live here if she decided to stay in Benson, considering she appreciated quality security.

The elevator let her out on the fourth floor. Edith's door number was twelve. She lifted her hand to knock, and it opened before her fist made contact. She saw dark hair and at first thought it was Eric. But it wasn't.

The man stepped out before she could enter, leaving the door open.

Stella frowned at his retreating form. He went in an apartment two doors down, without a key. Just twisted the handle and let himself in like he lived there.

Edith's neighbor?

"Are you going to stand in the hall?"

Stella smiled to herself, because that was exactly what her grandmother would have said. In a way, Edith reminded Stella a lot of the grandmother who'd brought stability to her teen years, even though the older woman hadn't had a clue what to do with an adolescent. Stella had come to appreciate what having her grandma in her life meant, even if she hadn't at the time.

Stella shut the door.

"Kitchen!"

She walked the short hall and looked in the kitchen, which was a guess, but the living room was to the right and the hall stretched in front of her.

Edith stood at the sink, rinsing two cups. Stella tried to absorb the homeyness of it. All she could think was that they'd known she was coming up, but the guy who'd been here didn't leave until she was at the door.

Which meant both of them had wanted her to see him.

And why would that be?

She was an FBI agent, so this could've been a test to see if she'd recognize him instead of just thinking of Eric. Or they wanted her to figure out who he was.

Maybe none of this had even occurred to them, and Stella just had an overactive imagination.

Edith placed two mugs on the drying rack beside her sink. A PG Tips teabags cube box sat on the counter beside an electric kettle. "How are you this—" She stared at Stella.

"It looks worse than it is."

"Those things usually do." Edith waved her hand. "Let's go sit in the living room."

Stella wasn't sure this needed to take that long, but figured sitting wasn't an awful idea. "I should've covered it with makeup."

"Not this soon. That would hurt far too much. You'll lose a couple of tears and have to fix your makeup too many times."

Stella blinked. "Bad relationship?"

"Nothing quite that pedestrian."

"Are you ever going to tell me the story?"

Edith studied her from the recliner where she'd settled herself. In this environment she appeared as the quintessential older lady. Refined. Somewhat mobile. Someone who would tell an amazing story from her life.

But Stella had seen her hop from that pedicure chair. She wasn't going to be fooled into believing this woman was like any other.

"Perhaps."

Stella chuckled. "I'd love to hear it. My grandmother used to tell me all kinds of stories. Before she had my mom, she lived a crazy life. After mom she quieted down, but it didn't seem that much. Until she was older."

"Is she still with us?"

Stella shook her head. "She passed a number of years ago."

"And your living family?"

Eric might've told her, but then again maybe he didn't talk about Stella with his grandmother at all. Who knew? It wasn't as if she'd mentioned him or what happened between them with anyone. Not even Kyle had heard about what was brewing, though he'd gathered that she'd met someone she was attracted to.

Stella pulled her thoughts back to the question at hand. "I guess it's going to get around sooner or later. My dad gets out of prison tomorrow, and I have to go pick him up."

Edith blinked.

Stella figured it was difficult to surprise this woman, but she'd managed it. "I haven't seen him since the sentencing, so I have no idea how it will go. And I can't think about it because I'm trying to work a case."

"Which is why you're here."

Stella nodded. Her head hurt, but she didn't want to give in to the pain. That meant the guy from last night had won. And considering she had no intention of doing what he said and backing off her investigation, she also wasn't going to admit defeat with anything else.

She said, "The woman from the spa, Bridget? Did you see her after I left, or exchange numbers with her?" She wanted to ask also if Edith knew her outside of that conversation but didn't need to overload her with a list of questions right away.

Edith shook her head. "You need to get ahold of her?"

"I tried calling the number she gave me, but it's disconnected."

"So *you* saw her after you ditched me for lunch."

Stella blinked. "I ran into her on the way out."

She'd looked up the woman's number but ran into a roadblock. She didn't think that was Edith's issue, though.

"I left before lunch because I wasn't going to be good company after my dad called."

Edith said, "I see. I'm sorry to hear that."

"I was, too." After all, this was Eric's grandmother. If this was another world or a different life where she had a relationship with him, this woman might've turned out to be family. But Stella didn't believe in any of that stuff.

In this world, that wasn't going to happen. Stella and Eric were a nonstarter. Edith wasn't going to be a grandmother figure to her, as a replacement for the one she'd lost.

"I don't know that girl," Edith said. "You're looking for her?"

Stella nodded. "She's related to a case I'm working."

One I was warned to stay away from. It had to be about this. After all, she had no other high-profile cases and for weeks this had been where she put all her energy.

Ever since she had laid her partner to rest in the ground.

"Does she have to do with that knot under your bangs?"

"Yes."

"And now you're bound and determined to get into even more trouble?"

Oh, yeah. Stella knew she could form a serious attachment to this woman if given half the chance. Astute, capable, and caring? Edith was the whole package, and until just now Stella hadn't realized how desperate she'd been for a mentor. A friend. Someone to confide in.

She needed a therapist.

Except she'd likely form an attachment to them. Not a good idea.

"How about you tell Addie all about it, get some backup, and then look for the girl?"

Stella bit the inside of her lip.

"I see."

She should go. Stella shifted to the edge of the couch about to stand.

Edith said, "I'll help you."

She frowned.

"I have the…skills. I can track her down and get close to her. Figure out what she knows about what you're looking into. If you read me in, that is."

"I'm not sure—"

"That's the beauty of it, dear. No one expects a classy older woman."

Stella narrowed her gaze on Edith.

"Yes, it could be dangerous," she said. "That's why I know about having backup, and I know how to take care of myself, Stell'. Women have to learn these things."

Stella thought maybe she'd learned more than just simple self-defense a woman might need to utilize to take care of herself. Which she'd tried, only to have her gun knocked out of her hand. She'd been disarmed and nearly knocked out.

That guy could have taken her with him anywhere.

Killed her.

She shot up out of the seat. "I'm not going to put you in danger. That's not why I came here." The fact Edith had used the nickname *Stell'* was a problem. Stella couldn't let it penetrate those empty places in her heart.

No one called her that now.

"I should go." She headed for the door.

Coming here wasn't a mistake when she'd gotten an answer to her question. However, she'd also been given a whole lot more. Or offered it, at least. But she couldn't accept. It would be too weird to be close to Edith when things with Eric were so strained and awkward.

The way he'd reacted to her being hurt made her want to fall into his arms.

Big mistake.

She was never going to get back the connection she'd lost when Kyle died. Or when everyone else died. The hope, the what-ifs and maybes. None of it would happen for her. Life just didn't work out that way—or it would've happened by now. She'd have a longstanding relationship in her life. With anyone.

The elevator descended while Stella leaned against the wall and tried to hold herself together.

When the doors slid open at the ground floor, she dug out the card to hand back to security. A man stood in front of the doors.

Dark hair. Not the guy from upstairs.

"Eric." She closed her mouth before more words came out and she sounded like an idiot.

He stepped a fraction closer, as though they were going to have a private conversation. "How's your head?"

She scrunched up her nose. "I didn't go to the gym this morning." And if she didn't watch what she ate for a few days, the ramifications weren't going to be pretty. She liked how she looked and didn't plan on that changing—at least as much as she could control it.

"Everything okay?"

She remembered her vow not to let her emotions connect her to these people and shored up her defenses. "Everything is fine. It's my day off, and I wanted to say hi to your grandma." He'd figure out where she had been soon enough. No point lying about that.

What would Edith tell him was the reason she'd been up there?

"That's good." He shifted his stance. "Uh, listen…"

Was he about to ask her out? Everything in her head screamed a warning. Her dad would be in Benson tomorrow. Eric would find out she was the daughter of a dirty cop, and she would have to see the disappointment on his face.

Before he could continue, her phone rang. Instead of thanking whoever was looking out for her that they'd saved her from an awkward conversation, she found herself wincing.

The shrill tone cut through the open lobby and bounced off the walls. "Sorry. I didn't realize it was that loud."

Addie was calling. Stella answered, "Davis."

"Hey, I know you're not working today, but you know Bridget O'Mara, right? She was Orlando Salvatore's girlfriend. It's in your report."

Addie had read her report? If she'd done that, she might've figured out the extent of Stella's drive to get answers. *Never mind.* Addie was a profiler. Of course she knew.

Stella said, "What about her?"

Eric shifted again, disappointed. And listening.

Addie said, "Her body was found early this morning. She's been killed."

6

Eric followed her to the site. She gave him directions like he'd make his own way there, but he stuck behind her just to be safe.

When he climbed out of his car, he had no better idea of what was going on in her head than he'd had earlier. He knew he wanted to protect her if whoever hurt her the night before came back to try again. She hadn't objected to his coming with her now. Was she going to open up? He doubted it.

Eric shook his head, caught the attention of the officer on the tape, and waved the guy off before he could ask what was up.

Eric stuck his hand out, sneaking a peek at the guy's nameplate because he didn't know everyone who worked when he didn't. Benson had several precincts, though Eric worked out of the downtown one.

"Dubois."

The guy nodded. "You're central, right?"

"Hummet," Eric said. "One *t*." He gave his badge number.

Dubois wrote it down. Eric figured he likely operated from Benson West, given they were currently in the industrial complex where construction had halted on what was going to be a new warehouse.

"What do you know about this?" Eric asked.

Dubois had a tan line on each side of his eyes, indicating he'd worn sunglasses outside for an extended period. When he squinted, the lines shifted. "Female victim. From the look I got of her, I'd say *she's dead.*"

"Astute and funny. It's a winning combination." He wanted to add *I bet your mom thinks so,* but he didn't know this guy that well.

"Be sure to fill out a card that says what a good job I did here and drop it to my sergeant."

Eric chuckled. Dubois slapped him on the shoulder as he headed toward where Stella stood with Addie. He didn't let on how heavy that hand was and only barely managed to keep the impact to himself.

He spotted two uniformed officers: Captain McCauley and a sergeant Eric didn't know. Addie stood with Stella, making it two FBI agents on scene—the only two Benson had. Not that they necessarily needed a male just for the sake of it, but bringing one in did make sense. Kyle had been here after all.

Eric had actually liked the guy. The fact Kyle was dead, and Stella had been hospitalized because of that incident, made him grieve. And it dragged up memories he didn't want to revisit.

Images of another woman lying in a hospital bed.

He shook off those thoughts. The loss didn't necessarily mean the FBI needed to replace him here in Benson.

The victim's body lay curled up against a wall, braced by two-by-fours. Hidden from view of the street. The local chief medical examiner was a redhead, currently crouched over the body. Dr. Sarah Carlton drew something from the dead woman's abdomen.

"Who found her?"

The FBI agents turned to him. Addie motioned to a construction worker talking to the sergeant. Eric nodded and shut his mouth. It wasn't like he had the position to be here. He wanted to be a detective, but it would take time and Eric had no intention of being pushy. Too many eyes were on the police department waiting for someone to mess up again so it could be splashed all over the media.

He should leave. He was halfway turned back toward his car when Addie said, "Hang on a sec."

Eric turned to her. Stella had moved to the medical examiner and spoke to the doctor beside the body. "What is it?"

"There's something I'm missing here, and I think you have a piece."

He shook his head.

"Yeah, I feel that way with Stella sometimes." Addie motioned for him to move away with her a couple of steps. "I think you might be able to break through to her where I can't."

Oh. That's what this was. "You think she might get in over her head going after the RPG and get hurt?"

Addie shrugged. "I'm her supervisor, but it's not a leash."

"Oversight isn't a bad thing."

"She reports to me as she should. However, in taking this office-boss thing a little more seriously, I'm thinking there's things she's leaving out of her reports when she writes them."

Eric glanced back at Stella and frowned. "Did she leave something out about last night?"

"You tell me. You were there."

"She didn't say much." Had her attacker said—or done

—something she'd withheld? "But I can find out. Or my grandma knows."

"She needs to stay here in town. Benson needs her." Addie frowned. "You know they were just friends, right?"

Eric didn't know what to say to that. "He took up space in her heart."

The way Eric wanted to take up space in hers.

Addie said, "Did you say your grandma knows?"

"That's where Stella was this morning. It's why we showed up here together." The doorman had told him Edith had a visitor.

"Okay, there's definitely more going on." Addie called out, "Special Agent Davis!"

Stella spoke quickly to the medical examiner and then came over. Captain McCauley took her place, assessing the body before it was transported to the morgue.

"Yes, Special Agent Franklin?" Stella had a look in her eye, and it wasn't good.

She had become such a huge part of his life in the last few months since she got here. Sure, it could be called a "crush," and it wasn't like they'd done more than hung out a few times. She'd opened up some, and he wanted to explore it more. They'd kissed.

Then the shutters went down, and now all he saw was grief. And secrets.

He started to ease away from them, since this was a federal conversation and he wasn't even working.

"Over here, Officer Hummet." Captain McCauley waved him over.

"Sir?" He couldn't help his curiosity and took a look at the body. She'd been shot in the chest and head. "Execution?"

"Looks that way."

The medical examiner frowned. "That is to be determined, after I get her back to the morgue for an autopsy."

Eric nodded.

The redhead said, "I'd shake your hand but I'm not removing my gloves until I'm done."

"Officer Eric Hummet."

She smiled. "Sarah Carlton."

"Yes, ma'am. I know."

The smile turned to a chuckle. "I like this one, Captain."

"Noted." McCauley frowned. "Being this close to a dead body doesn't freak you out?"

Eric hadn't even thought about it, but he guessed not. Though, as far as murders went, this one was relatively contained. "It's not the first one I've seen." And he wasn't talking about just on the job.

"You should come by and view an autopsy," Dr. Carlton said. "All cops should."

"I'd like that. Seems interesting."

McCauley said, "Let's let the ME work."

The two of them went into their own huddle, like the two FBI agents doing the same several feet away.

"Sorry if I overstepped coming here. I followed Stella since I was with her, and I wanted to make sure whoever knocked her around last night didn't try again."

McCauley frowned. "You're looking to put your name in the hat for detective, right, Hummet?"

He nodded. "Yes, sir."

"There's a taskforce post coming up. Joint, Benson PD and the FBI." He waved in the direction of Stella and Addie. "What do you think about signing up to hunt down stolen military weapons?"

Eric frowned. "Is this death connected?"

"We have reason to suspect it may be, and that it's connected to the death of Special Agent Kyle Averson."

"You said military weapons?"

"You want in?"

Eric said, "Anything to do with stolen arms it's likely my cousins know about it. They hang out with all those VA guys." Even though they'd never built up the gumption to serve, Ian and his dad, Aaron, liked to spend time with people who did. As if that goodness and nobility might rub off on them.

"Great."

"And Special Agent Davis will be part of it as well. So you can keep on keeping an eye on her." McCauley nodded.

Eric frowned. "As part of the taskforce?"

"You'll be working more closely together."

Why did it seem like everyone around him was determined to be a matchmaker? First Addie brought up Kyle, and now McCauley thought the fact he'd be distracted and pulling double duty as a bodyguard was a good thing?

"Look," McCauley said. "This police department got a soured reputation after Maxwell was found to be a murderer. We do what's right now. We hit all the checks and balances, promote good people, and take care of each other. That means the feds, too."

"And the fact Russ Franklin is the new police commissioner has nothing to do with it?"

McCauley chuckled. "I guess it's all in the family." Before Eric could say anything his boss continued, "You want to make detective? This will look good in your file when you put your name in the hat for the test."

Eric nodded. It was out there now. His captain knew what he wanted, which meant the spotlight would be on him. Watching. Assessing him to see if he made the cut. Eric had been one of the uniformed officers, no one special, for years. He'd liked that sense of camaraderie and being one of them. He was an only child with no living parents.

He cleared his throat. "I chose the Benson PD because I wanted to make the place I grew up better. I didn't want to join the marines, or the army, and make other countries free. I wanted to affect the place I live. People I care about."

He'd been told he was predisposed to attachment because of his upbringing. The police force gave him the family he didn't have anymore, except for Grams. "I'm not going to let us down."

McCauley nodded. "Good to hear."

If that meant keeping Stella safe, he was happy to do it. But at the expense of his job as a police officer? Eric would have to think long and hard about going outside procedure to the detriment of justice.

He couldn't let his nature become so enamored with her that he forgot what was important. He could do this—as long as he remembered the police force came first. They'd saved his life from being detached and purposeless, and he owed them.

Being a cop meant more to him than Stella ever could. Or should. That was all there was to it.

"Eight tomorrow morning. My conference room." McCauley wandered back to the body.

Eric spotted Stella and Addie wrapping up their conversation and he wanted to see if she needed to eat. Maybe he could persuade her to take the rest of the day off and let her injury heal some before work tomorrow.

"It's my fault." Stella ran a hand over her short hair. "She talked to me and now she's dead."

"You don't know that, and the taskforce is here to find out. It's all part of the same investigation, right?" Addie's voice held a gentler tone than she used with him. Likely because she knew how close to Stella's grief she was going. "It's a tragedy, but you didn't do this."

"It's on me." Stella's eyes filled with tears.

Eric said, "You can't know that. If she'd been in danger, do you think you'd have missed it?"

Stella sniffed.

"I don't think you'd have glossed over someone being in danger for the sake of anything. You'd have offered her protection. Right?"

She nodded.

"Let's go to brunch and talk it through. See what we can figure out."

Addie grinned. "Great idea. I'll get everything ready for the taskforce first thing tomorrow."

"I'm being railroaded."

"Yes." Eric grinned. "Into eating protein waffles."

"You fight dirty."

He chuckled and laid a hand on his chest. He bowed slightly. "I'll use all the tactics at my disposal."

"I'm leaving both of you and eating at the gas station on my way out of town." Her grin indicated she might not be entirely convinced of that being a good idea.

"Likely a good plan, given the possible repercussions of gas station food. You'd want to be well clear of populated areas."

"Go, you two." Addie ushered them from the scene. "I'll work this because I'm the boss. You guys have fun."

"She's serious." Stella leaned over and spoke quietly. "And she'll never let us live it down."

Eric grinned their faces close. He could do this. He could work the taskforce, keep her safe and not get sucked into everything she was.

He had to. Or he would wind up losing everything he'd worked for.

7

Stella might not be on the clock, but she showed up at the prison in her work suit with her badge clearly visible. She waited beside the car, checked her email, and listened to voice mails about her car warranty. The sooner she could get started on this taskforce thing, the better, even if Addie did think family came first.

Maybe for her, it did.

Stella didn't have a family like Addie, whose own was unconventional enough. Addie had a younger half-sister and an uncle who'd raised them both. She had a fiancé. Stella never had any of those things even when she did have a grandmother and a mom. Her dad had been gone so long.

Long enough she didn't even know the man who walked out of the prison toward her.

Bob Davis carried a backpack over one shoulder. Lean, a couple of inches taller than her. Short gray hair cut close to his head and clean-shaven. She didn't know if the smile was for her, or the fact he was free after twenty years.

A dirty cop seeing the light of day.

"Stella." He grinned wide and shook his head. "You grew up."

She pushed off the car. "I've got things to do, so we should get going."

"Doesn't matter what you say, or if you won't talk to me at all. Nothing can diminish this feeling." He pulled the back door open and tossed his bag in. For a second, she thought he might sit back there like a criminal, but he got in the front passenger seat.

She said, "Buckle up." Just in case he might not remember to do that.

Meanwhile she remembered a bunch of things. Like how good her father was about talking his way out of situations. How her mom blossomed into a different kind of person after he went to prison. Relationships did that. A person in love became part of something new, and when it was inevitably over, they got to be themselves again.

So why would Stella want to do that?

She'd never thought it was worth it to lose part of herself just to have someone in her life all the time.

"What happened to your head?"

Stella considered the fact he might not make a great father, but he could be a resource. A confidential informant even. Except that all his friends were from decades ago and this was the wrong state, so it wasn't like he could give her anything current.

She said, "I'm working a case. Someone didn't like me getting close to an answer, so they tried to discourage me."

"Did it work?" There was interest mixed with caution in his tone.

She glanced over and saw some familiar features she shared in his face. But there was nothing more than that between them.

Not anymore.

Bob Davis had betrayed the oath he took to serve and protect his community. She knew, because being a dirty cop was something she'd vowed never to let herself slip into. It was a simple fact of not compromising. Not letting her own selfish wants rank higher than the law and her own sense of integrity.

How he could've gone against everything he was supposed to believe was beyond her. What had possessed him to do it?

"Of *course* it didn't work." She sighed, wishing the halfway house where he was going to be living was closer to the prison. Not hours away, right in the town of Benson. "I got assigned to a taskforce that's looking for stolen military weapons, and these people are involved. Whoever attacked me? I'm going to find them and slap federal charges on them. They're never going to get away with this."

"I read about your partner in the paper." He started to offer halfhearted condolences.

She cut him off. "That's not on the table for conversation."

"Anything you need." He paused. "Anything at all, I want to be here for you. I want to get to know the woman you are now." Another pause. "I messed up. For myself, and for the people I was supposed to protect. I can't apologize to your mother. Hurting you two was the worst of all."

He thought he could make it up to her?

"Why don't you tell me what you've got?" he said. "Maybe I can help you think of an avenue that could net you a lead." He shifted, probably a shrug, but she was doing eighty on the freeway, so she wasn't going to look over at him.

"You want to work the case?"

"I'm a little rusty probably, but I was good at investigating back in the day."

Until he decided to take bribes and steal from the wrong person. He'd betrayed everything he was supposed to stand for.

"Never mind." He pushed out a breath. "It was a bad idea."

"I figure you'll be busy putting your life back together."

"I'm never going to be too busy for you."

Stella bit the inside of her lip. "Did they get you set up with job interviews?"

"Some company called Vanguard. Not sure what they want me to do."

She blinked. "They do private security."

It was on the tip of her tongue to ask what on earth he'd be doing for them—or if it was even legal for an ex-con to do it. Stella didn't need to harp on his chance for a fresh start, but she would be looking into it.

She didn't know much about the people at Vanguard Investigations, and she intended to find out. As soon as the taskforce job was over, Kyle was fully laid to rest.

Her dad said, "I'll hear them out and let you know what the offer is. You can help me decide if it's a good fit."

"Oh," Stella said. "Okay, that sounds good."

She pulled up in front of the halfway house and walked him in. Sure, she got a couple of funny looks from residents, but then she figured new people probably didn't often get dropped off by FBI agents.

The house manager was a slender African American man who smiled wide and shook her hand firmly. "We'll take good care of your father."

"Thanks." This whole thing was entirely too weird.

Her dad said, "Can I call you tomorrow?"

She frowned. "Do you have a phone?"

Her father blinked. Bob Davis looked a little lost, until the manager said, "The house has a phone you can use."

"I'll get you a cell." Stella headed for the door. "Bye, Dad."

That sounded even weirder than the fact he was back in her life. She pushed her way out the door and got back in her car. Since she was on this side of Benson, she figured she'd swing by Bridget's apartment. CSU was done sweeping the place for trace evidence, or anything that might indicate who had killed her.

Stella's stomach roiled. She looked once at the halfway house but figured she didn't have time to worry about her dad. He would either make a life for himself now or go back to ripping people off. Sure, it would hurt if he took that path, but short of forcing him to do what she wanted—which wouldn't work anyway—what options did she have? He was a grown man, and it was his life to live.

She didn't want it to have anything to do with her, but it did.

Still, she could work the problem of Bridget's murder and the missing military weapons—one of which was used to kill Kyle. She could ascertain if the gun used to kill Bridget was from the same batch of arms set to be destroyed. That meant a look around Bridget's apartment to see what she could find out.

Stella would work the problem she could fix.

Close the case.

She parked on the street and made her way up to the eighteenth floor of this downtown condo building. Bridget's place was high-end, so Stella needed to look into who'd paid for it. Though she had a sneaking suspicion.

Work the problem.

A woman like Bridget, with no inheritance and no employment, shouldn't be able to afford a place valued in the $800k range.

Stella used the building manager's key, but the place had

been left unlocked. Which was strange. She ducked under the police tape strung up across the door.

Inside the surfaces were covered in a layer of fingerprint dust. Drawers had been rifled through. Bridget didn't have many personal belongings beyond a few art pieces that'd possibly been put there by an interior designer. The closet looked like a showroom.

The place held little personal detail at all.

Stella looked in the kitchen and didn't even find a junk drawer. There was no desk. The floor in the hall closet was littered with sandals. All the heels were in the bedroom closet. She checked the clothes pockets even though the crime scene unit would've gone through it. Stella wanted her own impression.

And it was that the woman who'd lived here didn't really live here. This was a place, but it wasn't a home. The spot where Bridget slept, changed, and got ready for the outside world wasn't a refuge. It was a showpiece, and she likely never relaxed here.

Had she ever relaxed?

The amount of pressure put on Bridget wasn't something Stella liked the idea of. She wouldn't be able to live like that. Even though she didn't have a home either, this place was even less personal than her motel room.

Stella felt the prick of the hair on the back of her neck.

She turned around but heard nothing and didn't see anyone in here with her. She checked outside, through the massive windows. She did it staying behind cover. Just in case there was a sniper across the street. She didn't want to get shot before she even saw the person.

Even now, the idea she might be in someone's crosshairs made her body shiver.

Her head still pounded from last night. She needed to go home and take a nap so she was fresh for tomorrow. This morning's taskforce meeting had been long and necessary, but she was ready to get to work—not sit around talking about who might be behind the theft of military weapons.

Eric had clammed up at the mention of a militia group who lived outside town. She wanted to get him aside and ask him about that. Maybe he knew them or had some kind of issue with whoever it was. A run in of some kind.

Stella turned to head for the door, not willing to consider this had been a waste of time. She didn't think of it like win or lose, just what she'd gained. Seeing Bridget's living space gave her a window into the woman's life—which had been as impersonal as her death.

The same prickle on the back of her neck had Stella picking up her pace to the front door, deeper in the center of the building. Away from the windows and anyone out there who might want to harm her. She was definitely not dropping this case. Whether they continued to target her or not, she wasn't going to quit.

She opened the door.

The air sucked backward, blowing her bangs and the sides of her jacket.

A boom behind her sent heat rushing toward her. It pushed at her body, picked her up, and slammed her against the wall in one move. Flames exploded out the door, and she heard the distant sound of shattered glass and screaming. Heat licked at her back.

Stella descended into a world of darkness.

8

Eric stayed back enough that his uncle hopefully didn't notice a tail. He likely knew Eric's regular car, so he'd switched it out for an unmarked from the motor pool. That meant this had gone on record, as he'd had to tell his sergeant what he was working on. The conversation lasted a while but was worth it.

Kind of like how taking down his family would be worth it if they were involved in this.

"Because I'd take you all down."

If they weren't involved in stolen weapons, then fine. Everyone would go back to their corners, and he'd continue ignoring their existence like they did with him. Considering they saw Eric as the black sheep after he became a cop, that wasn't too much of a sacrifice.

He hadn't connected with his younger cousin Nigel, and wanted to, but that was different.

His uncle Aaron pulled onto a side street on the east end of town. Eric followed, thinking about brunch with Stella the other day. They'd laughed and told stories of dumb criminals they'd caught using zero police know-how, but only because the person who committed the crime had been tragically inept. Not a great example of stellar police work, but it made for lighthearted table conversation.

Since then there had been radio silence. He knew she picked up her dad today, and he wasn't interested in acting desperate to talk to her or see her when she was giving him nothing. This was a marathon, not a sprint.

Aaron drove through the streets like he knew where he was going, which put Eric at a serious disadvantage. Eric headed right so he could come at the back side of the building from a different angle. The complex used to be a furniture warehouse. Now it was a bunch of empty buildings, except for one where a new church fellowship was renovating into their building.

"What are you up to?" It occurred to him that he was talking to himself, alone in his car.

There might be somewhere to hide his car. He could sneak closer and see what his uncle was doing if the guy got out of his car. It looked like there was another person in there, but he hadn't been able to figure out who it was without getting alongside them.

Eric slowed around the right side of the building. He eased his car out far enough so he could see around the building and spotted Aaron's vehicle.

His uncle stood leaning against the closed driver's door. Waiting for something. Or someone.

Eric dug in his backpack for the camera he'd checked out of equipment and took a few snaps of the vehicle and his uncle waiting.

A second car pulled in and parked nose to nose with Aaron's. Eric didn't know where the other occupant of Aaron's car had gone, or if they were hiding. That could be problematic if he was unaware, focused on whoever this was.

The second car was a silver Lexus while Aaron's was an

older model American car, offering a hint at the disparity between these two men. Were they friends, or enemies? Business partners, maybe. Aaron likely didn't think he was beneath the other man in status.

Eric blinked at the suited man who climbed out of the back of the Lexus.

He zoomed with the camera and got a good look at the guy's face.

"Francisco Salvatore." The father of Orlando Salvatore, the man responsible for Kyle's death.

Eric hadn't been there when it happened, but he and Grams had sat vigil in the hospital waiting for Stella to wake up.

Everyone assumed the son had run the club before the police killed him. However, on paper it became clear that Francisco held all the strings. Orlando had been involved in a local ring that targeted women for sale any time someone caught the eye of one of their patrons. Regulars that had been rescued by the police a few weeks ago, and innocents targeted once and dragged into their web.

Had Francisco ordered the hit on Bridget to keep her from talking to the police?

That had to mean she'd known something they didn't want to get out. Why else would she need to be silenced?

Eric took photos as the two men greeted each other. How on earth did Aaron know Francisco? This wasn't good at all. If his uncle was tangled up with this filth, it didn't spell anything but disaster for anyone caught in the fallout of their business. Eric wondered if it was a new thing, or if they'd been partners in whatever this was for a while.

Something pricked in his awareness of the environment around him.

Eric lowered the camera and grabbed for his gun, but the

passenger door opened too fast. His cousin Ian slid in, holding a gun of his own. "Don't, Cop."

He said that word like it was the ultimate insult. Which to them, he supposed it was. Eric liked who he was even if his family thought being on the right side of the law made him the scum of the earth.

"Just doing my job," Eric said. "Which right now involves protecting myself."

Ian snorted and lowered the gun. "Cause you're gonna arrest me? Or shoot me?"

He should. He also wanted to. However, his sergeant had given him several workable scenarios. "Why is your dad meeting with Francisco Salvatore?"

Ian leaned back in the chair. "They're old friends."

"Yeah, right."

"It's just business?"

His cousin wasn't going to tell him. Eric switched tactics. "Where's Nigel at today? I've been meaning to get back with him."

Ian shrugged. "Who knows with that kid."

Nigel was twenty-four, but Eric would admit he still saw the guy as a kid as well. It was just the way Nigel was. Everyone in his life tried to shield him because it seemed like he needed it. "Maybe you could find out. So I don't have to."

They all said Eric's dad had been the same way, soft to the point he was malleable. Since his father had been killed when he was six, he never got to know the guy. He could remember a handful of things that had become permanently embedded in his mind.

He'd looked up the case file on the incident, but there wasn't much in the report that had told him anything about what happened that night. Edith had told him many times that the past was better left in the past.

"I need to ask you something."

Ian said, "As a cop, or as my cousin?"

Both. "Do you know anything about stolen military weapons floating around?"

Someone else could go after Salvatore. Though, it was likely to be Stella. Problem was, Eric had been ordered to focus on his family connection. While work on this angle kept him busy, she was unprotected in a way that didn't sit right with him. He needed to be able to do both because the choice between them didn't sit right.

Either way he lost something important.

Ian pushed out a breath. "Maybe I do. You gonna pay me as a confidential informant?"

"Do you need money?"

Ian laughed. "Hardly." Given that Eric figured everyone needed money or could use a little more, that was an interesting comment. "I've got something on. And it's bigger than a weapons deal."

"Yeah?"

Ian said, "Is that why you're here taking pictures? You really interested in weapons, or something more?"

"I should sign you up as an informant. Anything happens, it might keep you out of jail."

Ian huffed. Eric could play this off as being about Francisco and the fact that Aaron was here was just a coincidence. If his family thought there was heat on them, they could shy away from anything overt. Keep under the radar for a while. Go quiet.

Then again, Eric figured they didn't even know how to do that. "You might not care about jail, but Nigel will. And Grams."

Ian snorted. "She'll probably get a rifle and lay on a rooftop. The moment I head into my arraignment in chains she'll put a bullet in my head."

Eric bit his cheek. There was an unspoken family rule

when talking about Grams. Ian had just broken it. "All the more reason to stay out of cuffs."

He should've just called Aaron and asked to meet. Told him the FBI and the police were looking into their family with a microscope. Now there was a solid connection to Salvatore, still over there talking to his uncle, all the more focus would land on them. Who knew what would be discovered?

At least Grams' life would go undisturbed. She lived at that apartment complex, but the lease had been signed by someone he'd never met. An assumed name he'd run through his police database and found to be extremely solid.

Anyone who knew them knew she was their grandmother. Both of Eric's parents were dead, and no one knew who Aaron's father was. The whole thing was a complicated mess, but thankfully no one asked questions when she'd suddenly shown back up in their lives years ago. Right before his seventh birthday.

"What if I…," Eric started. "Never mind." He had to play this carefully, or it might backfire on him.

"What's going on?" Ian asked.

Eric set the camera on his lap. "You know what's been going on with the police department lately. Things aren't exactly fun right now."

"Thought that was why you joined. So you could get your jollies pushing around people you don't like."

Eric wasn't the one who was a bully. "There's too much heat now. Constantly being assessed and having every decision undermined." There was a chance Ian felt like this about Aaron, and they could connect over it. "It's exhausting having to live up to the pressure of being perfect all the time." He paused. "I'm kind of sick of it, if I'm honest."

"Understandable."

He felt sick just going in this direction, especially knowing how Stella might react when she found out. With her father's history she could run away screaming.

Eric didn't think he'd blame her.

He forced down the nausea. "It's not cutting it for me anymore. Not with the way things are now. I get no peace and…I'm thinking of getting out. Doing something different."

His phone started to ring in his pocket, but he ignored it.

"Sounds like you might need to make a statement on your way out. Let everyone know that isn't what you signed up for."

"Yeah?" Eric said. "What would you do?"

"You have to ask, we need to hang out more." Ian chuckled. "You should come out to the camp. We'll get Nigel there. Blow off some steam, family style. Like we used to."

Eric chuckled like he remembered the good times. But there was nothing good about what he recalled. Except that Grams had shown up several times just before things got so out of control, like she knew things were getting bad. Eric could only slip away and hide to escape the chaos.

"Same place?"

"Yeah," Ian said. "We're there a lot these days, hanging with friends."

"Sweet." It didn't sound good. More like Ian was trying to be a teenager again, mixed with what might prove dangerous if something went wrong.

But he'd needed that invitation.

Eric said, "I might bring my girl, too. If that's okay. She's pretty wild."

He could explain to Stella, but she'd worked undercover cases before so he figured she'd catch on quick.

Ian chuckled. "Sure you can handle her?"

"I don't need help with that. Just a little something that's going to give me back some fun in my life."

"Turns out I have just the thing." Ian grabbed the door handle. "Dad's done so get out of here."

Eric nodded.

"See you soon. And don't worry, we'll show your girl a good time."

"That's what I'm afraid of," Eric quipped.

Ian exited the car, laughing.

Eric's phone rang. He looked at the screen—and the laughter died.

A bomb had gone off downtown.

9

Stella groaned and rolled over. A woman's face swam into view, covered with the clear visor of a firefighter's helmet. Blonde wisps of hair. Green eyes that resonated with intensity.

Stella lifted her head. "Ouch." Her eyes wanted to roll back in her head. She forced herself to sit up anyway. She'd been lying here long enough already.

"Whoa, easy." The firefighter caught her and held her upright. "What's your name?"

"Stella." She figured it was easier to get it all out in the open. "FBI Special Agent Davis."

"Ah." The firefighter hauled Stella to her feet but didn't let her take her own weight. The woman held her up with impressive strength.

"You work out?"

"Girl, don't go thinking we're gonna be best friends. I'm leaving town in two days."

Stella frowned, but the firefighter apparently didn't take it too seriously. Obviously she worked out since she was a firefighter. She was leaving? Stella had no idea what was going on. Her head pounded, but the dead weight she made didn't seem to matter to this firefighter.

"You have a name?"

The woman tromped along in all her gear, hauling an FBI agent like she was a sack of potatoes. "Lieutenant Patterson."

"Special Agent Davis. Stella."

"Amelia." The lieutenant grabbed a radio with her free hand and held it to her mouth. "Eighteenth floor is clear. Bringing one out."

A garbled reply said, "Copy that."

Stella had to focus to see the hallway. Tried to remember what had happened. She'd dropped her dad at the halfway house, come over to…Bridget's. That's where she was. Nothing in the too-shiny apartment. No life. No personality.

Then, it had all blown up in her face on the way out of the door.

Literally and figuratively.

Stella muttered, "Trying to kill me."

The firefighter punched the handle to the stairs, and they headed down. "As long as I don't get caught in that. This is my last shift in Benson."

The smoke smell wasn't much less here than in the hallway. Still, the concrete was intact. Lots of people headed down, making a steady stream of residents getting away from the disaster.

"Did anyone get killed?" Stella was afraid to ask, but she had to.

The fact was, in trying to kill her they might've caught an innocent in the middle. Taken a life that should never have ended tonight.

"We'll find out, okay?" The firefighter shifted Stella against her. The woman's firm grip constricted Stella's ribs.

If they'd been more than bruised, that would hurt a lot. She'd probably have mustered some energy to complain.

The woman continued, "Windows outside exploded. There's a lot of damage, but the bulk of the blast was contained to that one apartment. There's likely a bunch of minor injuries, abrasions. Things like that. Anyway, did you set the bomb?"

Stella frowned. "No."

"Did you know it was there and neglect to stop it from exploding?"

"No." And the police had searched the house, so who had put it there afterward? Had it been meant for her? No one could know she would show up at Bridget's apartment. Least of all that she would do it tonight.

"Then I suggest you don't assume this is your fault, or that any deaths which result are on you. Because they won't be."

"Are you quitting firefighting to become a motivational speaker?"

Lieutenant Amelia Patterson barked a laugh. "Not hardly. Though, I get the job done with the guys on truck. I don't do slackers."

Stella could appreciate that.

"I got a new job. Open truck lieutenant spot in a place I need to be." Amelia huffed down the last flight of stairs.

Stella was about to ask more when a firefighter opened the door at the bottom of the stairs and Amelia handed her over. "Peters, get her to the ambo."

"Yes, Lieutenant."

Stella glanced back. The firefighter with LIEUTENANT on the back of her jacket jogged back up the stairs.

Peters said, "Don't get attached. She's—"

"Leaving. I know."

They headed outside, where an ocean of people and

vehicles with flashing lights filled the street out in front of the building. Stella tried to breathe. But the air got stuck in her throat, and she had to cough it out.

Addie ran to them. "I've got her!"

Stella was handed over yet again. "I can walk."

"Doesn't mean I'm not going to help you." Addie walked with her to the ambulance, and said, "She was caught in the blast."

"I'm fine. I just got knocked around."

The EMT studied the knot on her forehead and then looked her over. "I see that."

He had her sit on the back of the ambulance and started feeling around her skull. She tried not to let on that it hurt.

"We should be trying to figure out what that was," Stella said. "Were there any fatalities?"

"So far, no," Addie said. "A couple of critical patients from next door either side of Bridget's apartment. One is an elderly man." She frowned. "Do you think whoever attacked you outside the motel just tried to kill you?"

"I think they blew it because they could."

"So there was something we missed," Addie said. "Evidence in there?"

"No, the apartment was clean."

"So what's with the destruction? Why come back after CSU cleared out and blow it up later?"

"Misdirection." Stella lifted her hands and counted fingers. "Because you like to see stuff explode. Francisco ordered it. You needed to test your skills. We missed something." She didn't like that last one, and she'd run out of fingers.

Whichever it was, this wasn't good.

Eric slammed his car door and had to sprint the half mile through and ocean of first responders over to where Addie had told him Stella was.

Addie had told him she was all right, but considering she'd also used the word *bomb* in the same sentence he needed to see for himself.

Were they taking her to the hospital?

If she'd already left in an ambulance he might not get to see her before she…

His steps faltered and he stumbled against a black and white SUV, the chief's vehicle. There was nothing he could do but hang his head.

Take a few deep.

Fight the way that memory wanted to suck him down.

He squeezed his eyes shut. If he let it come, gave it a second or two of airtime and then let it go would he discover it had less power over him now? He needed that, but the risk of being wrong and realizing his past held him in a death grip even now wasn't something he could handle.

Stella was all right.

She wouldn't be pale, lying in a hospital bed. Bandaged. Cold to the touch.

He wouldn't have to listen to that relentless beep. He could still hear it as if it was right here with him, on the street. The way it slowed. Then the final tone that carried on as the line of her heartbeat flattened to a single drone.

He'd been shoved aside so that he fell to the floor in the corner of the room while they talked about her. He'd been too young to understand what they meant. The look on the doctor's face had been plain. No one was surprised when she was gone.

Eric felt his knees give out. He sank into a crouch and covered his face. Took a few deep breaths.

Twenty years. More than that now.

He was still right back there in that hospital room. The reason he hadn't been able to visit Stella in the room where she'd been lying there, just the same as his mom.

Dying.

His phone buzzed in his pocket, probably just an update. Eric used it to jolt him back to reality but didn't pull it out. He straightened and rolled his shoulders. The memories hung on, but he had to do his job first. Be the cop. Not the scared kid with nothing but a scary grandma he didn't understand. Lost. Broken.

Eric pushed away from the car and headed for the fire trucks, shaking off that episode the way he did with all the others. Exercise. The relentless pounding of a run or lifting until he couldn't do any more reps. Listening to music that drowned out everything and reminded him of who God was and what He had done. Finding solace where things were simpler. Where the past didn't need to hold him captive.

He spotted Addie and Stella at the back of an ambulance, talking while an EMT put a gel substance on her forehead.

Eric wanted to sweep her up in his arms. Things between them weren't that. He wasn't sure what they were, but it wasn't closeness and hugs. "Hey."

Her gaze shifted to him, and he saw relief in her gaze. She wanted him here?

"You okay?"

She winced up at the building behind him. "Yes."

"I'll leave you guys to talk."

Eric said, "I'll be filing a report for the taskforce, and I'll copy you in."

"Surveillance on your uncle?" Addie asked.

He nodded.

"I'll look for it." Stella tracked their conversation with her gaze. The EMT let her go, and Addie had gone.

Eric studied her. "Are you really okay?"

"Couple days rest, I should be right as rain."

He figured that might need to be a week but didn't say it. He glanced over at the building behind him.

"No—" She tugged on his arm. "You don't need to see that."

Eric gaped up at the building. "You're lucky to be alive." Not that he believed in luck but she knew what he meant.

Windows on this side of the building had shattered. The glass now lined the concrete at street level. Two fire trucks had stretched their ladders to windows, high up on the side of the building. Evacuating people. Another sprayed water in an open window, battling flames.

"They wanted to destroy the apartment, but I don't think it was aimed at me."

Eric glanced over. "Did you tell anyone where you were going?"

"If I'd have taken backup, they could be dead."

"You were that close, someone right behind you wouldn't have made it?" This was about losing Kyle. It had to be. She wanted to retain control and prevent anyone else from meeting the same fate. But that meant she went at things solo.

And Addie thought he could break through to her?

Eric had no idea what to do. He should be focusing on the taskforce and trying to make detective like McCauley seemed to think was a good idea. He needed to work the lead he had now from his cousin. And catch up with Nigel. Make sure his younger cousin was okay, probably while he followed up on his attempt to get them to invite him back in and see where that went. If he could find these stolen weapons.

No way was he going to take Ian up on his offer and bring Stella to the camp. While he tried to protect her, she'd be working alone trying to protect him.

Neither would work.

"What was that you mentioned to Addie, about surveillance?"

Eric shook his head. "It doesn't matter. Get checked out at the hospital, okay? Let yourself heal so when you go right back to work, which we all know you're going to do, you won't end up getting *yourself* killed."

He walked away, not wanting to be a party to that.

10

Two days after she'd nearly been killed, Stella banged on Eric's door when Bridget's house exploded. As if that was the point. She was fine, and he was going without her. After dropping the bomb that he thought she'd get herself killed. *As if.*

The door swung open, and he blinked. Halfway through putting his coat on he lowered his arms. The shoulders of the jacket snagged behind him. "What are you doing out of bed?" He stepped back.

"They only kept me overnight in the hospital because I lost consciousness. I'm fine."

He raised one eyebrow.

"What's up with you and hospitals, anyway?" Like that was the reason he hadn't visited her and not his parting words. It seemed like he was determined to leave her to it. By herself. But since a bomb went off when she did that, how was it going to go well?

She'd thought about it a lot at the hospital and decided working together made way more sense.

"I had to be at the scene yesterday." He shrugged his coat all the way on. "Investigating for the taskforce."

"I know what you're doing." She strode into his house, hiding the fact her hip hurt.

She'd landed on it hard, but doctors had good stuff to take care of things like that. They'd released her after that one night in the hospital, and now she was mobile again.

She turned and faced him down in a standoff. "I'm coming with you."

The FBI usually didn't give cops an ultimatum, but these were extenuating circumstances.

His expression blanked, an awful lot like it had at the scene of that apartment explosion. Right before he walked away. He'd decided she wasn't going with him now. Maybe he just didn't want to hurt her by shutting her out, but that didn't mean it wasn't exactly what he was doing.

Whatever that'd been, today was a new day as far as she was concerned.

"You think you're well enough for that?"

Sure, hit her with the big guns. "You don't know me, or what I can handle."

"I know you."

"You think?" She put her hands on her hips.

"Not as well as I thought, but better than *you* think I do."

Stella didn't even know where to start with that. "We need to focus. You're going to the camp, and I'm coming with you."

"Maybe I'm going to church."

She frowned. Was it Sunday? "You're going. I know it. Maybe after, but you still are. And I need you to understand how badly I have to do this. You can't cut me out."

"You read the report from my conversation with Ian?"

She nodded even though it made her head a bit swimmy. She didn't let injury slow her down. If it was a detriment to her performance, she should step out. That barb of his had hit home. She didn't want to end up getting herself killed.

But this wasn't that. Yet. For Kyle, she could withstand a little discomfort while she talked with backwoods guys. Heck, with the headache she had, she'd probably fit right in with them.

Eric said, "When did you read it?"

"This morning at breakfast." Before he could argue she continued, "I know you got an 'in' and I'm not being left behind."

"You're injured."

As if that was an issue. "I can handle this."

"And if we have to run ten miles because something happens?"

"What are the odds of that?" She was the kind of person who made sure she could as part of being a capable FBI agent. He did, too. They had to have a level of physical ability to do their jobs. Today was just an off day, that was all. Normally she'd be ready for whatever came at her.

"You nearly got blown up. What are the *odds* of that?"

Stella had no argument. "Well then statistically it's unlikely to happen again, right?"

Eric turned and hung his coat on a hook beside the front door. "Coffee?"

"You're skipping church?"

"It's Saturday."

Stella shrugged. "Okay."

"You need a day off. I can reschedule the visit for tomorrow, after church like you suggested." He wandered to the kitchen. "You should come with me to service."

Stella followed. "You just don't think I should be working today, so you're forcing me to rest."

"And?" He filled the carafe at the sink.

"Am I supposed to be grateful?" She folded her arms.

"No, I don't figure you would be."

"Because I'm a mean person?"

"I'm going to go with 'single minded.'"

She stuck her foot out and cocked her hip. "That's never been a problem before."

He paused pouring water into the coffee pot. "Every alarm bell in my head is going off. I think we should talk about something else."

He turned away from her and made the coffee.

Stella huffed over to the couch since his whole living area was open plan. The whole place was gorgeous, all natural light and clean lines. It had to be a rental. "Whose house is this?"

"Mine. I bought it while you were in the hospital a few weeks ago." He slumped down next to her. Blinking. "You were thrown out of Bridget's apartment by an explosion the day before yesterday. I'm having a little trouble with the fact you're here."

"Alive?"

"No. Sitting like this is just another day. You on my couch, about to have coffee."

Did he think this was going to be a date? They'd had coffee before, but never at his house. Most people thought she didn't like coffee. The fact was, she only drank it rarely. Stella didn't do vices, and she definitely didn't do addiction. She didn't even have a cup of coffee often enough for it to be once a week.

She wanted to enjoy it when she had some.

Stella looked away from those dark eyes that she could get used to, like a daily coffee that was more like a lifesaving medicine than a thirst quencher. All kinds of metaphors about what Eric represented ran through her head.

A mirage in the desert.

An umbrella in the rain.

"We need to focus," she said. "There's work to be done."

"It will still be there after you've rested."

"I got a full night's sleep and then some." Stella paused. "I was only admitted to the hospital because they were mad that I turned the EMTs down the first time when I wasn't even knocked out. They did it out of spite."

"Is that even true?"

She made a face. "Okay, fine. I inhaled some smoke, and there's a slight chance my airway could close up randomly. They wanted to *observe* me. Because they're nosy."

"I'm sure that's it. Not the risk of medical complications from being knocked unconscious because you were blown up."

"Why did you freak out and yell at me?" Stella realized after it was out that she'd said it out loud. Why did she do that?

Eric sighed. He rubbed his hands over his knees like he wanted to jump off the couch and run to the coffee even though it wasn't ready. "I don't like you being hurt."

"All the more reason to stick together."

"Do you have an answer for everything?"

"Usually, yes." He might as well know now. "Also, what on earth is this house?"

Eric blinked. "What do you mean?"

"Um, nothing, *Better Homes and Gardens*. It's, you know, nice and stuff." Like seriously nice. She wanted to get all her stuff now and move into this living room just to see how the sun hit the gleaming wood floor in the morning. She could lay her exercise mat out and stretch in the warm rays.

"Something is happening."

She cleared her throat. "Yeah, it's called work. And we need to get to it."

He shook his head. "I don't think that's it."

Stella didn't want to think about Kyle right now. Not

when the exhaustion and the fact she felt like she'd been hit by a bus—there, she admitted it—meant her emotions were closer to the surface than normal. Still, her eyes felt hot and filled with tears.

She sniffed and shook her head.

"So you like my house?"

She said, "Why is it *so cute?*"

Eric burst out laughing. "I'm glad you like it. Grams helped, and I told her it should still be a little manly but I don't think she listened. I go to my friends' houses. I don't invite them here."

She joined in his laughter. "I really like it."

So much she wanted to live here. It seemed homey, and she could use a little of that when she'd been rudderless for so long. No roots. No family. "Kyle was my family."

Eric nodded.

"He was my best friend and like an irritating older brother. He saved my life one time, and he *never* let me hear the end of it." She smiled. "Until I saved his and made it even. Then he had to shut up about it."

Eric smiled. Something unspoken remained in his expression.

She wanted to ask about it, but at the same time so much fear rose in her that she couldn't form the words.

"You want to go into the camp together?"

She nodded. "I want us to work this whole thing together as partners."

Maybe he worried she was trying to replace Kyle with him since she was missing a confidante. But since they had kissed before Kyle died, and they'd been making plans to go on a date, how could that argument hold water?

He'd have to see the truth that she cared about him, the way he cared about her.

They connected on so many levels.

"Kyle drove me crazy."

Eric gave her a small smile.

"I was thinking about the difference between him and you." She winced. "Not in a weird way. Just that I know it's different. With you."

He nodded. "I'm glad."

It seemed like he hesitated, so she said, "What is it?"

"At the risk of being redundant, I just can't believe that apartment exploded. With you in it." He ran both hands down his face. "That's twice now you could've been killed and I wasn't there."

"So stick with me." The answer was simple as far as she could see. But she couldn't say more because her phone buzzed. She slid it from her back pocket and he got up, returning with two mugs of black coffee.

Putting anything in it was sacrilege.

Stella looked at what had arrived and frowned. Her phone continued to beep with a stream of text messages. "I'm getting a bunch of photos."

"From who?" He leaned over so she showed him.

"Unknown." She tapped on the first one and three more loaded while the image filled her screen. "What does that look like?" She'd never seen anything like it.

"The inside of a tent and rows of cots."

"Military?"

He shook his head. "I don't think so. Keep scrolling." When she slid her thumb through a couple of similar images he said, "That's a Quonset hut."

"Which I *know* is a military thing."

"Yeah, but there's a decommissioned, abandoned base an hour outside of Benson. In the hills. That's what this looks like. It's the camp where my uncle and cousins hang out with their friends."

She frowned, but it hurt her head, so she let go of the

tension and rubbed her forehead. "But I don't see any weapons anywhere."

"Maybe that's the point," Eric said. "Someone went in already and did reconnaissance. There are no weapons in any of these pictures. Maybe it means what we're looking for isn't there."

So going would be a waste of time.

But who had done it for them and sent her pictures anonymously? She couldn't figure out who might know. Someone who took it upon themselves to help.

Stella needed a minute, so she handed him the phone and drank some of her coffee. Someone banged on the door. She sloshed coffee over her hand putting it back on his coffee table.

"One sec." He strode to the door and she heard it open. "Nigel? You okay?"

Stella knew that was his youngest cousin. The one he'd been trying to track down.

She heard a shuddering inhale. "I did something... I need your help."

The kid wasn't going to talk with an FBI agent there. She took her mug, headed for the kitchen, and stood out of sight. When they moved into the house and then the living room she ducked into the hall.

Eric asked Nigel, "What's going on?"

Nigel shifted, nervous and unsure. "I think I killed someone."

11

Eric tugged his cousin inside. The kid, as Ian called him, was twenty-four and rail thin even though Nigel ate probably twice what Eric did. He'd killed someone?

The kid's face flushed, and his hairline was damp where too-long strands fell over his forehead.

"Come on." Eric waved him to the living room and shut the front door. "Does anyone know you're here?"

Nigel didn't take a seat. Beyond him the living room was empty. Eric tried not to look surprised, but where had Stella gone? If Nigel thought about it, he'd wonder why there were two mugs on the—

She'd taken her mug? Only his remained on the coffee table.

Nigel shook his head. "I left early. I've been driving around trying to figure out what to do. Nearly got pulled over on Ravenswood, but I lost the guy." He backed up and slumped onto the couch.

Ian would've said *pig* when referencing a cop, but Nigel had always been a little nicer about Eric's chosen profession.

Had Ian and Nigel talked since the car conversation two

nights ago? Things had been delayed since Eric found out the apartment Stella had been searching literally blew up while she was there. She might have emerged unscathed for the most part, but Eric's heart had *not*. The last day or so was a blur. He could hardly process it.

After he'd left the surveillance operation with no more information about what Salvatore was into with Aaron than he'd had before he spoke to Ian, he'd been sucked into Stella's orbit again.

He couldn't even think about the fact she nearly died or he'd lose his ever-loving mind. Again.

He'd barely held it together enough to walk away. Now she showed up here, wanting to work this case with him? His heart couldn't take it. Stella threatened his composure. She put at risk every survival tactic he had.

Nigel ran his hands down his face. Eric took a seat in the recliner.

He studied his young cousin. "Whatever happened, you can tell me."

"So you'll stop being a cop for a minute?"

"Honestly? No, I won't. But I'll do everything I can to help you."

He wasn't going to compromise who he was, or the oath he'd taken. Ian would've asked him to. Nigel knew better than to put him in that position, even for family. Then again, if Ian and Nigel had talked about Eric being disillusioned by the police, right now he might expect Eric to cross a line in favor of helping. He didn't know what Nigel knew, though.

Nigel said, "You can't help me."

"There's a reason you came here." Eric didn't like the dejected look on Nigel's face. "And it's because deep down you know I can."

Stella would likely help, assuming she was somewhere listening and she hadn't bailed.

Eric continued, "Whatever you've done it doesn't matter. We'll figure it out."

A phone started to ring. Not his or Stella's, so it had to be Nigel's.

"Don't answer that," Eric said. "It's not important right now."

What was important was helping Nigel, which meant the kid needed to tell him what was going on and not keep being cryptic never saying anything.

Nigel shook his head and jumped up. He headed toward the front door, which took him past Eric, who got up fast enough to intercept. "Whoa, bro. Hold up. I can help you."

"No. You should arrest me, so I have to go."

"We'll work it out. Just tell me what happened."

He shoved at Eric. "You can't!"

Eric absorbed the hit. "Cool down. Just tell me what happened." He didn't move out of the way. Nigel stared him down. "You gonna hit me again?"

"You can't help me. No one can." Nigel lifted his chin. "Get out of my way."

The kid didn't have a weapon, or Eric figured he'd pull it and start waving it around. Trying to be the big man, hard criminal. Is that what'd happened? Had Nigel gotten in over his head trying to prove himself and it backfired?

"I'll still be here." Eric backed up. "I'll always be here, no matter what. I will help you if you need it but you've gotta trust me."

"Whatever." Nigel headed for the door. And left it open.

Eric took note of the car he was driving, but couldn't get the license plate as his young cousin sped away with a screech of tires and a cloud of exhaust.

"You just let him go?"

He turned to see Stella. She was not lying in a hospital bed, and she'd recovered. There was a slight hitch to her stride as if she had a few bruises she didn't want to admit to, but other than that his heart didn't need to do that squeeze thing where he had to sit and rub his chest until it went away.

"You terrify me."

Stella frowned.

"If you keep getting hurt, I'm not going to survive."

Her expression blanked. "So I should just go? Try not to die. Is that it?"

He didn't like that look on her. He wanted the light back in her eyes, and the warmth of her smile. The knowledge they had shared secrets. That they both wanted justice for this community.

She started toward the door.

Eric put his arm in front of her, and it connected with the warmth of her abdomen. He tugged her gently toward him and shifted as well until she was all the way up against him in a hug. Nothing more than that. Just the comfort of a warm embrace, where he got to put his head against hers and feel her heartbeat under the fingers he slid along her neck, into her hair.

Okay, it was a *little* more than a hug.

"You're very confusing."

Eric smiled against her hair. "It feels pretty simple to me."

Stella sighed. But she didn't let go of him.

He closed his eyes, and all he saw was her lying in that hospital bed even though he hadn't visited. "I can't believe you nearly got yourself blown up."

"Are you going to talk with me about your reaction?" She moved a fraction and lifted her face to his.

"I'd rather kiss you." Did she want him to do that?

Stella stared up at him. "We need to have that conversation first. I need to know what that was."

Eric's stomach clenched.

Stella stepped back. "Why did you let Nigel go?"

Because he cared less about whatever that was than spending time with Stella. Call it work, or not, he knew what he wanted, and it wasn't getting tied up with family drama. Nigel *thought* he'd killed someone? If the kid didn't want to talk about it, there wasn't much he could do for his cousin.

Eric shut the door.

"We should get to work, not waste more time sitting around." Stella waved her phone. "The morning taskforce briefing report just came through, and we know where Francisco will be today."

He didn't like the sound of that. "Resting isn't a waste."

"I rest between cases. We're in the middle of this one."

"That's how you get burned out." Cases always overlapped. She couldn't guarantee time between them to take days off. And what did she do when investigations lasted months, or longer?

"There are things to do." She shrugged. "If you don't want to come with me, then fine—"

"Of course I'm going to come with you. Where are we going?"

She grinned. "Francisco Salvatore is at the country club. Time for some recon." She looked down at his socks, then back up. "Do you have slacks and a polo, or just jeans?"

He would have to dig stuff out of the church clothes end of his closet. "We're going in?"

"Thanks to your surveillance of him when he met with your uncle, the taskforce has had its eyes on him. We're not doing anything so I volunteered us."

He wouldn't exactly describe what they'd been doing as nothing. "We can go check it out."

She frowned. Before he got argued with, Eric quickly changed clothes so she didn't get a wild idea and go without him. Half an hour later they paid the day fee for the country club—which had better be reimbursed—and signed up for a round of golf.

While they waited for their start time, Stella dragged him to the bar and ordered two drinks that looked like punch. Each had a tiny umbrella in the glass.

"I'd prefer coffee, but you've had your cup for the next two weeks, so I guess that's out." He needed to act enamored with her, so he smiled.

She returned the smile as though his attempts worked. "Coffee is so 'everyone' it's boring. Be unique already."

Eric wanted to talk about what'd happened, but that meant he needed to explain his reaction to her being hurt. Namely the fact it hadn't been about her injury. It was actually about potentially seeing her in a hospital bed, or dead. That would lead to talking about his mother—something he'd avoided for years.

Still, if he was going to tell anyone, it would be Stella.

He was about to tell her that, so she'd know he wasn't giving her the brush off, when she jerked his arm forward. Eric nearly stumbled but caught himself and managed to keep from spilling his drink.

"I feel like brunch. What do you say?" She dragged him by his elbow to the restaurant/café area. The inside room had an expansive domed ceiling with windows, giving them a view of the greens. French doors lined one wall, all opened onto the patio letting in a cool breeze with the morning sun.

"I could go for some eggs benedict." As if they had time for that.

He looked around and surveyed each patron and saw many moneyed people but no one he recognized except the guy who'd run against the governor in the last election. Probably drowning his sorrows still.

"Over there." She led them past a stammering waiter to

a tiny corner table. Two tables down he saw what she had. Francisco Salvatore in a discussion over lunch with two men in suits that Eric couldn't see because their backs were to him.

Stella gave him a pointed look, so he held her chair.

When they'd settled and the waiter left, he said, "We need surveillance equipment or we'll get nothing."

Stella pulled her phone from a tiny white purse she'd retrieved from her motel room. The sundress she'd put on made his mouth dry, and she'd paired it with flat white canvas shoes. She'd even brought along a visor for when they did golf.

He hoped they weren't actually going to play because he was terrible at it.

She tapped the screen of her phone and then inserted one Air Pod. She handed him the other. The second he inserted it in his ear, he heard a man say, "I'm sure we can come to some kind of arrangement."

That wasn't Francisco. Intel they had said the guy had a heavy accent his son Orlando had worked hard to eliminate. The father didn't feel the need to lose his heritage and become Americanized.

Someone muttered, "It is past time for that, and well you know."

"So now you're threatening me?"

Eric saw the guy lean back in his chair. Beside him, his associate bristled. Both of them were nervous.

"On the contrary, you're only causing further problems for yourself, Mr. Mayor." Francisco slid his chair back and stood. The screech of it on the floor cut across the audio.

Eric had to struggle to hide his reaction while Stella closed her eyes and sucked in a breath.

"You might want to rethink your strategy, or you won't like what happens next."

12

Stella pulled out her air pod. She took the one Eric held out to her and stood, sliding her phone into the ridiculous purse. The mayor hadn't left his seat, and neither had the aide. They still looked as shell-shocked as the mayor sounded on the audio her phone mic picked up, which worked for her because they might say more than they would otherwise.

She slid into the seat in front of the mayor at the square table. "I should've brought my drink over. Then we could have a real visit."

Mayor Wilton stiffened. "I didn't invite you to join me."

He was a man with a healthy middle and thick dark hair. His wife was far too slender considering she had zero muscle tone, something that had never made sense to Stella. She glanced around at the room and clocked how many patrons noticed them. How many staff.

They weren't causing a scene, but they also hadn't gone unnoticed.

"No, you didn't invite us. But here we are." She slid her

FBI badge from the purse but didn't reveal it yet. "How about Francisco Salvatore, did you invite him?"

Eric shifted beside her. The aide looked like he wanted to run away…or drag her from the table and start a fight. Loyalty, but no backbone. As if he could take her? She nearly laughed out loud.

Stella looked back at the mayor. "Mr. Wilton?"

Dark brows reached for each other. "Who are you?"

She slid her badge onto the table. "It's D-A-V-I-S. For when you write out that complaint."

Stella figured he'd probably get that far, writing it all down, but would likely never hit send. After all, the repercussions of his conversation with Salvatore going on record weren't going to look good for him. Right now he had a choice to make.

Several theories regarding his involvement with a known criminal were workable. Some held more weight than others, like Salvatore and Wilton being co-conspirators with the recent group brought down just a few weeks ago. Stella had been in the house when a woman caught up in that was rescued.

She'd also arrested someone who it turned out wasn't related, but Lyric Thompson had accepted her apology. They were good.

"I'm Officer Hummet." Eric motioned between himself and Stella. "We're part of the recently formed taskforce that is looking into Salvatore, among other things."

"I'm well aware of the taskforce," the mayor said. "Just not why one conversation should put me in your crosshairs, Officer Hummet. And I know who you are. I know all about your family and their dangerous hobbies."

Eric didn't let it show how he felt about that. "Doesn't mean I'm part of it. I serve this city."

Stella didn't give away her feelings either. Wilton wanted

them to know he had ammo on them, just in case they thought they had some to hold over him?

"And I'm unable to say the same about myself?" the mayor asked. "Because I'm in politics, I suppose, so that makes me automatically corrupt. As though I must have a hidden agenda."

Eric leaned back in his chair. "We'd like to ask you a few questions."

Mayor Wilton said, "A man I don't know sat in front of me, disturbing my meal. Much like the two of you are now doing." He spread his manicured fingers out. "What's there to ask?"

Stella wasn't going to let him off that easily. "What is the nature of your relationship with Francisco Salvatore?"

Wilton turned to his aide. "Retrieve the car. I'll be ready to leave momentarily."

The aide scurried away, and Stella spotted their waiter talking to a suited man who looked distinctly managerial. She lifted her badge so they could see it—and hopefully get the idea not to disturb them.

She knew it was pushing the boundaries of her authority to force the mayor of Benson into a conversation. Her jurisdiction didn't extend past federal matters, but if the mayor's business conflicted with the taskforce investigation, he would need to come in and make a statement.

"If you're aware of the existence of the taskforce, I'm sure you'd have wondered when we would get around to speaking with you." Stella let him talk, hoping he'd say more now he'd dismissed the aide.

"Unless I've never met the man and have no ties to him."

"Why would he bother to threaten you if you have no connection?" Eric asked.

Skin around the mayor's eye twitched.

She didn't mind that he'd let it slip they'd been listening

in. It was one of several tactics they could employ, and given it was the plain truth she wasn't going to object. "Why does he consider you to be in over your head?"

"Naturally you see me as the root of some sort of conspiracy." The mayor sniffed. "How cliché would that be?" He tried to chuckle, but it didn't work. "As if I'd work this hard to get where I am only to be taken down in a scandal before I can complete the things I set out to do."

He certainly wouldn't be the first liar to be elected to some kind of office, or other position of power. But considering how vocal he was about weeding out corruption, she figured he had a point. She wanted the police department to be free of officers who abused their authority, same as with federal law enforcement.

Cops couldn't do whatever they wanted, not even to pursue justice. And if she was going to hold other people to a standard, it would be one she also held herself to.

Stella spread her fingers on the table, then linked them back together. "So what was Mr. Salvatore referring to?"

Wilton fingered his water glass and turned it in his hand. "Unfortunately, there's a certain criminal element of this town who don't agree with my attempts to clean up the police department."

He paused long enough Eric said, "Shocking."

Wilton gave a half smile. "I've been advised to dial back my enthusiasm."

"They're putting pressure on and threatening you?" Stella asked.

"As if I'd back down." He shrugged one shoulder. "I knew this wouldn't be a popular choice, but only from those threatened by the prospect of a better police force. Some would have me scrap it altogether. Others care nothing for police brutality. I choose what's best for this community."

"Good," Eric said. "The police department can assign

officers to protect you if necessary." Before Wilton could argue he added, "It's not worth waiting until after you're targeted physically to make sure you're guarded."

"Trust me." Stella pointed at her forehead, which still kind of hurt. "I learned it the hard way."

"I shall take your advice to heart." The mayor stood, smoothing down his tie. He gave a slight bow. "Thank you for your consideration."

He seemed diminished as he left.

They watched until he disappeared through the lobby, then Eric glanced at her. She spotted the heat of his attention out the corner of her eyes.

"I know."

Eric said, "Because you read my mind, so you know what I was going to say?"

Stella rolled her eyes. "Let's get out of here before the manager flips out. He's ready to call security."

"We should be following Salvatore to see who he's harassing now." Eric huffed, pushing both their chairs in so far they bumped the table. "Every time I turn around this guy is meeting with someone right in front of me."

Stella nodded. They trailed together through the hall in the direction Salvatore had gone but didn't see him. The manager wasn't going to answer questions. He was busy glaring at them. She said, "I wonder if the guys from homicide have found the gun used to kill Bridget."

She stepped outside, and they walked around the building, looking for Salvatore. He was nowhere. They could get a warrant for the surveillance tapes. But that would take time, and Francisco would be long gone before they figured out what car he was driving and where he'd taken it.

"You think the mayor knows more than he said?" Eric asked.

"I'd argue he's in politics, so yeah. But he basically just

schooled us on assuming he's corrupt just because he's in office, so maybe I can't jump straight to that conclusion before I have proof." She sighed.

"I'd defend a police officer accused of corruption for the same reason, which amounts to bias."

"Which is basically pride, because you think you know something others don't, or just have more knowledge of the situation than anyone else. And instead you have no proof. Just supposition."

They climbed in the car, and she reached for her phone but didn't draw it out yet. "I've been doing the same with my dad, I think. Except there was proof because he was convicted."

"And now that he's served out his time?"

"He's considered rehabilitated. He accepted the consequences, and now he gets to live the rest of his life free—provided he doesn't break the law again."

Her dad had been right, though. They didn't know each other.

She'd never visited him, even after she was old enough that she could decide for herself if she wanted to go or not. Something kept her from reaching out.

Eric drove. Stella took a few minutes to close her eyes and think through everything. Instead of Salvatore, Bridget's murder and the taskforce investigation all she could see was her dad's face when she left him at that halfway house. The fact he'd so clearly wanted to have a relationship. Get to know her again.

He was the only father she was ever going to have.

She opened her eyes. "What was your dad like?"

His foot slipped off the gas. "Why do you ask?" Eric's voice was tight.

She'd stepped into dangerous territory and needed to walk it back. "I was just thinking about my dad, so I wanted to ask about yours. But it's okay if that's an out-of-bounds topic right now."

She hoped one day he'd tell her. Getting to know Eric better seemed so right, like pieces of a puzzle that fit together because they were made that way. She wanted to feel the comfort of his arms, the way she had in his foyer. Spend more time in his house. See where things might go.

Was the inevitable end Thanksgiving dinner with her dad at the table?

A ring on her finger.

A family of her own.

She knew what she wanted out of life, but had always been too discouraged to hope with all of her heart. She'd left it to the tiny corner of her heart that refused to give up.

The part that wanted a dad who was a good guy. Maybe Eric didn't have that any more than she did.

Eric reached over and squeezed her hand. "It's a longer story than we have time for now."

She figured that meant he intended to tell her, which she couldn't argue with. Her energy had been depleted. That wasn't surprising, given everything she'd been through the last few days. Wherever they were going, she was going to close her eyes and do some of that resting he'd advised she should on the way.

She let out a long breath.

Eric's voice was barely audible, but she heard him say, "It's a tragic story I don't want to tell you."

Her heart broke at the pain in his voice. It made her want to reach out to him and her father.

For the first time in her life she had the power to ease another person's pain in a way only she could. Not just as an FBI agent, but as her.

Just Stella.

13

Eric drove all the way to the camp from memory even though it had been years since he'd been out here. The place hadn't changed much, though April rains had washed out the road leading to it from the highway in a couple of places. Overgrown on the sides. The dirt track snaked up the mountains, then down the other side where the camp resided out of sight of civilization.

She'd slept so long he had pulled through a drive-thru, fueled up, and sat in the parking lot, eating his meal and writing a report on what happened at the country club.

He'd sent that in along with a note saying where they were headed this afternoon.

Up until the early '60s, the camp had been a working air force base. A decade or so after it was abandoned, the locals reclaimed it, and no one bothered to tell them they weren't allowed to squat here. Once in a while the state police drove by, and sometimes they stopped to chat.

Mostly Eric figured they'd been paid to leave again. No questions. No reports.

He had never heard of Aaron, Ian, or Nigel being

wrapped up in a crime before to the extent they were named in police files.

Considering he knew the better half of what they got up to, that meant they were good enough to keep their noses clean to have gone this long without being targeted by an investigation.

But that time had run out.

Whether he liked it or not, the truth of what they did out here was about to be brought to light. It made sense, and it was the right thing. But the fact it was happening now when the police department had a tarnished reputation was interesting. He could potentially add fuel to the fire when his connection to his family was revealed in the media. It would be a juicy story, and one made even more juicy for any reporter who dug far enough into Eric's past to get to the tale underneath.

The last thing he needed was for everyone to find out.

Stella he could *maybe* handle knowing. He would never refuse to tell her, as that wouldn't be fair. They didn't need a relationship based on half-truths. Even if he wanted to keep it to himself. Keep them apart.

The fact was, he considered nothing insurmountable. After all, God had put her in his path. Why would He do that and then add obstacles He couldn't overcome? Impossible.

"Just because I can't see a way, doesn't mean there isn't one."

Stella stretched and blinked her eyes open. "What was that?"

Eric pulled to the side of the one lane road, just in front of the old gate. "Nothing, I was just talking to myself."

At least she hadn't heard him earlier when he'd spoken aloud without realizing it. The last thing he needed was for her to ask when he wasn't ready to tell her.

She looked around. "This is the camp?"

He nodded. A couple of cars and a few more trucks than that were inside the gate, parked in haphazard rows. The camp stretched for a good mile with people milling around. Enough they might blend in if they were careful, but he wasn't going to bank on it.

"You could stay here in the car if you'd like to rest more?" The second he said those words he cringed.

As he figured, she twisted around in her chair to glare at him. "What did I say about us working together?"

"Are you always this moody when you wake up?"

Her eyes flashed with fire. "I guess you'll never find out."

She shoved out the door, dressed in her country club clothes. Eric let out a loud sigh. She turned around and came back to her still-open door. "I'm going to stick out like a sore thumb."

"No kidding." He lifted a bag from the passenger footwell. "Here."

It was her things from before they'd changed to go track down Salvatore. Jeans and a T-shirt, because she'd shown up at his house expecting to come here.

"And I'm supposed to just strip out here? Someone will see."

"Go find a tree to hide behind."

She glared at him.

"I'm going to do the same. In the opposite direction." He knew she'd ditch him. "Meet back here as soon as you're done. Do *not* go in without me. You don't know these people."

She strode off to the trees, jogging hopefully unnoticed by those in the camp too far away to see. He'd parked decently out of sight behind a group of trees. Far enough he couldn't see the entrance from the car.

Eric jogged in the other direction to get out of his golf clothes, then put on the jeans and T-shirt from his gym bag.

He shouldn't worry nearly as much about Stella as he was.

Maybe it was all the residual effects of hearing she'd been injured. He could still be feeling the sheer terror of her in a hospital room, even if he knew it was illogical. She had been nowhere near death.

She was a trained FBI agent. She hated corruption as much as he did. Sure, she would totally go into the camp without him if he didn't hurry it up, but she could handle herself.

The woman was as capable as he was. And she likely had greater skill considering her training versus his. Their knowledge and ability could pool into something more if they worked together.

The fact they might fit in a way he hadn't expected but was amazing to consider made him stop and thank God that she'd come into his life. That they had this chance to work together. He prayed for protection and guidance, and that they would discover not only who'd killed Bridget and supplied Orlando with the weapon that killed Kyle. But also that they would learn who had taken the photos of inside this camp that'd been sent to Stella.

She strode out of the woods at the same time he did and tossed the purse in the car. She pulled a jacket over her holster. Eric slid his on the back of his belt so he could keep it out of sight, though he figured most people in this camp would be openly carrying.

"Ready?"

He nodded and they strode through the gate. "Maybe this is pointless. After all, those pictures showed no weapons."

"We know your uncle isn't unconnected." She glanced around. "Do you think he's here?"

"If he is, he'll be in the main hall," he said. "So let's check some of the outbuildings first."

"What are these people up to?"

The handful they could see walked with purpose. Over to the right, in a stretch of pitted asphalt clear of trees and buildings—probably the old parade ground—a couple of guys loaded wood in a stack that was up to their waists.

Right. It was Saturday. "They're getting ready for an influx of people. You smell that?"

"Barbecue?"

"Around back." He waved at the building to their left. Offices turned into residences, mattresses on the bare floor, and a central hall where the kitchen was. "They'll make a fire, and the party will go until the early hours. They'll have a church service when they all wake up tomorrow hungover. Like doing that wipes it all away."

It had taken him years to walk back what he'd learned as a kid and get his theology straight. He'd been unable to believe these people worthy of grace for a while. But neither was he, which was why it was such an amazing gift. Eric still hadn't completely forgiven his father. It was more like sometimes he forgave his old man, and other times he didn't. Then he'd have to work his way back to being able to live free of the pain of his dad's actions.

Did she feel the same about her dad? It seemed like she was interested in extending grace, but they hadn't talked about faith much. Eric wasn't sure he'd be so receptive to it if his dad was around.

Although, if he was alive there was reason to believe he'd be still in jail.

And he would *never* get out.

Eric spotted a guy who noticed Stella and headed toward

them. He reached over and pulled her to his side, one arm around her shoulders. "Act like I just said something fascinating."

She chuckled, looked at him, and slid a hand up his chest to touch his lips.

Heat rushed through him.

The guy broke off. Deterred.

Eric said, "We're good." But the words came out throaty. He cleared it and tried again. "We should check the gray building."

They angled toward it.

Anyone who watched would think he was showing his girl all the firepower here to try to impress her. Eric and Ian had broken in through a tiny storage door so many times as kids. Just so they could gape at all the weapons stored here.

If the photos were to be believed, it had all been cleared out. Given there was no lock on the door, Eric pushed the handle down and they headed inside. "Huh."

"What is it?"

He waited until the door shut and they were standing in the empty concrete entryway with only the light coming through the cloudy windows.

"This place is usually locked up tight."

She headed for the inner doors first. "Let's check it out."

Eric pulled his gun. The comforting slide of it releasing from the holster calmed him more than the feel of it in his hands sometimes. He'd fired it outside of the range maybe a half-dozen times in the years he'd been an officer. The last thing he wanted was to assume he didn't need it and end up dead—or worse, with Stella hurt again—because he'd been complacent.

The room had been completely cleared out, like a church hall on a Monday but without the stacked chairs. "This is weird. Something is definitely off."

A couple of pallets in one corner had been leaned against the wall, but that was literally it.

"Maybe they knew the taskforce was coming and hid everything." She spoke over her shoulder as she wandered the empty room. Nothing was behind those pallets, so why bother looking? But if she checked, he wouldn't begrudge her.

He shook his head. "There's nowhere to put stuff I don't know about. We can check everywhere, but that will take time and this is where weapons are kept."

Plus they would be seen if they spent too much time here. It wasn't worth the risk just to find out what they already knew from those pictures.

He racked his brain to figure out if there was anywhere else the weapons could possibly have been hidden.

"I'm inclined to just track down my uncle and ask him what's going on, why I'm suddenly finding them in the middle of everything." He lowered his voice even further than it had been. "Use the same line as I did with Ian and claim I want in."

He turned to the door to leave but looked back for her. Stella was now completely out of sight. What on earth? "Are we going to—"

"What is this?"

Eric spun to the door and the guy stand there. "Uh, hey bro."

"I'm not your 'bro,' and you shouldn't be in here." He pulled a Desert Eagle from his belt and pointed it at Eric. "Get to steppin'."

He lifted his hands so the guy could see his gun.

"I'll take that."

Eric had no choice but to give it up. He gritted his teeth. Where had Stella gone? That was twice now she'd made herself scarce when he was confronted. He just hoped whatever this was didn't take long.

And she didn't get herself into trouble in the meantime.

"Let's go." The guy jabbed the gun in his back and shoved him out the door.

14

Stella pushed against the man holding her. The echo of a heavy door shutting rang through the empty room. "Get off me."

Her words were muffled against his hand.

He let go a fraction, and she shoved his hand away from her mouth. "What was that? And where are we?"

It was nearly pitch-black.

She tugged out her phone and unlocked it, because the light of her screen was brighter than the flashlight.

The man who'd grabbed her and dragged her into wherever this was stayed completely still. "Talk."

His lips flexed into a flat line, then he said. "Fine. Don't thank me."

Stella blinked. "Is there some reason I shouldn't be seen?" Whatever it was he'd felt the need to drag her back here whether she liked it or not. She didn't want to reveal her occupation, but it might be necessary if it saved her life.

A lot of criminals drew the line at the heat that would come from killing a federal agent. Some cared nothing for who they murdered. She needed to know what kind this guy with his dark hair and long nose was.

So far he'd said nothing else. Stella said, "Talk. Or you and I have problems."

"You already have problems. You don't want to know what they like to do with women here. You'd be wise to leave before dark."

"I'm not leaving without Eric."

"Don't worry about Eric." The guy shook his head. "Worry about you."

"Who are you?" She shifted her phone to get a better look. "You were at Edith's house. You left when I arrived."

"Congratulations, you figured it out." He lifted both hands and clapped silently. "Now you need to get out of here."

"Yeah, no," Stella said. "Keep talking."

The last thing she wanted was to be stuck in some closet or between the walls, whispering with some stranger. Years from now, she could end up being discovered, a skeleton hidden here after she was murdered.

A shiver ran through her, and not from the cold.

She might be a fully trained FBI agent, but it wasn't like she was immune to fear. Sometimes it swallowed her—usually when she was alone. But that didn't mean she needed to latch onto the first capable person she found. She'd kind of already done that with Eric, after she was left adrift when Kyle had been killed. Even if he kept the story about his father from her, she knew she wanted to be in his life as much as he allowed her to.

Which meant getting back to him.

She had a gun. She could defend herself. Maybe not against a whole camp full of backwoods guys, but she could do some damage before she was overcome at least.

This man wasn't part of their group, so maybe he would help her out. The two of them could help Eric.

He sighed. "You asked Edith to help you."

Her eyes narrowed. "You were the one who took those pictures. Who are you?"

"Apparently my name is Joseph now."

She frowned. "In this camp?"

He shook his head. "Anywhere."

"You don't look like a 'Joseph.'" She had no idea what he did look like, but it would be more threatening than that generic, forgettable name. Although maybe that was the point.

Was he here hiding?

The guy cocked his head to the side. "Do I look like a friendly ghost?"

"No. What? No."

He chuckled. "Never mind." The words had a slight edge of an accent to them. It disappeared when he said, "I'll show you how to get out of here."

Stella wondered if she'd even seen that shift in him. Who was this guy?

The fact he thought she would leave—and leave him to her investigation—was interesting. "So, Joseph." She folded her arms. "You took those pictures and now you're still here, looking for something? Or you live in these walls?"

She heard a breathy inhale, the start of another chuckle. He slid his finger down her phone and tapped the flashlight icon. "We are in the walls."

She waved the phone around and saw that this opening between the interior room and the exterior walls ran up to the ceiling. Above them there was a structure, the framework of ladders and gangways that led to openings high in the walls.

"It's for fixing the lights, or running stuff across the ceiling since it's so high. This way you don't need to rent a lift. You just send someone in here."

She shivered.

"Yeah. There's a stain behind you. I think someone fell a long time ago."

"What is this place?" She had a sense that this camp had been here forever, yet it only just got on the police radar. Eric had to know more than he was saying. "I need to find my friend."

"Your friend is fine."

And she was supposed to just take his word for that? "Fine, then tell me. Have you found any weapons yet?"

He said nothing, so she turned the phone from the gangways above back to his face and frowned. "Talk."

"I'm still looking."

"Then why send those pictures like there's nothing here to find? The taskforce could have written this whole place off as not involved and moved on to another lead."

"To keep you away while I figure this out."

Joseph, or whatever his name was, spoke so matter-of-factly. Stella couldn't figure out what it was about this guy that made her want to agree and leave him to it. Something about him just seemed so capable. As if she needn't worry over the outcome, he'd take care of it. She could get on with her job satisfied she'd delegated wisely.

But was that just part of the ruse?

"Why should I stay away and let you do this?"

His gaze zeroed in on her forehead, where she'd tried to cover the knot with her bangs.

"Talk."

"I was bored?"

Stella said, "How do you know Edith?"

"She's my neighbor."

As if that was all it was. "I don't need another guy sidelining me because I need to 'rest.' I can tell for myself what I can and can't do."

He lifted both hands. "Okay, but you're worth something to the FBI and the people you know. If you get hurt again. They'll worry about you, right?"

"And no one will worry about you?"

He shrugged. "I'm expendable."

"I don't believe that. No one has zero value."

He made a tiny *huh* sound in his throat.

"So you think the weapons are here somewhere?" She looked around some more. There was maybe two or three feet between the interior wall and the exterior. Enough if she stretched her arms out she'd be able to touch both. It was pretty cramped. She didn't mind it for a few minutes, but if she got stuck in here, things wouldn't progress well.

Stella much preferred open spaces.

He pointed over her shoulder. "That way. There's a door to outside."

Stella started that direction but said, "Answer the question."

From behind her he said, "There's something going down here. It might be bigger than missing military weapons."

"Stolen. Not missing."

"Whatever that is, this is bigger. If the weapons are on this property, I'll find them. But no one here will react well to a swarm of police serving a search warrant. And whatever they're planning will get lost in the mix of the military recovering what they should've kept better track of in the first place."

Stella swiped away a spider web she had no desire to get all over her. She made a face it was good he didn't see or he'd wonder if she was a professional. "Any idea what else they're up to."

"They had some meeting earlier. Closed doors, only a select few. Very hush-hush." Once in a while his accent slipped a fraction. She heard the edge of what might be British when he was frustrated. "I caught a few words but nothing to say what they're up to. Afterward the lot of them were squirrely. They're nervous."

"Outside they've got people setting up. Eric said there will be a big party thing tonight, with people coming in." She wondered if they could make their way through that crowd unnoticed. Find some people to question, preferably when they were too inebriated to realize they overshared. Get intel they could look into. Evidence. A warrant.

This could lead to a result.

Even if he'd said she shouldn't be here after dark. Stella didn't put herself needlessly at risk, but she would do her job if it was necessary.

"I'll take care of that. And your friend Eric can help, depending on how that meeting with his uncle goes."

Stella stopped moving and turned back. "His uncle?"

"Aaron Hummet runs this place. He and Eric's dad used to do it together, back in the day. Now it's just the one and everyone he runs with. Most of the guys here figure he'll give the mantle to Ian pretty soon."

"What's your read on Nigel?" The guy was much younger than his brother Ian, and he'd seemed pretty distraught when he'd shown up at Eric's house. If Nigel was willing to provide evidence, she could have him get her information.

If this Joseph guy doing it didn't get a result.

She had no problem working more than one angle.

"They want him in the fold, but he doesn't have the stomach for what they do. Nigel is going to get swallowed up by it." He didn't sound sad exactly, more like this was a fact of life so often and he knew it well.

"I can get him out."

"Do it in a way they don't know it's happened. They'll go to ground if they think something's up."

"With Eric in the mix, they have to know the police have eyes on them. He's a cop and suddenly he comes sniffing around?" She'd wanted to watch out for him, as much as he was determined to do the same for her. But this guy had dragged her out of the room so she couldn't.

"Seems like he's done pretty well so far convincing them he's disillusioned. Might not last long though." Joseph shrugged.

"He shouldn't be here when things go south."

"So get your cop out of here. Let me take care of this."

She found a door at the end of the wall, basically a hatch. "And trust you to solve all my problems?"

"It's what I'm good at." He stalled her with a hand on her shoulder. "Don't doubt the cop. Keep the faith."

He reached past her and shoved her out. Stella stumbled onto the grass behind two trash cans, and the hatch closed behind her. She heard the snick of a lock engage.

Stella crawled far enough to look around the trash cans. Since she couldn't see anyone, Stella got up from her crouch and crept along the back of the building. Whoever that guy was, he had some interesting ways of getting the job done.

She checked her phone just in case Eric had messaged her but had nothing from him. A new report had come in for everyone in the taskforce, but she'd have to read it later.

Between this building and the next was clear. She headed around to the front, moving as casually as she could to see if Eric was still at there.

She peered around the front and looked everywhere she could see for him. "Where are—"

A man stepped in front of her.

Stella stumbled back half a step but he grabbed her.

"I guess you didn't learn your lesson the first time." Ian grinned. "But don't worry, I'm a thorough teacher."

Eric's cousin shoved her against the building and pressed his body against hers.

15

The slap came out of nowhere. The crack of a palm against a cheek cracked through the room and the man who'd brought him in here fell to his knees.

Eric braced.

Aaron turned from the guy on the ground and stared down Eric. "Something to say?"

His uncle birthed a feeling in Eric's chest that he also felt staring down the barrel of a gun. Literally and figuratively. Something inside him saw no difference between the imminent loss of his life, usually in an ugly nightmare kind of way, and looking at his uncle.

The older man strode over. His jeans had grease stains on the thighs, and a leather vest covered his long-sleeved denim shirt. He reached up and squeezed the back of Eric's neck. "It's good to see you, kid."

There was no warmth in his eyes. Eric had to fight not to flinch.

It was definitely *not* good to see Aaron up close. Not at all. Eric needed to realize his uncle was behind all of what the taskforce was investigating and quit kidding himself.

He tried to smile. "Been a while."

Those were all the words Eric could choke out. He wanted to run back to that room and work out where Stella had gone. Was she really hiding? He couldn't help thinking something bad had happened. He needed her to be okay, because the thought of her being in a hospital bed again wasn't something his heart could handle.

He couldn't think of her right now.

Aaron walked back to the man he'd slapped, who'd gotten up. The guy backed away and left the room. Cowed by his superior and the authority Aaron wielded. All because he'd put his hands on Eric. Even though Eric was a cop, evidently he was still considered to be under Aaron's protection.

Maybe this guy had no idea Eric was police. Could just be that Aaron seized an opportunity to assert his authority and Eric's presence was just an easy way to do it.

Aaron smirked. "What brings you home?"

Eric let out a sigh, like the way he'd been treated was an affront. He smoothed down his shirt. Now that they were alone, he could say what he needed to.

Then again, he could also kill his uncle, and who would know? Except for him and the Lord. Which was the crux of the reason why he wasn't going to take out his dad's brother.

Eric had other family members whose tactics leaned in that direction, but he knew himself.

"You know about the police investigation?" He didn't say anything about stolen weapons, hoping Aaron would fill in the gaps.

His uncle made a dismissive motion.

"There's only so much I can do. We're all on a short leash right now."

"So if you weren't on a leash, you'd be pitching in?" Aaron said.

"Do you need people? Seems like you've got plenty of guys here."

"They're not family." Aaron wandered to an empty metal desk and sat on the edge.

The room was partitioned off by office cubicle walls, making Eric wonder what was on the other side. If it was weapons, whoever had snuck in would've gotten photos of it. Still, he couldn't remember any of the pictures looking like the inside of this room.

"There might not be much I can do," Eric said, "but that doesn't mean I'm against what you're doing."

Aaron said, "What am I doing?"

"All the cops know is that a shipment of military weapons set to be destroyed were stolen." Eric shrugged and didn't mention the apartment explosion. The prevailing theory had Francisco as the responsible party. "I can make sure it stays that way."

Aaron nodded slowly. "Is that right?"

"Things at the department are stupid," Eric said. "Too much oversight. Too many rules, and everyone's pointing fingers at everyone else. Trying to be the one who finds the next dirty cop." He figured Ian had told his dad about their previous conversation.

"Is that why you're all up in my business?"

"The taskforce is." Eric paused. "I could keep you apprised of their movements, if you want to be one step ahead of the investigation. Just in case."

"And you think I need you for that?"

Eric didn't know what to say. Aaron had an informant in the police department? That wasn't good. How long had there been someone sympathetic embedded in the Benson PD? The fact Aaron did that instead of trying to turn Eric into a mole said a lot about how he viewed Eric. It would take some convincing to make a believable turncoat.

"Right now they only care about missing weapons." Eric slid his thumbs in his pockets like all this was no big deal. "Whatever else you might be up to? They have no idea. It can stay that way, rather than just alerting you to what they have I can also make sure they don't discover anything you don't want them to."

Aaron studied him, and that knot in Eric's stomach got bigger.

"If you told me where to find the weapons, they might even be persuaded to believe you had nothing to do with the theft. The PD will never know I made a deal with you."

"You think they'll believe you just happened to find them?"

"Give me someone to pin it on. Some veteran with the know-how to pull it off, you can send him with me as a scapegoat. Someone who owes you a favor." Eric shrugged, as though destroying someone's life also meant little. "I'm sure there's enough guys here you can lose one and not suffer."

"You'd play it like that, all to keep me out of prison?"

Eric figured the guy would never allow himself to get anywhere near a jail cell, let alone a trial. However, the expression on Aaron's face was completely inscrutable. Eric had to wonder if he felt the impending sense of doom because of the threat Aaron represented, or if it was because he reminded Eric so much of his father.

Memories from the shadows of his mind drifted to the surface, like dark whisps rising out of that place where he'd locked them down tight. He'd heard the counselor tell Grams he didn't remember anything. That it was probably for the best. But that wasn't true.

Aaron said, "Maybe I can send a few jobs your way. For old times' sake."

"I can be your eyes and ears in the taskforce."

"I'll worry about that. You worry about you."

Eric frowned. "What does that mean? I thought family looked out for each other."

"We haven't been family since that old bag murdered my brother." Aaron spat the words out. "And did the police do anything about it then? No. Of course not."

Eric flinched. Not because of his uncle's words, but because the lid on his memories slid open just a little more. He realized he'd taken two steps back.

Aaron pushed off the desk and closed in. "Whatever you think you remember? It's wrong. Only I know the truth of what she did. One day I might even tell you the story." He huffed out a breath. "You should know where you come from. Because that poison is in all of us." He lifted his hands. "Why do you think we are the way we are?"

"Because of Grams?" Eric forced out the words, needing to know the truth.

"She's already destroyed us all. She's just too stubborn to admit it."

Eric had to get a handle on this. His breaths came fast, making his head swim. Memories swirled. He had to get this conversation back on track. "Where are the weapons?"

"You think I'm going to give them up to you?" Aaron was close now. Too close.

"It'll get the cops to back off, even returning some of them and not all. The rest could be lost forever."

Aaron's mouth curled into a semblance of a smile.

"I'll write the report myself."

"Maybe the scapegoat could be Nigel. He's basically useless at this point."

He would sacrifice his own son? Of course. This man was no better than Eric's dad, who'd been a monster on a good day. The fact he'd been left unchecked for so many years. Up here doing whatever he wanted. It terrified Eric to think of all the destruction that man had gotten away with.

And what else he had in mind.

Eric managed a shrug. "Where is Nigel? I can take him in with the weapons, but do you think he'll tell the right story?"

His heart broke for his young cousin, even while he didn't know what Nigel might have done. He could be looking at jail time anyway. Without taking the blame for this.

Who knew why Nigel had shown up at his house, freaking out? Whatever was so bad that he'd done might mean Eric could convince him to testify against Aaron in exchange for a deal. Did the kid know what his dad was up to?

Maybe Eric could find out that way.

"Find him," Aaron said. "Call me, and I'll tell you where the weapons are."

"And after that? I want to be able to keep the cops off your tail. They don't need to get in your way."

"I'll let you know."

The door flung open and hit the wall behind it, rattling the front end of the Quonset hut they were in. Stella entered first, a pinched look on her face. Lips pressed into a thin line until they had virtually no color.

Behind her was Ian.

She clocked the fact he was with Aaron but looked at Eric. She touched her forehead where the knot was and then pointed at Ian.

"What's going on, Ian?" Aaron didn't sound happy. He sounded like a boss with too many unruly employees.

Eric's stomach flipped. The guy who'd shoved Stella against her car and threatened her had been his own cousin. He didn't even know what to think about that—while at the same time it made perfect sense. His family were no better than gangsters and criminals. Why wouldn't they have deliberately hurt and threatened a federal agent?

That meant Ian knew exactly who she was. Something he'd figured but now had confirmed. They wouldn't be able to talk their way out of this. It was entirely up to Aaron how things went down. But at least both Eric and Stella were armed.

Whether he liked it or not, his family was linked to the death of a federal agent. Except for the question of whether Ian took jobs of his own on the side, or if they were in business. Given Aaron met with Salvatore, he figured they were both all in. Maybe Nigel as well.

"Yeah." Eric lifted his chin. "What is going on, *Ian*?"

"Caught your girl outside snooping around." He shoved Stella toward Eric.

She stumbled two steps, and he caught her in his arms, tugging her close to him. Who cared if they knew he had feelings for her? He would protect her, and they needed to know the extent he'd go to do it.

"I was *looking* for *Eric*." She put a hand on her hip. "I didn't know y'all had him in here or I wouldn't have been lookin' all over. Would I?"

Eric lifted his brows and gave Ian a pointed look. "Cops gonna be cops, you know? What did you expect?"

Aaron said, "How about the two of you don't come around here anymore. This isn't the kind of place for police or feds. Got it?"

Whatever his uncle thought about what Eric had told Stella, it probably wasn't that he'd have no secrets with her. At least, he wouldn't after he forced himself to say everything out loud. What Edith thought he remembered and what she thought he didn't.

Aaron turned to Ian. "It's time for our taskforce friends to be escorted out."

Eric said, "And you'll let me know where Nigel is?"

Aaron's face was again inscrutable. "You want your cousin? Find him yourself."

"Let's go." Ian pulled a gun and motioned with it to the door. "Get to steppin'."

16

Stella stepped out first. Despite the sun high in the sky she felt a chill down to her bones. This trip hadn't gone exactly how she imagined. Even though she wasn't sure what she thought the outcome would be.

Eric reached out and snagged her hand.

She squeezed it and held on. Who cared what anyone around them thought the relationship was between the two of them? Whatever they guessed was probably right, at least as far as her feelings were concerned. They'd only kissed twice.

She quit that train of thought before it snagged on what number three would feel like. Where it would take place. How he might...

Focus.

A couple of people stared at them. She glanced over her shoulder and saw Ian close behind. Pointing that gun at her. Better than him pointing it at Eric, though she had no doubt he would kill his cousin. Stella needed to stop Ian before that happened.

Away from this camp.

She tried to calculate how fast she could draw her weapon. Not fast enough considering the others who closed in.

Ian said, "Take their weapons."

Before she could argue, someone snagged her gun from its holster. She reached for it and the next second Ian pressed his gun to her forehead. "Try me. I'd love to blow away some federal brains." Ian glared at her. "One less problem for us to worry about."

"You think killing me gives you less problems? You don't know the FBI very well."

"Because I'm gonna worry about Addie Franklin?" He laughed. "Get moving. Or I kill you *and* anyone who comes at me. Though it'll be a shame you don't get to see it."

Eric tugged her hand. She hadn't realized she was still holding on.

They walked to his car, where she quickly realized they weren't just being escorted to it.

"Eric in the back," Ian said. "Stella, you drive."

"Where are we going?" Eric asked.

Ian swung out and slammed his gun into Eric's temple, causing him to crumple to his knees and gasp out a breath. "Any more questions?"

Stella opened the driver's door and climbed in.

"Good." Ian hauled Eric into the back seat, and when Stella tried to see if he was all right, or even conscious, Ian stuck his gun in her face. "Don't, okay?"

She blew out a breath. If he planned to kill them, he should just do it here and now, and get it over with. Clearly that Joseph guy wasn't going to help. He would do whatever he thought was fun, even if apparently it was doing favors for Edith. Or working for her. "Your grandmother is probably ashamed of you," she said. "I know she's proud of Eric, so it's not that much of a stretch. I'd change everything if I ever thought my grandmother wasn't—"

"Shut up and drive."

Stella shoved the car in reverse and hit the gas.

"If you crash this car, Eric is the first to die!"

She hit the brake.

Sadly, Ian didn't slam his face into the dash. In the back Eric rolled off the seat and slammed into her chair.

"Turn around and go."

Stella drove. After a few miles of highway, headed back toward Benson, Ian shifted. Relaxed in the seat. He lowered the gun so his wrist rested on his knee.

"Where am I going?"

"Where I tell you to."

She didn't know whether that was to leave them in the middle of nowhere and make it impossible to get to help easily or go all out and kill them, she didn't know.

Stella said, "Just because we're cops doesn't mean you need to do this. We don't know what you're up to." When she knew he'd glanced up at her face, she said, "I heard about something 'happening' but that's all I know."

"So the heat will be on."

"Not from me. I can't investigate when I have no clue what something even is. As far as I'm concerned there's nothing at the camp. No stolen weapons, nothing else."

"Huh."

She had no idea if she was getting through to him. A glance at the dash screen of Eric's car told her he had no signal on his phone. Was it here, or back at the camp? She couldn't call for help without navigating the menu—and even if Ian didn't stop her could she actually make a call?

Did he have that system that dispatched you through to a call center in an emergency? Her smartwatch was out of battery since she forgot to charge it last night. So that was no help to get them aid if needed.

She always relied so much on technology that she would have to figure out how to save their lives the old-fashioned way—with sweat and probably blood.

Swerve suddenly and crash? Ian could still shoot them.

Swing out her arm and hit him. Try to knock him out and not crash the car at the same time? He could still shoot them.

Wait him out and figure a way to get free?

"Take a left."

Stella gripped the wheel. If she reached up and jabbed the button on the rearview mirror, would it even be connected? Ian could tell whoever answered that they were fine. No problems here.

If she was about to die, Stella wanted answers.

"If you're the one who warned me off the investigation into Orlando, then did you kill Bridget?"

He said nothing.

"Just because I talked to her?" Stella huffed. "She told me nothing, by the way. She didn't have to die."

"Quit rambling."

Stella said, "I want to know why you killed her."

"Who says I did?"

She shook her head, navigating the canyons between the camp and Benson. So many places to sail over the edge and plummet to their deaths. She couldn't bring herself to do it when it wouldn't solve the problem of getting them free of Ian. It would only be suicide. "Of course you did. Who else would it have been?"

She heard a low voice in the back. "It was Nigel, wasn't it?"

Ian shifted in his seat. "You should've stayed knocked

out. This would've been a whole lot more pleasant if you had."

"You forced Nigel to kill her." Eric's voice sounded lethal.

"As if the kid is so innocent. You cops are all the same, looking at everything like it's black and white when it's far from that. Everything is gray." Ian waved the gun around. "That's why I don't care I'm gonna be the one who kills you."

"You don't have to," Eric said. "No one else is here. It's just us."

"So? Like my dad has so much influence on me I can't make my own decisions. He's not a cult leader, bro. He's got plans and I'm gonna be a part of them. We just have some business to take care of first."

"Clearing the way for what's to come?" She spoke carefully, inviting him to share more. He might since he thought he was going to kill them. "Who are we gonna tell?"

"True." Ian chuckled, low and mean.

"I'd like to say it's a surprise that you're like this, but it's not," Eric said. "You were always mean as a snake. I've felt sorry for Nigel his whole life."

"Surprise, surprise the golden boy disapproves." Ian scoffed. "Everyone always knew you couldn't hack our life. That's why we let her take you away."

"You think I wanted to be part of your sick family?"

"You weren't even when your daddy tried to beat it into you." Ian huffed. "There was no hope. Might as well have let her take you out like trash."

Stella held herself very still.

Ian added, "Considering how you turned out, she should've killed you like she killed him."

She bit her lip.

Eric's dad had beaten him and tried to condition him.

Someone female had killed his dad. She thought first of

Edith, but was that possible? She had only known the woman as a spry, older lady. The kind who had a neighbor conduct a recon operation into a dangerous camp.

Stella needed to investigate Edith some more.

"Maybe she should have," Eric said. "It would have saved me all this grief."

"You mean coming into our camp, *Officer*, and thinking we'll tell you anything?" Ian laughed. A hollow sound she didn't like at all. "Like no one saw through your story about wanting to sign up."

"It's my job. Investigating trash like you and bringing justice."

Ian swung back with the gun. She heard it slam bone. Eric grunted, and Ian rounded the gun on her. "Pull over. Here's as good a spot as any."

"Here?" There was nothing around them. Just a tall mountain on the left side of the street that the highway snaked around. To the right it dropped off to a river. Far too much space between the road and the icy cold snow runoff.

Stella bit her lip.

"PULL OVER!"

She hit the brake and sprayed gravel onto the shoulder, a slim space between the white line and the edge. She was halfway in the lane still, and a truck that had been behind her honked as it passed.

Help.

Her silent prayer went unnoticed. By the truck driver at least. Her grandmother had been a devout follower of Jesus. She'd never called it a religion but told Stella it was a relationship. Not a "have to" but a "get to." A life of thankfulness, not obligation.

Stella needed some of that hope right now. The unwavering faith her grandmother had died with. Afterward Stella railed at God that He had taken everything good from her life. He'd done it again so many times. The most recent one was Kyle. Maybe even Eric.

She'd hardened her heart toward Him.

But now Stella realized that maybe God was precisely what she should need when she had nothing. Not the one she should blame and push away.

She put the car in park. "What now—"

The gun came out of nowhere, cracked against her head, and Stella's world went black the way Eric's had done.

When the world came back into focus Stella sucked in a breath. Everything was numb. Her entire body was frozen, half submerged in water. "Eric!" No sound came from her mouth. She sucked in a breath. "Eric!"

The car shifted. Pushed along the river by the force of the current. Icy cold water lapped at her.

Get out.

Stella reached with numb fingers to unlatch her seatbelt. Her fingers glanced off the buckle and pain shot up her arm. She tried again, got nowhere, and tugged against the belt. It wouldn't move.

"Come on. Come on."

She needed to get to him. Eric was in the back. Get him and get out. Get dry. Safe.

Ian might have thought this would kill them, but he'd find out quickly how wrong he was. And how bad things would be for him now.

Her lips spread in a sneer. "I'm coming for you."

Stella sucked in a breath. She worked her hands down the seatbelt slowly, inch by inch, hardly able to feel sensation in her fingers. She pressed against the latch. It popped free.

"Eric!" She hauled herself up using the steering wheel for leverage. Got a knee in the seat.

She screamed out all her frustration and pulled herself onto the seat. Half her body was now out of the water.

Where was Eric?

The back door on the passenger side was open. Water rushed in.

Where he'd been lying was completely submerged. Had he drowned while she had sat unconscious in the driver's seat?

Terror erupted in every fiber of her being.

Stella screamed.

17

The echo of a scream drifted to him. Eric didn't know where it came from. He sucked air into his lungs and leveraged himself out of the freezing water.

Pain tore through his left arm.

He cried out and face-planted back in the river.

Get up.

Eric planted his other hand and forced his legs to cooperate. Got his knees under him. Pushed up to crouching. The river's muddy bank was an arm's length away, but he had to figure out what was going on first.

He glanced around and saw a car. His car. Back door open. Eric's head swam as he scrambled to stand in the knee-height water.

Above him on both sides of the river were high banks. He could hear intermittent traffic pass—a single vehicle at a time. Wind battered his body as the breeze raced down the valley with the river at the bottom. It was too high to climb up.

Metal scraped rock. The car shifted toward him.

A woman screamed.

"Stella!" Eric waded toward the car.

It shifted again. The sound of metal on rock screeched in his ears and echoed off the hills on both sides. How on earth were they going to get free of—*no*. He needed to get her out of the car first, then they could figure out the next step.

Eric waded to the car. It slid down the river, pushed by the force of the water.

He stumbled as it came toward him. Panic stalled out everything, but he grabbed the door with his hand that wanted to work and looked inside. "Stella?"

Her face was completely pale, dark circles around her eyes. Her mouth opened, but she said nothing.

"Come on." The car shifted, and he had to move with it. If he climbed in and it was swept away, he'd be as much in need of rescue as her. "Can you climb back and get out?"

Her fingers gripped the headrest.

The car shifted.

She let out a short scream, then swallowed through a flash of gritted teeth.

"You can do it. Come on." Eric had no idea what was downriver, and he didn't want to find out. "Come on, Stella." He moved around the open rear door to the front passenger door and got it open.

The car slid several feet, then bumped against a rock.

Eric said, "Can you toss me that backpack?"

Stella climbed into the passenger seat and passed it to him. She looked at the water between them, just a couple of steps, and then downriver.

"Just take my hand." He'd have to let go of the door, but she had to take the step.

Stella shifted.

He held out his hand, and he steadied her as she stepped into the river. "Are you hurt?"

She inhaled a sharp breath and shook her head. "Cold."

Eric slung the backpack onto his useless shoulder, then onto both so he didn't have to hold it in place and it wouldn't slip.

Think.

"Come on." He grabbed her hand.

They traversed rocks and the silty bottom of the rushing ice-cold river side by side. On the opposite bank snow had gathered in patches, where the sun never hit it. They climbed out of the water, then Stella turned to sit on a rock. Eric took the grass beside her and laid his left wrist in his lap.

"Are you okay?" she asked.

He winced. "I'm pretty sure it's broken."

But not the same way he remembered it feeling when he was little. An experience he didn't want to recall in the slightest, considering everything else that happened that day.

Eric felt the touch of her fingers in his hair. Sure, they were cold as he was. But the gentle thread made him want to lean into her. He closed his eyes as she ran her hand along the hair from his left temple to behind his ear.

"Thank you," she whispered.

Eric couldn't see what she might be thanking him for. After all, the woman was only in this predicament because of his family.

"It wasn't your fault."

He didn't want to get into that, so he shifted enough to tug the phone from his front jeans pocket and look at the screen. The thing had been submerged, but thankfully still worked. Why own a phone you couldn't dunk in a river?

Eric said, "Do you have any bars? I've got nothing."

"Probably all the dirt." Stella kept her gaze on the road high in front of them. Across the river. Up what from down here looked like an impassable hill. "We need to get higher so we can call Addie."

"I'm thinking a helicopter would be nice." All the energy

seemed to drain from his body. Eric leaned back and laid his upper body on the grass, his knees up. He let out a long sigh. "Give me a second."

"So I shouldn't tell you there's a beetle right by your head."

He narrowed his eyes on her.

"There's no way I'd get that up close and personal with nature. Not even when I'm camping."

He wanted to laugh, but it seemed like that would take too much energy. "How are we going to get up there?" The words were a long groan. Hopefully they made sense.

"Don't pass out." She shifted on the rock and nudged his hip with her shoe. "I do not want to be alone."

He closed his eyes, just to rest. All he could see in his mind was Nigel, pointing a gun at them. He'd hit Eric on the head and… Eric didn't even know.

He shifted and opened his eyes so he could see her. "What did he do to you?"

Stella sighed. "Made me pull over. Knocked me out." She touched her head.

"I'm sorry."

"Why? It wasn't your fault. Your cousin's actions don't have anything to do with you." She shook her head.

Eric knew what she was saying. In his head he understood that he was a cop and his cousins were criminals. They weren't the same. But in his heart, where his blood beat the same as theirs? Different story. He couldn't separate himself from bearing some responsibility for their actions. Especially when it got Stella hurt.

"Ian was the one who knocked me out a few days ago, outside the motel." Her voice was low, like she didn't want him to know how she felt about his family.

"That piece of trash." He gritted his teeth and sat up,

not really wanting a beetle in his shirt collar—or anywhere else. "Let's figure out how to get out of here."

He managed to get to his feet, certain it looked capable and manly and not like he was an invalid. Even if he had to fight his body's urge to shiver. Thankfully it was a hotter day today. The sun felt good on his face—and his wet clothes.

Stella got up off the rock and laid her hand on the T-shirt over his abdomen before he could move. She raised up to the balls of her feet and kissed his cheek.

He started to ask what that was when she spun around and said over her shoulder, "Let's go."

Eric stared at her. Stella made her way along the hill, careful with each step, sticking parallel to the river.

A few feet away, she turned. "Are you coming?"

"Sure."

"Because you have nothing better to do."

He followed her. "Do you have any idea how to get to the road?"

"I saw a bridge before your cousin had me pull over."

Eric winced again.

"I'm just glad he didn't sail us off the edge at high speed. Who knows if we'd even be alive if we'd hit the riverbed at fifty?" She shook her head. "I should probably say thanks to God for that, but I don't really know how, you know?"

"Thank You, Lord," he said. "For both of us."

"Amen to that."

Eric felt the edges of his lips curl up. He also felt like he'd been hit by a truck. Things were complicated right now. Aside from the state of his life, he wouldn't mind hiking with Stella. Any other day, at any other time. For any other reason.

Still, he could hardly let go of the fact that his family had dragged them into this.

If his uncle hadn't met with Salvatore.

No, it was even before that. If his cousin wasn't the one who'd threatened and hurt Stella.

Eric had followed the truck from the motel and seen it at the bar where his family hung out with all their thug friends. Nigel had acted all cool and calm. Someone else had driven the truck away. Coordinated efforts to keep him from putting the pieces together.

Now they'd tried to kill him and Stella. Two cops.

Because they'd come too close to discovering what his family was up to at that camp?

Eric said, "Did you find anything?"

"Other than Joseph?"

He stumbled but caught himself. "Uh, what?"

"Joseph." She slowed a bit so he could catch up. "I think he's a friend of your grandma's. Anyway, he was at the camp. He's the one who sent us those photos, and he's still looking."

"Then why send us the pictures if he's not done?"

"That's what I said!" She glanced over her shoulder and they shared a smile. "He wanted us to stand down while he found what they're *really* hiding, or what they're up to. Because he thinks they've got something bigger in the works. And we should leave him to it, or something."

Eric made a sound with his lips that wasn't entirely intentional.

"Pretty much. *As if.*" She sighed. "Wow, that bridge is farther than I thought."

Eric moved so he was close behind her. The urge to slide his arms around her waist and pull her back against him flared up and he flexed his fingers. But he didn't reach for her. They were both freezing, drenched, and injured. His arm did not feel good.

Wasting time with comfort didn't get them out of here.

Stella glanced over her shoulder. "To the bridge, or higher until I can get a signal?"

"Either way we have to get to the road, so bridge."

She nodded. "You okay?"

"I will be when I'm showered, in my sweats and eating a pizza."

"And if I want to join you?" Her eyes flared. "For the pizza part."

He wanted to kiss her now, kind of like she'd done with him. "Dinner together sounds great."

"Good, because who knows what would happen to you if I wasn't around to keep you safe."

His laughter echoed through the canyon.

She turned away, and he focused on following her. It wouldn't be good if either of them fell. Although, they were already in a sorry state so it wasn't like they could get wetter.

He moved his arm and had to swallow the gasp. He'd probably have to go to a doctor before the pizza happened, but he was going to make sure it did.

Stella led the way to an old bridge that stretched across the river. As soon as they stepped onto it, she looked at her phone. "Here we go." She swiped the screen with stiff fingers.

Eric squeezed her shoulder with his good hand. She shifted and leaned against him so that they stood together shivering.

He laid his cheek on her forehead, and she put the phone to her ear. He heard someone answer, but not what they said.

"Addie." Stella exhaled against him, and he pulled her a little bit closer. "Eric and I need help."

Her words were as comforting as them standing together. But underneath the surface all he could think of was that his family were the ones at the heart of this. He'd grown up as one of them until Grams got him out.

Deep down inside, where he'd been made the person he was now, it was the same as them. Those formative years.

The things he tried to overcome and change about himself now. The blood in his veins. They were poison, and he'd been infected with the same thing before he could even do anything about it.

And Stella could never know.

18

The car bounced over a speed bump out of the hospital parking lot. Beside Stella, Eric let out a hissed breath.

After waiting for Addie to pick them up, they'd been in the hospital getting poked and prodded for hours. Since they were both released, they were headed for her motel first. Stella had another prescription—she'd turned down the pain killers and opted for a low-dose sleeping pill she was on the fence about—and Eric had a temporary cast on his arm that was basically a bandage. His wrist was very swollen.

"Sorry." Addie looked at Stella in the rearview.

She nodded, even though that was probably for Eric more than her. It was becoming clearer that he didn't like hospitals. This time he hadn't come to see her. Considering how he'd been the last time that was probably for the best, and he'd been getting treated himself anyway.

"Do you guys want an update since you were admitted?"

Stella said, "Sure."

Eric stared out the window. Maybe just exhausted, or in pain. She didn't feel great but had no new injuries apart from bruises. Eric had saved her. They'd stood close, hugging while they waited for help to come.

Aside from needing a huge mug of hot water to drink, she was no more worse for wear than she'd been earlier.

Addie said, "Police and fire were dispatched to pull your car out of the river. Captain McCauley took your statement to a judge and got the sign off on a warrant for Ian Hummet's arrest. He's not getting away with what he did to you guys."

Stella had told Addie that Ian was the one who'd attacked her, as well as the one who tried to kill them just a few hours ago. She'd been thinking about it the whole time she was in the hospital, trying to put the dissonant fragments together in her mind.

Bridget.

Salvatore.

Aaron Hummet.

Joseph.

How it all fit together, she had no idea. Yet. But she planned to figure it out, and she hoped Eric would still be beside her to do it.

"So he's being arrested?" Eric shifted in the seat, grunted, and let out a breath. "Right now?"

"McCauley's got the warrant in hand. He's taking a couple of officers up to the camp first thing. No one wants to start a standoff, so they're hoping keeping it quiet will help."

"Could be dangerous for them."

Stella glanced over, wondering what he was thinking. She wanted to be there for him. It couldn't be easy having his own family in the middle of this. Plus, there was that thing he'd wanted to tell her, maybe even wrapped up in his reaction to her being in a hospital the last time.

She wasn't going to dig into his past on her own, so Eric was going to have to tell her.

The irony that she'd do that with him hit her. While with her dad she'd read all the case files and court transcripts and refused to speak to him. She figured at some point having Bob Davis in her life now meant they'd have to talk it through. But what was there to say when he was a dirty cop.

That part of his life had nothing to do with her.

His actions had no bearing. She refused to take that on, even when people at school—even the teachers—had acted like what he did meant she was bad as well. Like tattling on people, when she'd never done that, was the same as taking bribes and breaking the law.

Eric's family didn't have anything to do with the kind of man he was. Or his ability to be a great police officer, and an honorable guy.

"You guys worry about resting," Addie said. "Tomorrow we can have a meeting first thing and run down everything the taskforce has. McCauley will interview Ian and get to the bottom of whatever they might have planned."

Stella nodded.

"I don't suppose anyone would let me be the one to do that?" Eric asked.

Stella glanced at him, wondering if they could do it together. Before she could suggest that, Addie said, "Considering you're the one he tried to kill? I'm thinking I have a few things to say to him."

Eric's expression softened.

Stella knew they'd met before she came to town. Addie and Eric had formed a friendship, and now he hung out with Addie and her fiancé Jacob. Maybe the four of them could go on a double date.

Was that a crazy idea?

Dating seemed so benign after everything they'd been through. But it still sounded good. Like what a real couple could do, rather than the wasteland her love life seemed to have always been. "Do you know I've never been on a real date?"

Eric frowned. He started to speak but Addie's phone rang, and she tapped the dash screen. "This is Special Agent Franklin."

"This is Officer Gutierrez. I'm looking for Special Agent Davis and Officer Hummet?"

"They're here."

Eric spoke up. "Hey, Pablo."

"Oh…hey, dude." His voice filled the car speakers. "Listen, my partner and I responded to a call about a woman in distress. She's older. Says she's your grandma."

Stella reached over and touched Eric's fingers at the end of his bandaged arm. He shifted his hand like she'd burned him.

"Are you at her apartment?"

"No." Gutierrez rattled off an address.

Addie pulled over and typed it into her GPS. "Got it. We'll be there in a couple of minutes. Is she okay?"

"A little rattled by the look of it, but she'll only talk to Stella."

They signed off, and the guy hung up.

"Why does she only want to talk to you?" Eric asked.

Stella glanced at him, wondering what that tone was. "How should I know?"

"You knew about that Joseph guy being at her house."

"She's a nice lady."

He studied her.

Because he thought she had some kind of ulterior motive for going to his grandma's house? As if she would, when he was the one who'd pursued her. She'd only wanted to know if Edith spoke to Bridget at all. Did he think she'd been there fishing for information on his cousins? They hadn't even been on her radar yet.

Stella turned to ask Addie, "Did we find the gun used for Bridget's murder yet?"

Addie said, "We did. When her apartment exploded, I forgot to say. It was in the taskforce briefing the next morning though. Maybe you missed it, but the same gun used to kill her was listed with the stolen weapons. So we know it's the same batch, we just don't know who took them and where the rest are now."

"Could someone be planning to use them?" Stella recalled Joseph's words again.

Since he didn't have any idea what they were up to, she didn't either.

And how could they figure it out when Eric's cousins and uncle weren't going to let them in the camp.

Joseph could find out. Like some kind of inside man.

Stella figured her father also likely could. He certainly had the skills to infiltrate a place and feed back information. However, it was a condition of his parole that he wasn't supposed to associate with convicted criminals.

She'd have to trust the unknown. Until Edith explained who the guy was, and why they should trust him.

Stella tapped her phone on her leg. The minutes stretched long, but then they pulled into a strip mall parking lot.

Addie headed around the back.

"There." Stella pointed to where the black and white was parked at the far end between the store buildings and the fence on the other side. Wide enough two cars could pass, but barely. And only between the dumpsters.

Addie pulled over.

Stella and Eric shoved their doors open. She wondered if he would start running just to get there before her and frowned as she walked after him, feeling every one of her bruises. There were several hours until dark. She wasn't sure if she would make it until then before she had to go to sleep.

"Grams?" Eric crouched.

Stella heard an inhale. She looked over his shoulder and saw Edith Hummet sat with her back to the wall, on the ground in the alley. "Do you want to stand?"

She rounded Eric and held her hand out.

Edith frowned. "What happened to you two?"

Stella glanced at the cops and mouthed, *Ambulance?*

The cop said, "She refused our offer."

Given everything that'd happened this week, Stella still figured she was making the medical staff and first responders earn every penny of what they were paid. "Edith, do you need to see a doctor?"

"No, dear." She gave Stella a small smile. "I'm not the injured one."

Eric said, "We're fine."

"So Ian didn't try to kill you?"

Eric closed his mouth.

Edith said, "Mmm."

Stella crouched. "Can we help you up?"

"I didn't fall. I was just sitting, hiding here. Peeking around and listening."

And now she needed help to get up? Stella held Edith's elbow and assisted her to stand. While Edith got up Stella said, "Did you discover anything interesting?"

Eric held her other elbow with his good hand, frowning. She couldn't figure out why he looked kind of mad and kind of disappointed. He needed to get over whatever it was pretty quickly or they were going to get distracted. Edith wouldn't open up if she thought there was something up with Eric that she needed to sort out—because she was the kind of grandma who waded into her grandson's issues.

Probably with guns blazing. After all, she was out here, wasn't she?

"Actually, I did," Edith said. "I'm not sure how much it's going to help though."

"Do you want to sit somewhere and tell us."

"I was sitting, dear."

Stella smiled. "I won't make you get in the back of the police car."

"Might be fun. You think they'd arrest me so I can take pictures? My friends will get a kick out of it."

Eric's expression shifted a fraction. "You want them to take a mugshot and get your fingerprints?"

"Maybe not." Edith frowned at the cops, now talking to Addie.

Stella couldn't hear what they were saying. "Addie's car?"

Eric nodded.

Stella said, "Did you know your friend Joseph is at the camp, snooping around?" When Edith said nothing, she continued, "Is that why you're here? What were you doing?"

"I'll get to that," Edith said. "Let me sit."

They walked with the older woman, not really helping her. Stella figured she'd just been stiff, unable to get up on her own. She might have fallen but didn't walk like she was hurt. Someone had called the police—or Edith phoned with an anonymous tip about herself just so she could get them to come rescue her.

Eric pulled open the door. "Did someone hurt you?"

Edith shook her head.

Stella gave her elbow a tiny squeeze. "Where's your purse and phone?"

Maybe she'd been mugged but didn't want to admit it.

Edith said, "My phone slid too far under the dumpster."

Stella got her sat in Addie's front seat, sideways so her white sneakers touched the ground. She went back to the dumpster and laid down. She could just about reach the phone and tried to hide all her aches and pains as she got up again and brushed herself off. Considering she was still wearing the same clothes from the crash, mostly dry when she put them back on at the hospital, more dirt didn't factor that much.

Edith took it from her. "Thanks. I got a recording I can send to Addie, since it was still going when it slid under the dumpster."

Stella said, "A recording of a conversation?"

Edith nodded. "I couldn't see their faces, but I got audio. They were talking about a bomb."

Eric swayed. Stella reached for him, but he moved to lean against the car. "Grams, did you just say *bomb*?"

One had already gone off.

Stella said, "You mean *another* bomb."

19

"I know you got a recording." Eric watched his grams as he settled onto the couch, closest to her recliner. Sure, she said she was fine, but it wasn't like he would take her word for it. "But I want to hear you tell it. The doctor isn't here yet."

"I don't feel well." She closed her eyes.

"Am I supposed to believe that?"

She opened her eyes, but they narrowed on him. "I didn't have to let you stay."

Eric blew out a long breath and eased back. He laid his head back and closed his eyes.

"Maybe *you* should talk about someone we know, and what all that stony silence was in the car."

"I think a bomb is a bit more pressing."

"Men always want to avoid talking about relationships."

"I'm not—" He caught himself before he lied. "It's complicated."

"What's the problem with you and Stella?"

Eric reached up with his good hand and swiped it down his face. "It's never going to work."

"Because you've decided that. Not because you gave it a chance and then found out there are problems afterward."

"So we avoid the pain? What's the big deal?" It seemed like a far better idea to him than going through misery and a breakup. "Can we please talk about the bomb now?"

He wanted to ask why she'd been out there investigating. It certainly wasn't happenstance that she'd stumbled across a terror plot on her afternoon walk…twenty-six miles from the apartment.

"There were two men. They walked past where I was hiding, and they mentioned the bomb."

"Just by coincidence?" Eric asked carefully, not with judgment. Since Addie and Stella had brought up his lack of experience questioning people, he'd been more aware of his deficiencies than ever. Not to mention the "victim" status he seemed to have been saddled with despite his position on the taskforce.

Eric was fast losing the grip he'd had on what he wanted. It felt like he'd taken more steps back than forward lately. Even with everything that had occurred between him and Stella. Namely the kissing they'd done. How he'd effectively made his feelings clear, and she hadn't flat out turned him down. In fact, she'd leaned into him when he invited it. Taken solace in his arms.

He had to contend with being the cousin of the men the taskforce was trying to take down. Soon enough she was going to realize he was their family, and all that meant. She would ask around, or dig into his background. If he didn't tell her. Stella was going to discover he had lived at that camp until he was six.

Until Grams came and got him, and his mom was finally taken to hospital.

"Of course it wasn't coincidence." She huffed. "I

followed the older one for six blocks until he met up with his younger friend."

"You're sure they knew each other?"

"They spoke comfortably. I'd guess they at least respect each other, although the younger definitely deferred to the older."

"Did you recognize their voices?" He wondered if the younger was Nigel.

She shook her head. "Neither were familiar, but I don't get out much."

"Sure. That's why you were at the spa the other day, and across town today. Are you going to still be trying to convince me of that next week when you're on vacation in Aruba?"

Edith chuckled. "You always did have a sense of humor."

He was about to object when Edith's phone beside her chair rang. No one had a landline these days, except residents in this building. Mostly it was only for the security guard downstairs to call up announcing the arrival of a guest, though he'd heard other residents used an app.

Edith only had a flip phone. He was only slightly convinced it was due to her age and not that she thought a burner phone with no GPS tracker was better than a smartphone that knew her every move and recorded everything she said or did. She'd been adamant about that. Eric hadn't had the strength to mount a full-blown argument with her.

"Thank you, dear." She hung up. "The doctor will be here momentarily."

Eric had never met Edith's doctor who did house calls. She refused to be taken to a hospital. A private lab was the only people who ever saw her blood, if her doctor didn't do the tests himself. Her life was something he'd grown accustomed to.

Once, in the middle of the night after he'd awoken from a nightmare, she'd explained a few things to him. How he couldn't ever tell anyone what he'd seen. How the way she lived was for their protection.

If he told Aaron, or his cousins, they would likely laugh. But then they'd never cared what was right in front of their faces.

Maybe they just didn't want to see.

Edith—and everyone she cared about—would be in serious danger if they did.

There was a knock on the door. Eric strode to it and nearly grabbed the handle before catching himself and using his good hand. He'd refused a sling for his casted arm, but maybe that was a bad idea.

"Hey."

The doctor looked down him, then up. "Eric Hummet?"

"Yeah, but this isn't about me."

Dr. Windermere, Edith's personal and private doctor, frowned. "And her condition?"

"Much better than mine." Eric smiled. "Thankfully."

He stepped back, and Windermere entered. The man had gray hair and a distinguished air to him. He wore a suit and expensive-looking shoes but didn't come across as uppity. Which was good, because Eric didn't like people who thought they were all that. Usually they were hiding insecurity, or criminal activity. In his line of work it was usually both.

Eric caught a look at the two men in the hallway.

The one with huge shoulders and ice-blue eyes lifted his chin. "We'll stay out here."

The guy next to him had light-brown skin and was dressed like those cargos, boots, and T-shirts were a uniform. Neither of them was men he'd want to meet in a dark alley. At least not without a SWAT team behind him. Or in front of him.

The blue-eyed one lifted his chin.

Both turned to Grams' neighbor's front door and knocked, odd looks on their faces. The door opened and the occupant launched out the door. Eric braced for a second, thinking a fight was about to erupt.

The big man grunted. The blond, his grams' neighbor—Eric thought his name might be Isaac, though he'd never met the guy—gripped the big guy in an intense bear hug. The dark-haired one wrapped his arms around both of them and laughed.

Eric got the feeling he was intruding, just watching them greet one another like long-lost brothers or one of those videos of military heroes returning home and surprising their families.

He closed the door so he didn't get caught watching, even though he'd never had a moment like that in his life.

He likely never would unless Edith took on one of her old jobs and went on a mission. As if that was a good idea. Not that she couldn't do it. Just that…

Eric shook his head. It had been more than twenty years since she did that.

He needed a nap. But then at this point he was going to dream of Stella returning from war and the two of them having a hot and heavy reunion.

Not a good way to wake up.

He trailed to the kitchen and poured a mug of coffee. In the living room he said, "Coffee, Doc?"

Windermere smiled. "I'm good, thank you." He lifted a stethoscope to his ears and Eric turned to the couch.

He sat while Grams got her lungs listened to. The doctor did a few other things, like checking her wrists and elbows by rotating them. Shining a light in her eyes. He watched her take a few steps to check her mobility, and Grams even did a couple of squats with her arms out straight in front of her level with the floor.

Eric said, "Did we waste your time?"

Windermere shook his head and sat on the couch. "It's never a waste checking on my favorite patient."

Grams motioned to the doctor's left hand. "When did that happen?"

"A few months ago." Windermere smiled. "Maggie finally agreed to make an honest man out of me."

"She had a long road. A woman like that? She's worth the wait."

"Yes." Windermere nodded. "She was and is."

Eric felt his eyes drift closed. He hadn't realized he was so exhausted, but it didn't surprise him that it caught up to him.

"How's he doing?" Windermere asked.

"In a similar predicament," Grams said. "Maybe he's unaware, but everything he's been through is causing him to hesitate. Question when he should make the leap and let love catch him. The way Maggie had to find the strength to do with you."

"This woman of his is worth it?"

"Definitely." Grams chuckled. "She's an FBI agent."

Windermere chuckled. "He'll have his hands full."

"That's why I was helping out. They're into something big." She sighed. "There's another bomb in play here in Benson. I don't know what the target is, but this could be bigger than a taskforce."

"Do you need the boys to help out?"

"I thought they were just here to surprise Isaac."

Windermere said, "They could stick around for a day or two. Do some digging."

"I have some additional help I can employ. We should be fine, but thanks."

Eric tried to fight his way from sleep, but the fatigue dragged him into its depths until he couldn't swim anymore.

When he awoke, he was alone.

Eric felt like an old man, trudging to the bathroom and back. The clock on the microwave said 03:27, so he didn't go looking for Edith.

He heated coffee in the microwave and looked out the window. The thickness of the glass blurred his vision until his eyes crossed and he had to struggle to focus. But he could see a van parked on the street. So far below, maybe it wasn't anything but an ordinary van.

Eric wasn't going to leave anything to chance. He could call downstairs, but it would seem silly to make a big deal out of it if it was nothing. It wasn't like he'd seen anything suspicious, or they even knew what kind of vehicle they were supposed to be looking for, or anything about another bomb. It was likely nothing.

He found his shoes and hit the elevator, sipping from the mug of coffee. Thinking about what his Grams had said about coincidence. She'd gone out looking for an answer to what their family was up to. Taking the onus on herself to help because she could.

Kind of like Eric was doing now.

And why not? She'd taught him exactly that when she raised him to take care of the people around him. To step in when it was needed and do what was right.

The night security officer at the front desk was reading from a hardback book. She looked up as he approached. "Help you?" She blinked. "Officer Hummet, yeah?"

"Yeah. I don't know if it's anything." He headed for the glass lobby doors. "Might be nothing."

"Your instincts flaring?"

"Probably just the remnants of a bad dream." He stared out through the glass at the white van parked across the street. "How long has that vehicle been there?"

"I'll check the cameras." She headed back to her desk. "It wasn't there half an hour ago when I looked."

Eric took another sip. He turned back to look at her feeds as well.

The explosion hit the front of the building. Glass shattered. The blast battered his back, and Eric skidded for a couch. He ducked behind it, shielded from the debris long enough he could catch his breath. "Call 911!"

20

Stella straightened, let out a long breath and surveyed the street in front of her. She ran her hands through her hair and realized she still wore the gloves she'd been using for evidence collection.

The sun had risen enough it reflected off the glass of the bank building, but she couldn't see it above the high rises of downtown.

People milled around everywhere. Fire department trucks had sprayed the whole area with a foam to put the flames out and contain the chemicals spread by the blast. Who knew what contaminants the explosion had blown out onto the street? But that wasn't her purview.

Stella was here to figure out who had left a van with a bomb in it on a city street. The same person—presumably for now—who had done the same with Bridget's apartment.

Addie strode up to her, looking as grimy as Stella felt but far more put together. "Anything new?"

Stella said, "Plenty more fragments of the bomb we can add to the collection headed to the lab for testing."

"Still no organic material?"

Stella shook her head. "There was no one in the van when it went off."

"That's good, I guess."

"Or it was purposeful."

Addie shifted and lifted a hand in a wave. Stella glanced over her shoulder and spotted Addie's fiancé behind the police tape in the crowd of onlookers.

Stella said, "You need to go?"

"I might say hi for a second, but I'm not leaving. He knows I'm in the thick of it."

Addie's fiancé, Jacob, was a photographer famous for a coffee table book. He had a flexible schedule and seemed content to drop by the FBI office whenever the desire arose —usually when Addie had planned a lunch break. He'd brought Chinese takeout once when they were working a case late into the evening.

Addie attended church with him, the same one Eric went to.

Stella didn't want to think about the curiously absent police officer right now. He'd been in the lobby when the bomb blew, but she knew he was unhurt. Eric was thrown by the blast the same as she had been—something she didn't like.

Though, why it mattered more that it happened to him she couldn't say.

The fact Addie and Jacob were making a relationship work had more to do with the fact they'd been through the worst of experiences together. They'd fought their way to being together and wouldn't let that be pulled apart for anything.

Maybe it worked because Jacob wasn't a cop, or anything to do with that life.

Stella wandered through the explosion site again while Addie went to talk with Jacob. Behind the tape on the far side she spotted Lyric Thompson, a cabin owner Stella had mistakenly arrested—and apologized for. She stood with Isaac, one of Addie's confidential informants.

Lyric and Isaac leaned against each other, and he had his arm around her. They spoke with two men. Big guys dressed like private security, or the kind of guys she'd seen working as military contractors in Iraq and Afghanistan when she'd done a couple of investigations overseas a few years ago.

Whoever they were, they were both tall. One had big shoulders. The two of them made her think about Eric, mostly because she preferred his lean build. He wasn't intimidating the way these two were.

Stella returned her attention to the bomb since that was more important right now than her love life. Or lack thereof.

She headed for her duffel and pulled out the tablet she carried with her. No point packing a laptop all the time.

Stella did a web search and looked at the buildings around her on both sides of the street. The van had been parked in front of a bus stop that shattered with the blast, sending a shockwave of Plexiglas into a coffee shop.

Around them were the residential building owned by Jacob, Addie's fiancé. A couple of companies, including a startup for a new app that tracked spending. An investment firm. A couple of empty floors that used to be a cybersecurity company. A law office.

Considering the time of day the bomb had gone off, not that many people were at work. Mistake, or intention?

The target could've been Jacob's building and the residents in there—like Edith Hummet. And Eric himself. This could have been an attack on them, or a warning.

Did the bombers know Eric had stayed overnight?

Still, a better bomb would've been more strategically placed. Not that she wasn't grateful no one had been hurt.

All the damage was structural. Mostly this was a giant inconvenience.

However, it could point to a suspect with the means and motive to do this again in a way it would cause far more damage. Even loss of life.

Could they be looking at a serial bomber?

Captain McCauley came over at the same time Addie returned from talking to Jacob. McCauley said, "Did you get anything we can use to find these perpetrators?"

Stella blinked. "I wasn't aware we had proof it was more than one person."

"They must've mistimed the explosion." McCauley rocked back and forth on his shoes. "Or they could've killed someone with this, but thankfully they didn't, so now all we've gotta do is catch them."

Before Stella could say anything, Addie said, "Have your people found anything in their interviews of witnesses and local residents?"

"Got a janitor in the north side building." He pointed at the high rise above the decimated coffee shop. "He was cleaning the law office when the blast happened. Got knocked down but didn't see anything."

"And Officer Hummet?" Stella needed it to be natural that she asked about him. The last thing she wanted was for it to be obvious she was desperate to know where he was and what he was doing. "He was a witness as well, I believe?"

McCauley nodded.

Eric had been scarce already by the time she managed to drag herself out of bed and get here. She couldn't imagine how he was feeling considering he'd been in the lobby of Edith's building when the van exploded. He already had a broken arm from their trip into the river. Was he okay?

Addie said, "He was seen by Edith's doctor, who said he desperately needs rest. He's asleep right now."

McCauley nodded. "As soon as he wakes up, we'll get to the bottom of this. He must've seen something, or someone. Or why else would he be in the lobby?"

Stella winced. "I hope he can give us some information, but it's okay if he doesn't remember. Or didn't see anything. Who knows what drew him to the lobby? The security guard I spoke with said Eric came down because he had a weird feeling. That doesn't sound like witnessing something even if you can see the street from up there."

"When he wakes up, he can tell us."

Stella remembered the warrant. "Did you serve the arrest warrant for Ian Hummet?" She glanced between Addie and the captain, so it didn't seem like she was singling him out.

McCauley said, "We showed up, and he wasn't there. None of the Hummets were. The guys at the camp let us look around and said they'd call in when Ian showed up." He snorted. "As if we're going to believe that."

Stella said, "Now he knows we're looking for him."

If they thought they could find him before, they could kiss that goodbye. Ian would stay under the radar to avoid being caught by the police and hide until the heat died down. All the police had to do was wait the guy out and be ready for when he reappeared.

Addie looked around at the scene. "Do you think the Hummets had anything to do with this?"

"We still need to look at the surveillance cameras," Stella pointed out. They'd had to rush evidence collection because there was a rainstorm coming before lunch according to the local weather radar.

"Let's do that now." Addie motioned with her head to the front doors of Jacob's building.

Stella tried not to think too hard about the fact Jacob was so wealthy he owned the whole property, just from writing one coffee table book of photographs and stories about Native Americans, including his grandfather. Sure, he'd done other books since. And was apparently working on something different, about what he and Addie had been through.

She wasn't going to begrudge anyone else's success. Still, dwelling on it would wind up with her concluding things weren't fair. Nor were they supposed to be, so why be bothered by the inequalities that occurred naturally when people had all kinds of upbringings? Every child in the world had different opportunities and resources than even the child right beside them.

Then again, it was better than thinking about Eric.

She glanced over at Addie as they reached the building. "Is he really sleeping?"

Addie nodded. "The doc didn't want to give him something to make him sleep given his injuries, but he should rest."

"Good."

Addie squeezed her shoulder. "How about you?"

"Maybe the doc can give me something I can take tonight. Or after we figure out who did this and what on earth is going on right now." Stella shook her head. "Because I am so confused."

"Agreed. The camp? The Hummets, and Salvatore? Now another bomb? There's no way it's completely unrelated. Unfortunately it's more likely a portent of things to come."

"None of us wants a serial bomber setting explosions off around Benson." Stella bellied up to the front desk, where the security guard blinked at her. "Hey, you were in here when it exploded, right? How are you feeling?"

"Oh." The woman shifted a little taller on her chair. "I'm okay, thank you. They haven't said I could leave yet. Is that guy okay?"

Stella nodded. "He's resting. You should, too. I can make

sure they release you soon." Unless she was involved, of course. In which case she'd be resting in a holding cell.

Stella had often been told she assumed the worst in people and then looked for evidence to change her mind and prove her wrong. Instead of innocent until proven guilty, she forced people to validate their innocence, always assuming they were up to something.

For the first time in a very long time, she had opened herself up to the idea of a relationship. Right now she couldn't do anything about it. Eric had effectively shut her out. She didn't know what he was thinking, but he'd given her the cold shoulder after being rescued.

Stella had to just do her job, worry about her own health. Finish the investigation and solve the case. After that, hopefully they would both still be around and available to have that conversation.

For now she was just going to fall back on work. She knew how to do it well, and there were no emotions involved to get tangled up in.

Addie pointed at the computer. "Do you have surveillance feeds of the street in front of the building, where the van was parked?"

The guard nodded. Stella half expected her to say no, that it had been lost or they didn't have that angle. But the guard pulled up the video. "That guy asked the same thing, and we were looking at it right before the explosion."

The two of them came around the desk. Addie got herself a cup of coffee from the pod coffeemaker while the security guard pulled the digital video back to before the van arrived.

Stella said, "What time is that?"

The guard leaned in. "Time stamp says just after three in the morning."

"We're going to need a copy of this. Can you email the file, or burn it to a disk?"

The guard said, "I can have the security company send you the original. I don't have access to do anything but view it."

"Thanks." Stella smiled at her. "We appreciate it." She played the video, and they watched the van pull up. "That's a few minutes before the explosion. It was only sitting there undisturbed for a few minutes?"

The guard shrugged. "Meter maids don't get on until five."

Stella frowned. She'd already gotten several parking tickets in this city, mostly outside her gym.

The driver's door opened, and a guy got out. He beeped the locks on the van and strode away, like he was supposed to just leave the vehicle there and never come back.

"Do we know him?" the guard looked between Stella and Addie, eyebrows raised.

"Maybe." Addie frowned. "He looks familiar."

Stella knew exactly who it was. "Thanks for your help."

She and Addie headed for the front doors, now just a giant opening where the bomb had blown out the glass. "Seems like they wanted to make a statement. A warning."

"You don't think the bomb was a miscalculation?"

"I think they're warning someone to stay away." And she thought she might know who the intended target had been.

21

Eric tugged on his jeans and the clean T-shirt he'd found and headed to find out who was banging on his door. The wrist he'd had bandaged and splinted in place didn't feel good. Showering had been a pain. Once it was in the cast he hoped it felt better than this.

He tugged the door open.

Stella stood on his doorstep, her face flushed. She looked down at his bare feet. "You'll need shoes if you're going to come with me."

"Last I heard the FBI rushed off to follow up on a lead." That was when he'd woken up, just before lunch. He'd caught a ride with a couple of uniform officers he usually worked with on their lunch break and persuaded them to take him home on their way back to the precinct.

The normality of it had been stark after the last few days. Not just how they treated him the same as they always had. Even though it was now common knowledge that his family was the target of the taskforce, they didn't see him as anything but the cop they knew. It weirded him out as much as it was reassuring.

Eric had an email in his inbox that he'd been given a week's leave, but he'd just ignored it.

He should probably get kicked off the taskforce altogether. Talk about a conflict of interest. But McCauley hadn't called him back yet, so he had no idea where he stood.

Getting kicked off the taskforce and out of the police department altogether could get him into the camp, undercover of course. He didn't want to be the guy who was fired and then tried to get in with people who'd tried to kill him.

For the sake of justice, he would take the hit to his reputation.

Maybe that was the answer for the police department. Just being good cops, and doing the right thing, rather than continually trying to persuade the public they were better.

Stella waved a hand in front of his face. "I think you need more coffee."

"I was just about to get some." Eric needed to know why she was here so he could go back to resting without her filling his head with conflicting ideas. Getting him all twisted up about how she could possibly think he was a good guy after his cousin tried to kill them.

"Put it in a to-go cup and get your shoes."

He turned and headed for his kitchen. The front door closed and then her shoes tapped the floor behind him as she followed.

"Do you have two to-go cups?"

"You need some?"

She said, "Addie will be there."

"I'm supposed to be on leave." He pulled two thermal cups out of the cupboard below his coffee pot. "Where are we headed?"

"Where are your shoes? I'll get them for you."

"They're in the hall." He turned. "Stella, explain what we're doing."

"We haven't found Ian yet, but the taskforce is serving a warrant on Nigel."

He screwed the tops on both, then headed for his shoes. "Talk."

His laces were already tied, so he stuck his foot in and then wiggled it back and forth while she said, "Surveillance video from your grandma's building and a pharmacy a block down show the driver of the van that exploded was your younger cousin Nigel."

He stopped wiggling and looked at her. "You found him?"

"We got lucky. There's a BOLO out on him and Ian, and the officers sitting on Ian's house spotted Nigel climbing in the side window. They're sitting on the house until we get there. But at this point they'll probably have served the warrant before we show up."

"We're not on duty."

Stella shrugged. "And yet I seem to have been working today."

And that was his fault. Or, at least, the fault of his family. Which from where he was standing felt like the same thing. "Let's go."

He locked up his house, and she walked with him to the car, only glancing over once. She could've left him out of this, so he figured he shouldn't ignore that fact. As he buckled up he said, "Thanks for coming to get me."

She pulled away from his house. "I figured you wanted to be the one to talk to Nigel first."

"I can't believe he was the one who left the van there."

She shrugged one shoulder. "Maybe he didn't know what was in it. The bomb went off after he walked away from the van, but it doesn't look like was the one who did it. He's on surveillance walking away at the time. Hands by his sides."

Eric squeezed the bridge of his nose. "None of them has the experience to craft a bomb."

"It's not that hard to find plans on the internet." She glanced over. "You know what, maybe this was a trial run. Though with Bridget's apartment it would be the second test. Another explosion just to test what they made and see what happens. This could be someone learning."

"Great." An amateur could make more mistakes than someone who'd been an expert for years. "Or that was what Aaron was talking to Salvatore about. Does the club owner have someone in his employ with a background in making bombs?"

"Put that on the group thread." She motioned to his phone, tucked under the side of his leg.

Eric grabbed his coffee cup and downed half of it. After he got into the thick of this he wasn't going to have time to drink, or he'd be sick to his stomach unpacking what happened. "I'm so glad no one was hurt."

"It's a miracle. If you're inclined to believe in those things."

"Are you?" Eric said.

Stella shrugged one shoulder. "I've always thought it would be naïve to assume there was nothing more than what I can see and experience. There should always be some mystery in the world."

"Grams took me to church. It always made sense to believe that I was a sinner in need of a Savior." He'd felt the stain of sin even as a little kid, with all the things he'd seen and done. Even though he'd been in elementary school he'd wanted to be better. To accept forgiveness and belong to a new family. That had stuck with him, even while he tried to find a place he fit here on earth. First with the police department. Hopefully at some point with a wife and a family of his own.

"My mother would've called herself 'spiritual,' but it was like she believed so many things that none of them had any veracity. When I went to live with my grandmother she took me to her church. It seemed so foreign from anything else I'll admit I had a hard time with the structure, and all that time having to sit still when I'd rather have been outdoors. Getting all polished up on a Sunday to pretend you were good enough, and then you could do or say whatever you wanted all week."

"That's not Christianity."

"I'm getting that," she said. "And being around Addie, Jacob. You. Even Russ. It's helping me see that faith is just being honest about who you are, how you've failed, and how we all need help."

He wanted to talk more, but she pulled onto the street where his cousin's house was. The whole street was nothing but chain-link fences and weeds instead of lawns. Cracked sidewalks and aging houses. He didn't begrudge people what they could afford. A low income did not correlate with a person's ability to make the world a better place by being kind. If it did, a lot of people were in the wrong tax bracket.

As for his cousin, Eric figured the people in this neighborhood probably appreciated him as much as Eric did. They were probably looking for a way to get rid of him.

"He doesn't live up at the camp all the time?" she asked.

Eric shook his head. "Aaron does, but he has a cabin as well. Ian wanted to be closer to town and work at the garage, so he bought this place. Actually with his girlfriend at the time, but she left a few months after. Nigel has a place he crashes with friends, but no job and not much in the way of assets. I think he tends bar where they all hang out, though he's barely legal." He blew out a breath.

"How did you manage to make something of yourself?" She paused. "You could've been sucked into it so easily, but you're a good man who's nothing like them."

He blinked at the way wonder seemed to ring in her voice.

"Let's go. They're about to head inside." She was out of the car before he could say anything.

Eric shoved the door open at the same time armed police officers kicked the front door in. Addie, with her vest on, followed right behind them. A few seconds later the screen above the front door was kicked out. Nigel climbed onto the roof above the garage and looked around.

Eric saw him register exactly how many cops were here.

The kid had a pistol in one hand.

He was going to get himself killed.

Eric jogged over, feeling every one of his aches and pains and the shooting pains in his arm. He tucked the bandage against his stomach. Cops surrounded that section of the roof, most yelling for Nigel to throw the weapon and come down.

He eased between. "Hold your fire, guys." Eric called up to the rooftop. "Nigel, look at me."

His cousin shook his head, eyes wide. Swinging that gun around.

"Look at me, kid. It's Eric. You need to look at me." Eric eased forward a couple of steps, heading to where the path to the front door was. If Nigel moved to the other side of the garage, he wouldn't be able to see him or talk to him that well.

Eric prayed the kid would listen to him.

Prayed for the officers, and the outcome of all of this.

For everything in that moment, spoken and unspoken. All his hopes and dreams. Everything Nigel should get to do, and who he could be.

"Listen to me, Nige'." Eric hadn't used his cousin's nickname in a long time. "We can talk this out, but you're making all these cops nervous, so I need you to leave the gun on the roof and sit down. Talk to me."

He didn't even care if Nigel got down. Eric thought about climbing up there, but with one arm that wouldn't work.

"I can't. It's not..." Nigel paced the roof, but stayed close to Eric. "I can't get arrested."

"Why do you think I became a cop?"

"Because you're better than us."

"No. I decided to wear a police shield because I knew you'd need my help one day. That you'd need me to protect you. Because I wanted to be there when that happened." Eric paused. "I can help you. I just need you to trust me. The way I trusted Grams could help me."

Nigel wasn't born yet when Grams had rescued him from the camp. But he'd heard the story judging by the shift in his expression.

"Come down and let me help you."

Nigel stilled but didn't move.

Eric said, "It's why I'm here."

Nigel's gaze drifted to the other cops, who'd thankfully taken a step back with their lowered weapons.

"Leave the gun and come down, Nige'."

Nigel sat on the edge of the roof, set the gun aside, and hopped down twelve feet.

Eric stepped back to give him room.

A SWAT team member slammed into his cousin and tackled him to the ground.

Nigel squirmed, his head turned to the side as he glared up at Eric. "You lied to me! Liar!"

Eric shook his head. "I'm going to help you. That's not a lie."

Nigel screamed at him. "I don't need anything from you."

22

"Do you understand these rights as I have explained them to you?"

The young man leaned across the table. His lip quivered. "Yes."

Stella didn't let on how she felt about the sudden change in him. Nigel Hummet had been spewing all kinds of things since cuffs were slapped on, mostly in Eric's direction. Now the bravado had slipped. Or whatever drove him to fight against law enforcement had burned hot and fast. Now he had nothing. He was alone in police custody, with no one to support him.

Eric was in the viewing room with the new interim police commissioner. Listening to everything because he wasn't allowed in here—on either side of the table.

This was his family. She knew how she'd feel about it if it were her family being interviewed as possible terrorists. After all, her dad had gone to prison for what he'd done. Even if she'd been in elementary school at the time she understood what it would mean professionally for him. Her dad's partner had wound up resigning.

There was no way Eric should have to do that when his cousins and uncle were involved.

She wanted to suggest ways it might be turned into an asset but wasn't sure he was ready for that conversation.

"Good." Stella didn't open the file on the table in front of her.

Nigel Hummet was twenty-four. He worked part time, drove a brand-new pickup truck and had no steady relationship. His social media was a mess of party photos and dirt biking trips with his buddies. He was like a seventeen-year-old with the means to fund whatever he wanted to do.

The guy he was online didn't match the one who'd shown up at Eric's house, crying and desperate for help. Not surprising. It also didn't match this man—defiant and determined to keep his mouth shut.

"Why am I even here?" Nigel leaned back in the chair, looking like a high school kid who thought he was all that—and knew everything. Trying to pretend.

"That's a good question," Stella said. "Why do you think you're here?"

She was surprised he hadn't asked for a lawyer. Surely his dad would've coached him to handle a police interrogation like a pro. But he seemed to think he could handle this himself.

Nigel blew out a breath that kicked out the hair falling over his eyebrows. "Because I broke into Ian's house? Or the gun I had?"

"Maybe it's registered to you, and you were legally carrying it. Plus, I'd assume your brother is fine with you crashing whenever you want, right?"

Nigel shrugged. "You'd think so, since he's my brother."

"He doesn't let you?"

"I'm supposed to call first. Like I care what he's hiding." Nigel rolled his eyes, but Stella saw the hurt he couldn't hide.

"Could be he just doesn't want you to get picked up and questioned about what he's doing. You can be charged as an accessory." Stella kept her voice friendly. "He's probably trying to save you the hassle of being taken down with him."

"Like he would let himself get arrested?" Nigel said. "Eric wouldn't be able to trick him into coming down off that roof. He'd have gone out in a blaze of glory."

"Sounds like a good way to get dead. Not do what could save your life."

"And end up in jail for, like, ever?" He made a face.

Stella shrugged one shoulder. "That depends on what results from this conversation."

When she was in here, she had to leave everything outside this room beyond the door. She couldn't bring her personal feelings or issues into the interrogation room. Kind of like how Eric's feelings about what happened to his cousin couldn't factor. The same way how she felt about her dad didn't come into her work, or her dealings with the police department.

As much as she could leave it behind, anyway.

One of her family members was a convicted criminal—who wanted to get to know her, starting with dinner tonight. Same for Eric, if charges were filed against Nigel, and if they managed to find and arrest Ian. She had no doubt a hunt for Aaron would follow. His uncle would not emerge from this unscathed unless he'd made provisions to keep himself clean. There was still no way he wasn't dirty.

She'd lost her partner. Stella wasn't sure that Kyle's death would ever not factor. All this had started with finding out who was behind the attack that led to his death. She'd been injured as well, and no one could argue this wasn't personal.

And yet, the moment she started to dig a woman had been killed. Now things were far more complicated.

Was there really a terrorist attack in the works?

"So ask me questions." Nigel shrugged.

Stella wondered how extensively he had prepared to defend himself. "Sure you don't want to ask for a lawyer?"

"So I can get screwed over? No thanks."

She flipped open the file. "I'm not going to mince words here. I'll speak plainly, and I'd like you to do the same." She slid over a photo of him getting out of the van that came from the surveillance footage of the street in front of Edith's building. "This is you parking a van containing an explosive device outside a building where your grandmother lives."

He reacted to the last part where he'd had no reaction to the rest. "That old bag isn't family."

Stella shrugged. "So you had no qualms trying to blow up her building and kill her, then?"

If she could prove attempted murder it would only add to his charges. Then again, there were enough just with the terrorism. But she was under no dissolution that this guy was the mastermind behind it.

Nigel shifted in his seat like he wanted to jump up. "I didn't blow that van! I didn't even know there was a bomb in the back of it!"

When he didn't continue, she said, "So you drove it, but I'm supposed to believe you didn't even look in the back."

"That compartment was closed."

"And you didn't peek? At all?"

He said nothing.

"You just do whatever they tell you?"

Nigel swallowed.

Stella watched his throat bob.

"I didn't set off that bomb."

"And yet you knowingly participated in a terrorist attack."

His eyes widened. "That's not what it was!"

"So tell me. What was it?" Stella studied the minutiae of his reactions, knowing the video footage of this interrogation wouldn't show tiny detail like the flicker of the muscle under his eye.

Nigel looked to the side. He swallowed again. "Fine. I did what they told me."

"But you didn't want to."

"I think I was supposed to be in the van when it exploded. That's why they're ghosting me now, because I should be dead but I'm not. I've been cut loose. Shut out."

Stella bit the inside of her lip. This was what her father had gone through. She couldn't help the empathy for her dad, or for Nigel. No one should feel alone, even if they had done wrong. Especially if they regretted it.

She didn't care much for the sociopath. After all, why waste emotion on a person who felt nothing?

A scared kid was different.

Or her dad, who'd lost everything because his choices caught up to him.

"Why would they do that?" Stella wondered if it had anything to do with him showing up at Eric's, and then Eric and her being nearly killed when their car was pushed off the highway into that river.

Cleaning house? Maybe ahead of whatever they had planned.

Nigel groaned. He leaned forward and touched his forehead to the table.

She gave him a minute, and when he offered nothing she said, "When you showed up at Eric's, upset, what did you want to tell him?"

He sucked in a breath and sat back, tears in his eyes. "I messed that up."

"What happened?"

"I tossed the gun. How was I supposed to know Ian wanted me to bring it back so he could deal with it? He just told me to shoot her."

Stella forced herself not to react. She sat there, like he hadn't just admitted to murder.

Was it Nigel who had killed Bridget?

"Where did you toss it?" she asked.

"In a dumpster the trash truck missed, a couple of blocks away."

She imagined whoever was in the viewing room jumped up and went to instruct officers to search for the murder weapon. Stella said, "Did the gun come from the batch of military arms?"

He nodded.

"Did you shoot Bridget Caston?"

He stared at her, like he was deciding whether or not to say anything.

She found she was actually glad he did that. When the silence continued for a minute, Stella said, "If you perhaps had information I might be looking for. Something useful to the taskforce investigation currently underway. You might be able to bargain with that information. Make a deal in exchange for a reduced sentence for a murder I'm guessing was performed while you were under duress. Because your family forced you to do what they wanted and kill an innocent woman."

Surprise flared in his eyes.

She'd felt the same when she first heard about grace. She understood well the way it seemed almost too good to be true.

Nigel said, "Information like about the bomb?"

"No one was killed, so you can't be charged with an additional murder. You might have left the van there, but you didn't knowingly commit murder."

"I didn't want to know if there was a bomb in there or not, so I really didn't look."

Unfortunately that didn't mean he couldn't be charged. Stella said, "I can get the DA to talk to you about a deal in exchange for what you know about the camp. About what your dad is up to."

That Joseph guy—she didn't believe that was ever his real name, and even he indicated that—had told her they were up to something. He might be investigating as well, but she had her own methods.

"I could tell you about the other bombs."

Stella's stomach clenched. There were more? She swallowed. "I'd like to hear about them."

"And you'll get me off the murder charge?"

"That will be up to the DA at the end, I can make a strong recommendation based on your cooperation. Saving multiple lives will go a long way to compensating for shooting Bridget, if that's what you did."

"I only killed her because Ian told me I had to."

She wasn't entirely sure how true that would turn out to be. He could simply be a fantastic actor, and this was precisely how he'd been coached to respond to police questioning. Act like a young man who'd been browbeaten his whole life. Come across as sympathetic. Pretend like he had no idea he could make a deal.

For Eric's sake, she would do what he had done and give Nigel the benefit of the doubt. Extend some grace in the sense that she could try not assuming he was a guilty liar.

"Why did Ian need Bridget Caston to be killed?" Stella asked.

Nigel shrugged.

"I can't argue extenuating circumstances unless I'm aware of what they are." Stella shifted a couple of papers and slid over a photo of Bridget taken by the medical examiner for the file. "If you killed this woman, I need to know why."

23

Eric paced the hall, waiting for Stella to get his cousin to sign the written statement and come out so they could talk through everything Nigel had said in there.

He could hardly believe half of it. More bombs? Not only that, but Nigel was the one who'd killed Bridget.

He reached the end of the hall, tucked his arm against his front, and turned back. *More bombs.* His brain spun as he tried to work out what on earth Aaron planned.

"You gonna do that all day, Son?"

Eric quit moving. "Sir?"

Russ Franklin, the interim police commissioner, had shown up with his old prospector beard in full bloom, wearing khaki pants and a denim shirt. Not precisely what Eric would expect a man with his occupation to wear. But considering the former US Marshal was doing the mayor a favor in taking the position, maybe it was fine.

"Look, we all know someone we wish we didn't," Russ began. "Don't matter who it is, there's someone hanging on we should probably get rid of."

Eric frowned.

"So you don't like what your family does." Russ shrugged. "We do what we can to minimize the fallout if that's what's right, or we cut them loose to face the consequences."

"What did you do?"

Russ shrugged. "My sister's been the way she is since she turned ten. Never could figure out what was wrong with that girl. Seems like every time she had a kid, she thought it would settle her down. As if that's the cure for what makes her wayward. So I raised Addie, and I'm almost done raising Mona. Why would I complain? It was never easy, but the thought of those girls on the road with that woman?" He shook his head. "I never would've let that happen."

"So you stepped in and saved them?" Eric asked. When Russ nodded, he said, "That's what Grams did with me, getting me out of that camp. She saved my life."

The door to the interrogation room opened, and Stella came out.

"I've seen the file," Russ said. "Read everything I could on the history of that camp." He laid a hand on Eric's shoulder. "I'm sorry for what happened to you and your mom."

Eric's mind flashed with an image of his mother, tucked into the blankets in a hospital room. His ears rang with the unmistakable tone of a heart monitor flatlining. He took a step away from Russ and Stella, nearly stumbled, and fell against the wall.

Stella gasped and Russ started to speak.

But Eric held up a hand. "I'm good." He didn't need them coming any closer to him.

Frowning, Russ shifted his weight from foot to foot. "I'll leave you to it." He turned the corner at the end of the hall a couple of seconds later.

Stella spoke to a uniformed officer, probably instructing

him to return Nigel to a holding cell, then turned to Eric. "Come with me." She held out her hand.

Eric shook his head. "I don't want to talk about it."

Her hand lowered.

"Not here. Somewhere else." He winced. "I feel like I'm waiting for the right time, but maybe there isn't going to be one." He took her hand and held it in his. "No one needs to be around when I tell you. That's the only reason I'm pushing you off."

"Again." She gave him a pointed look. "This isn't the first time you've avoided talking about it."

Eric closed his eyes for a second as she squeezed his hand. "I'm sorry." He could argue things had cropped up every time he thought about telling her. Maybe he shouldn't put it off any longer.

He tugged her back into the viewing room and clicked the dial on the wall so they wouldn't be distracted by what was happening with Nigel.

There were two chairs, so he sat in one and waited as she settled beside him. Eric squeezed the bridge of his nose. If he told her, she would finally see that there was nothing down deep in him that was any good. She would walk away.

"What happened?"

Eric stared at the floor. "I grew up in that camp." He had to exhale a long breath. "My dad ruled the whole place like a king. No one crossed him." Edith had filled in some information when he'd gotten older. Eric incorporated it, so he wasn't telling the story from the point of view of a child. "My mom started informing on him to the DEA. The agents were apparently gung ho. My mom paid the price. My dad never forgot her betrayal."

She squeezed his hand. "I'm sorry."

"She would've liked you." He lifted his gaze to hers. "But she'd have needed you more."

Stella nodded, a soft expression on her face. But not pity. He didn't want to see that.

"When he found out what she was doing, he beat her nearly half to death. I don't know when Edith found out what was happening—or how—but he was wailing on me by the time she got there."

"She saved you."

"She shot him."

Stella gasped.

"Yeah. I might've been half unconscious and bleeding all over the place. Two broken ribs and a broken leg from where he stomped on me. But I saw her."

Eric could remember it all as well as any other indelible childhood event. Though normally he pretended he didn't.

"She stepped over me, a gun in her hand. She shot her own son." He shook his head. "Who knows what Aaron did with his body. But Grams got Mom and me to the hospital. Mom died a couple of days later. She was bleeding in her brain."

"And you went to live with Edith."

Eric nodded. "She already lived in Benson. Had for years ever since she quit..." He nearly said *CIA* out loud. After telling Stella everything else, it seemed natural to continue the story and just tell her all of it.

"There's more to the story?"

"That part isn't mine to tell."

"I'm sorry he was awful to you."

"That wasn't the first time," he said. "For either of us."

"How old were you?"

"Six."

Stella pushed out a breath between her teeth.

"Aaron wasn't much different with Ian, and then Nigel. But Grams couldn't get them out. Ian didn't want to leave, and they kept Nigel where she could never get to him." Eric didn't want to get into the weeds of it.

"Any idea where Aaron and Ian might've gone?"

Eric shrugged one shoulder. "I gave the captain all the information I have, and I know he talked to Edith, but I don't know how much she knows now. They were careful to keep her from the cap, and I barely saw them all these years."

His broken arm ached, but Eric felt the need to get up and move. He didn't want to be stuck doing nothing. Wallowing in the horrible past he'd had, and how he managed to turn out a halfway decent man when Ian was just like Aaron—and maybe Eric's dad. Eric didn't know how bad he was. They were working on infecting Nigel with it.

The interview room was empty now, but Nigel was in custody. That meant he wasn't too far from who they'd raised him to be. And yet, there seemed to be something in Nigel that they'd never managed to break.

He sighed. "I'd love to get out of here."

Stella looked at her watch. "I'm supposed to meet my dad for dinner in a couple of hours."

He could use a nap. "I've got an idea for after, if you want." When she nodded he said, "We have to talk to whoever is sitting on Salvatore, find out where he is."

"You want to talk to him?"

Eric nodded. "I want to know what he thinks about the fact my uncle took out a hit on Bridget. See what he has to say about her being a threat to the camp. He might know if she knew what they're up to."

"There could be a connection between her and your family. Maybe through Orlando Salvatore." Stella frowned. "Or he's going to retaliate when we tell him it was them. If he knows where Aaron or Ian are, we could follow."

"Exactly. Get the drop on him before it happens."

They headed back to the floor where the taskforce operated. Russ, the commissioner, was ensconced in McCauley's office. Eric glanced at Stella as they crossed to the white boards where they'd gathered all their information.

"So now we can put the motive with Bridget's murder." She looked at him after she spoke, and he saw warmth on her face. Not one ounce of recrimination for the stain of his past.

He hadn't explained all the ins and outs of the two days it took for his mom to succumb to her injuries, and the fact he hadn't left her side because Edith had been dealing with the police and social services. She'd even had to meet with a judge so she could work on adopting him officially. He had no idea what she'd told them about where his dad was, or the fact he was dead—though she'd likely omitted the part where she'd been the one who murdered him.

Stella got a whiteboard marker but didn't move to write the motive down. There was a question of whether the murder was even related to the taskforce case, so the information was off to the side. Relegated to peripheral beside stolen weapons.

Including enough components to make a bomb?

Now they knew for sure since uniformed officers had recovered the gun and it was being matched to the bullet.

She turned to Eric. "Thank you for telling me what happened."

He nodded.

"I'm sorry your family is caught up in this. That can't be easy." Stella turned away and made some notes. She'd have to write a full report of her interview with Nigel and what her recommendation was for charges that should be brought and everything for the DA to consider.

"Do you…" She turned, a tentative expression on her

face. "Do you want to come with me to dinner, with my dad?"

"You want me there?" Eric wasn't sure what that said about their relationship—whatever it was between them—or if she just wanted a buffer. He shrugged. "'Cause I could eat."

She glanced around, then moved closer. "I would like you to go with me and meet him. Since he wants us to get to know each other, you might as well be there." Her fingers tentatively touched the T-shirt over his hip.

Eric wanted to kiss her. He wasn't about to do that in the precinct.

The skin around her eyes flexed. She felt it, too. The attraction between them hummed in the air. Like it had in his foyer when he'd kissed her.

Eric wouldn't do it here, but the need swept through him anyway. "Later?"

Stella chuckled. "So sure of yourself." She replaced the whiteboard marker. "Dinner. Then Salvatore? It'll be a busy evening."

"We can make time."

Stella's chuckle burst to full out laughter he hadn't heard since before Kyle died. He saw the feeling, and the realization wash over her.

"It is okay."

"I know." She nodded and had to swipe away a tear from the corner of her eye. "Things are moving on, and it's good."

He was glad she thought so. He wasn't past the worry of how she—or anyone—might view him when his family was so wrapped up in this. But now that Stella knew the worst thing about him, he felt a little lighter. The knots around his chest a little looser.

Things might actually turn out okay.

If they could find that bomb and end this.

24

"What else did he say?"

Stella leaned back in the booth seat, feeling the flicker of amusement tug at her lips. As if there was anything funny about this situation. Her dad had jumped into learning about her life. She'd glossed over Kyle, not wanting to make dinner about her grief.

Instead, she and Eric had laid out the case when it seemed her dad wanted to also jump into helping them think it through.

Eric said, "Just that there were bombs."

Her dad wrote the word on the napkin he was using to make notes. He underlined the S. "The apartment and the one in the van, or more than that?"

Stella said, "We don't know."

Beside her on the bench seat Eric shifted. He had his bandaged arm in his lap, and his movement reminded her just how close to her he was. She liked it a lot. Things were happening between them. She didn't exactly know why she'd invited him along, except that having a buffer made seeing her dad a whole lot less scary.

As did talking about work.

"Do you miss it?" she asked.

Her dad scratched at the stubble on his jaw. He didn't seem anything like the man she remembered from before he went to prison. "Sure, I do." His smile was hesitant. "I actually wrote to a couple of newspapers with tips about cold cases they reported on. Kind of pointed them in the right direction."

"Really?"

He nodded. "One wrote back. Said I cracked the whole case."

Stella felt her eyebrows rise.

Eric nudged her. "That's great."

"How did it go with your job interview?" She realized she'd forgotten to ask.

Her dad grinned. "I figured they'd shut me out when they put it together who I was. But I guess it's something they do, giving people second chances."

"What company?" Eric glanced between them.

"Vanguard Investigations." Her dad grinned. "So it turns out they heard from one of the reporters what I did. They take a lot of cold case investigations, missing persons, and stuff no one else can solve. Things with no leads, or the investigation was corrupted." His smile widened. "They want me to start Monday, and if it works out, they're going to have me head up a whole department. Put together an investigative team."

Stella said, "Wow."

Eric didn't react the same way.

She continued, "That's great, Dad. I hope it goes really well."

"Me, too, darlin'. It'll be great to get back to doing right again."

She wondered if Eric had dealings with Vanguard Investigations before. Maybe he knew something about them that she didn't, because while everything she heard was good, she also hadn't heard much. Right now there was no time to dig deep on them. She'd have to look into it soon if she wanted to know.

In the end, it was his life. Kind of like with Eric and his family. They couldn't make or break his career because that wasn't fair to him. He had to own his life, and if that meant taking them down, he'd do it because he was a good cop.

"I could do some digging on this." Her dad tapped his index finger on the napkin. "Ask around, see if I can find out anything."

"We actually have a plan to do the same tonight." Eric's tone wasn't entirely flat, but it was clear he didn't think they needed her dad's help.

She said, "We'll let you know if anything comes up."

Given the fact Aaron and Ian had gone to ground, and no one knew where to find them, even Eric couldn't go in and try to draw them out. Everyone was now far more concerned about the prospect of another bomb. If the first ones really had just been a test, that was a scary prospect. Whoever set it intended to bring more destruction to Benson. No one wanted to see innocent lives lost. A community targeted and torn apart.

Her dad nodded. "Sounds good. I don't start work for a couple of days, so I'm free."

"Thanks, Dad." She wanted her dad in her life. He was her only shot at extended family.

But getting her hopes up had never helped her before. She'd rather be firmly rooted in reality. It probably had a lot to do with how she viewed faith in God. She'd been hesitant to trust because of her track record of things she put her hope in actually paying off.

"We should head out." Eric slid from the booth and held out his hand to her dad. "It was really nice to meet you."

"You, too." Her dad didn't call him Son or anything else. He just kept it light, friendly, and respectful.

Stella got up. She moved to stand beside her dad's seat, put her hand on the table, and leaned down to kiss her dad's cheek.

He seemed surprised.

"I'll see you soon?" She decided his tactic was a good one.

"Sure, darlin'."

"Bye." Stella tucked her hand into Eric's elbow, and they headed out. Before they got to the car she said, "So what do you think?" and braced for whatever his reaction was going to be.

Eric beeped the locks on his truck. "I think I don't want you to get hurt. I want to go slow and see what he's like, get to know him." He stopped by the vehicle and turned to her. "Before I trust him fully. Because there's no use getting your heart broken."

Stella lifted to the balls of her feet and kissed him. "Thank you."

He frowned. "For caring?"

"Not that many people have. Not about whether or not I get my heart broken." She scrunched her nose. "Kyle did, but more like an irritating older brother who threatened to break legs if I was hurt."

Eric smiled. "He was a good guy."

She let out a long breath. "Yes, he was."

The intel they'd gotten from the officers surveilling Francisco Salvatore indicated he was currently inside the club. Probably taking care of things since Orlando had run the place—though her impression of the guy was that he'd been more flash than substance. Maybe the older Salvatore was fixing his dead son's mess.

Either way, they needed to go in if they wanted to talk to him. And a club meant they had to change.

Half an hour later when they entered the club, Stella had on a tiny black dress and sky-high heels she hated because they were already painful. And the low-key irritation of hurting feet meant she was irritated before she even checked her coat at the desk.

The only good part was that Eric had on dark jeans and a pressed blue shirt. He opted to keep on his jacket, probably because it mostly covered the fact his arm was in a splint and bandaged.

"You gonna stare at me, or are we going in?" A smile played on his lips.

"I'm not going to answer that. We'll get no work done."

He slid an arm around her waist and whispered close to her ear. "So I don't get to tell you how I feel about that dress?"

Stella chuckled. "If you ever want me to wear it again instead of just throwing it out, sure."

"That'd be a crying shame." He kissed her.

She didn't mind, since it solidified their entry as a couple and not as two cops. Members of a taskforce.

They needed to get past security, through the crowd on the dance floor and the bar, which was four people deep with customers. The place might actually be more popular since Orlando's death.

She turned to Eric and slid her hands over his chest to link her fingers behind his neck. "Over there."

"Care to be more specific?"

When she could feel his body pressed against hers? They were going to have to be careful when the attraction flared like this between them. She knew how he felt about morality, and how his faith meant he lived life in a way that would seem contrary to so much of society these days. But the fact was, his traditional values were a huge part of what she liked about him.

Stella closed her eyes and pictured the room. "My eight o'clock. Employees only door."

"The one guarded by two security guys?"

She opened her eyes. "Yep."

"Guess we need to make a scene. Draw them away."

"Without you getting in a fight and getting hurt more than you already are." When his expression started to change, she realized that made it seem like she thought she had to baby him. "Neither of us needs more injuries."

"True."

"I've got an idea," she said. "How much cash do you have on you?"

"For this? I packed heavy."

"Okay, let's go flash it around and see what business we can drum up."

They waited until one security guard wandered off. She sashayed up to the other guy, drawing his attention from Eric to her. "Hey, baby."

She held onto Eric's good hand, needing that tether, and got real close to the guy. "Where does a girl go for a real party?"

The security guard said, "Depends what you're looking for."

"I wanna feel shiny. But I've got an after party at my house later, so I need enough for everyone. So all my friends can have some." She needed not to get directed to someone selling hand to hand on the club floor. She had to get in this hall.

The guy keyed his radio. "Two coming in."

"You should come to my party."

He opened the door for them.

"I'll save you some of the good stuff." She kept up the sashay, tugging Eric along with her into a dark hall. The door clicked shut, and the noise from the club muted. Dim lights lit the long hall.

Stella tugged her gun from the holster on her thigh.

Eric watched, his eyebrows raised.

"Where else was I gonna put it?" Before he could comment and get them both in dangerous territory, she said, "Let's go."

The door on the left started to open. She grabbed the edge of it and shoved it wide. The thump and exclamation told her she'd hit whoever was coming out. She shoved it again, hard and fast, and heard them slump to the floor.

Then she worked her way down the hall, opening doors and clearing rooms. Looking for Francisco.

He was behind the desk in the last office.

"Guy like you might want to hire more security."

He lifted a gun from the desk. "Why would I need to do that, Special Agent Davis?"

Okay, so he knew who she was.

"And Officer Hummet." Francisco motioned with the gun. "Both of you, do come in. Shut the door and put your guns on the floor."

No way was she going to do that, and no cop she knew would ever do it either. She returned hers to its holster. Eric slid his back in the holster in his jacket.

"Clip it down."

Eric fastened the strap, securing the weapon. Francisco could shoot them before they drew their guns, so he'd probably believe he had the upper hand here.

She said, "We need to talk to you."

"That's why you broke into my club? You could have called."

Before Stella could start in with her questioning, a massive boom rocked the building. Dust rained from the ceiling, and it seemed to list to the side.

For a split second she just stood there. Then she twisted around to Eric, who looked as wide-eyed as she felt.

"What is happening?" Francisco yelled.

Stella, Eric mouthed. Then he said, "Bomb."

25

The building seemed to take a breath. Then after a second of dead silence where he could've heard a piece of paper fall to the floor, the whole place began to shudder. The aftermath of whatever shockwave just slammed into the building now trembled in the walls and the ceiling. Eric's brain began to assimilate what had just happened.

Another bomb, here at the club.

He sprinted across the room and grabbed the door handle, the altercation or whatever had been with Salvatore forgotten in the wake of what was happening outside this room. They'd come here for answers, but all that went out the window if people were injured or hurt.

The lights in the hall flickered and went out, plunging everything into darkness.

He felt Stella's touch on the back of his jacket as he looked out into the hall. The door to the club at one end of the hall bowed in, cracked down the middle by the explosion. Beyond it he could hear screaming. Crying. The music had shut off, but the sound of the building groaning replaced it, almost reaching the same decibel level. Behind that door sounded like a nightmare.

He moved toward it.

Still in the office, Francisco yelled out, "The phones are down. Surveillance as well. We don't have any cameras." He shoved his way past them into the hall. "The exit is down here."

Eric grabbed the back of the guy's shirt. "Not so fast."

Francisco whirled around. "You can't possibly think we're going to stay in here!"

"You're sticking around to answer a whole lot of questions," Eric said. "So don't think for one second about running off."

"He's right," Stella said. "You're with us." She turned to him. "Should we see if we can get in there?"

Eric shook his head. "I don't want to open the door and risk a structural collapse. Not without the fire department here." He dug out his phone and called 911, but the line was busy. "I'm guessing they know. Let's get outside."

Stella moved to the door for a peek in. She turned, her face pale. "There are a lot of hurt people in there."

"Come on." He led her and Francisco to the door, and Stella pushed out first. His arm hurt, but not enough he needed her to do the heavy lifting for him.

They jogged around the building to the front. When they rounded the corner, Eric pulled up short. Stella put out a hand and touched his front, whispering words he couldn't hear for the rushing in his ears.

The front of the club looked like a warzone. Bodies, debris from the building, and destroyed cars littered the asphalt in front of what had been the doors.

A fire truck with a ladder on top bumped into the parking lot. The lights cut through his head like a migraine, and his ears suddenly registered the sound of sirens. He went to the closest person, knelt, and touched two fingers to the guy's neck to check for a pulse.

Nothing.

Given the guy's injuries, that might have been for the best.

The world rushed back into focus, and he realized he could hear chaos. Screaming. Sirens. People shouting.

Salvatore was ten feet away. Leaving.

Eric rushed over, grabbed his arm, and spun the guy back.

The fist came out of nowhere.

After just barely getting his head out of the way before Francisco's punch connected with his cheekbone, Eric retaliated with his good hand and slammed his fist into Francisco's stomach.

The older man doubled over.

"You're not going anywhere." Eric wanted to get inside, but the firefighters were already headed to the doors to go in. They had the expertise and the equipment.

Another fire truck, this one with no ladder, bumped into the parking lot.

Eric shook his head. "Who would do this?"

"You don't know?" Francisco paused. "Maybe you're not very good cops."

Eric continued, "So you're at war with my uncle?"

Stella shifted closer to his side, her face still pale. Maybe more than before. Was she in shock?

"You think I'm a target?" Francisco sniffed. "I'm still alive."

"They wanted to destroy your business, is that it?" Stella got closer to the guy, rallied by her drive to do her job. She often fell back on that mode, and he didn't think that was bad. She was good at what she did. If it kept her going until she was in a place she could fall apart later, that was fine.

Eric moved so he could get between them if he needed to. As soon as some cops arrived, he was putting Francisco in the back of a police vehicle and then going to help everyone inside. Later he and Stella could cling to each other while they worked through the emotions they had to stuff down right now.

Francisco huffed.

Stella asked, "Was there anyone of note inside the club who might've been the primary target?"

"How should I know?" Francisco replied.

Eric spotted something in his expression, besides the distaste for her questioning. "You know. Who was it?"

This person could have been the target here, rather than the club itself or people in general with the bomber going for the maximum casualties possible. Unlike the previous explosion, this one had surely killed a lot of people. Injuries. More would be added to the toll in the next few days.

The target can't have been Eric, Stella, or Francisco.

"Talk." Eric pointed at the club. "So we can get in there and *help save people's lives.*"

"I'm not going in there."

"Then talk." Stella set her hands on her hips.

"The finance guy for the mayor's office was inside." Francisco turned to Eric. "You tell me if he had some beef with your uncle. I don't see why I'd know, so don't bother interrogating me or whatever you call this farce of policing."

Stella snorted. "And the fact you threatened the mayor at that country club?" She paused. "Or did you think we didn't know about that?"

Eric said, "I'd worry a little more about the fate of innocent people than what's going to happen to you in the next couple of days." This guy was going to jail, and whether Eric was on duty or not justice would be done.

"You think I care?" Francisco laughed. "You might think

this is terror, or a tragedy, but it's barely an inconvenience to my bottom line."

A black and white pulled down the side of the building. Eric waved them over and got Francisco secured in the back of the car. He didn't have them take him away. Eric wanted him to witness exactly what happened in the aftermath of this—the culmination of his choices.

Once the door was shut, Stella said, "Boy, that guy is a piece of work."

"Let's get inside."

"Hold up." She touched a hand to his chest. "We don't have safety equipment, and I'm not dressed for rescue and recovery."

Before he could argue she continued, "So we focus on what's happening out here, okay? There are people who need help walking, people who need to be medically treated. We might not have that training, but we can help out, right?"

There were already two ambulances to one side. He spotted firefighters carrying a man toward them. He and Stella headed over. He wished they had their badges to show who they were, but chances were he knew these people in this town. Or some of them.

Eric caught the attention of a firefighter. "Peters!" He jogged over. "We'll take her."

"Hummet." Peters blew out a breath.

"How is it in there?" Eric asked.

"Not good. We should get back to it."

Eric nodded.

"We've got her," Stella said. "And anything you need, we're here to help."

Peters blinked at her.

They took the woman from him and helped her walk to the area the EMTs were setting up.

Eric held on as best he could with one arm, mostly just

letting the lady lean against him as they walked. "What's your name?"

"Rebecca." She gasped, tears in her voice. "I was here with my friend."

"It's not much farther." Eric didn't ask what happened to her. Instead, they walked her to the spot the EMT motioned to and had her sit on the tarp that had been laid out. That's when he realized it was Trey Banning. "Hey, man."

"Hummet. You okay?"

"Yeah." He nodded and let the guy get to work on the gash on the woman's head.

For hours they walked injured people from the firefighters over to the triage area that had been set up. The medical examiner and a couple of other doctors showed up and got to work helping treat the injured. The EMTs went back and forth, transporting people to the hospital while Dr. Carlton tagged people according to severity. It was gruesome business, especially when the firefighters pulled out a couple of really young, probably underage girls, from the debris. They were immediately covered with sheets.

Stella stuck beside Sarah, helping with bandages and checking vital signs. He figured she needed to focus on people who could be helped. Eric wanted to get inside and find people, but the EMTs and even a couple of police dogs were at work digging victims out of the rubble.

He headed for the opening the firefighters had made in the front of the club, now leading right into what had been the dance floor.

A man stumbled out, blood pouring down his face.

"Hey, whoa," Eric said.

The guy lurched forward.

Eric caught him with both hands, pain slicing up one arm. He gritted his teeth and swallowed back the cry. "Come on. Let's get you seen to."

"Not a good idea, mate. Can't be seen."

The guy was more articulate than Eric would've thought. And he had a British accent. "You need a bandage. You're injured."

Eric got him over to the triage area. "Doctor Carlton!"

She spotted him and headed over with a fast stride. The woman had powered through hours at this, and they were still pulling out victims.

The guy stiffened, then shoved away from Eric, who watched as the man held his arms out. "I could use a hug from a beautiful woman."

Sarah eyed him. "Because I want your blood on me?"

He clutched both hands over his heart. "You wound me."

"You're already wounded, dude." Eric motioned toward her. "She's a doctor, and she's going to treat you."

He turned to Eric and held his hand out. "Hey, thanks, man. I appreciate it."

"Uh, no problem." Eric shook his hand. "Go get your head looked at."

"Will do."

Stella wandered over, eyeing the man. "Did that guy have a British accent?"

Eric nodded.

"That's Joseph, the one who was looking into things at the camp."

"Huh. I wonder what brought him here."

Stella blew out a long breath. "Eighteen dead. At least fifty injured, and I heard they're still pulling people out. There are so many in there. It was packed with people—nearly a hundred."

Eric pulled her into a hug. "We do what we can. Like we have been."

Stella nodded against his chest.

He didn't want to think about his family's involvement in

this. Not when it was so horrific. It wasn't much of a comfort that Nigel at least wasn't part of it, considering the destruction. Whoever planned to get back at Salvatore. Or slow him down, get him to back off. They hadn't cared one bit about who would be caught in the crossfire.

So many dead.

Eric buried his face in her neck and gave himself a moment.

And when it was done, he would get back to the search. Helping any way he could. Until it was finished, and everyone had been recovered.

And then they would find the person responsible.

26

Stella leaned against Eric and sipped her coffee.

At the front of the conference room, the police commissioner, Russ Franklin, stepped up to the podium. "I'll make this fast. I know you're all tired and busy, but I wanted to gather you all and say thank you. Every single one of you did a fantastic job working the scene at the club."

He scanned the faces in the room. "I'll be meeting with the fire department and other first responders who were on scene as well. But I wanted to touch base with you first and tell you that before we get into working the investigation."

From the row in front of them, Addie glanced back over her shoulder. Her gaze flicked between Stella and Eric while a small smile played on her lips. Stella wanted to push off from leaning against Eric, but that would require energy she didn't have.

They'd been at the bomb explosion scene at the club until the early hours before they headed home for some sleep with orders to report to a taskforce meeting at eight in the morning. Eric's vacation status had been revoked, given the circumstances.

"Fragments of the bomb that have been recovered were sent to the lab for testing, so we will know in a few days if they match the signature of the bomb that exploded two days ago. However, for now we are assuming that it is the work of a single bomber." Russ glanced at Addie, then Stella. "Is the FBI interviewing Nigel Hummet?"

Addie nodded. "And we will also be interviewing Francisco Salvatore. I'll keep you apprised of what we learn."

The Commissioner said, "Good. The sooner we can find Aaron and Ian Hummet and get to the bottom of what's going on, the better."

She felt Eric stiffened beside her. Stella didn't blame him. Even if he was actively distancing himself from them, and doing his job the way he had sworn to do it, it still couldn't be easy when it was his own family. Now that she knew how they had treated him, she understood why there was no question he would ever sympathize with his cousin and uncle.

Stella wondered if Eric saw a little of himself, and the way he'd been treated, in his cousin Nigel.

If they needed to question the guy further, it would probably make sense to have Eric be the one to do it. After all, they might be able to use the family connection to get him to open up and possibly tell them where his brother and dad might be hiding.

The taskforce broke up, each team with their own assignments.

Addie came over to the two of them, weaving through people. Stella shifted her body away from Eric's.

"Do we want to ask for a team of agents from Seattle?" Addie asked. "And thinking about it, but I'd love to know your impression."

Stella had worked at the Seattle office of the FBI for over ten years. She knew the people who worked there, as well as the culture. "We would have to read them in pretty quickly. And we'd be pulling them from other investigations. It would take some time, when maybe we should focus on investigating ourselves." Knowing how that might come across, she added, "Not that I'm trying to do everything myself. But right now it's a time crunch. The quicker we can get to the bottom of this, the safer everyone in the community will be."

Addie nodded. "I was thinking the same thing. But that means we're going to be working nonstop until that happens."

Stella said, "I'm all in to do that."

"Good."

"I think Eric could be an asset talking to Nigel."

Addie said, "If you guys are both free to do that, I'd get on it."

"Will do." Stella turned to Eric and saw both his eyebrows were raised. "Okay, so what do you think about having a chat with Nigel?"

"Let's do it."

They headed over to the holding cells where his cousin was being held. Eric tugged on her arm, the motion for her to stay where she was in the hallway. He didn't want to go to an interview room? She leaned against the wall and watched him walk to the holding cell.

Definitely not a bad view.

She stared longer than she probably should have at the way his shirt hugged his upper body. There was a lot to appreciate about the way he took care of himself. Knowing he'd been that hurt, scared little boy rescued by his grandmother from a father who killed his mother? That only made her appreciate even more what he had overcome.

She didn't feel the same way about her own history. There was so much loss in her life she hardly wanted to think about it, especially in favor of what was right in front of her in the present. Then again, that made her want to grasp what she had now. Probably too tightly.

One day she might be able to relax and realize she could trust that what she had wouldn't suddenly be snatched from her fingers. She wasn't sure when that day would be, or if she even wanted to let go that much.

Both Eric and Addie would probably tell her that she needed to trust God more than she should trust the future, or what power she had over her own life.

Now that she had seen what could happen so quickly, torn and broken in the rubble of that nightclub, it made her want to take a moment and contemplate what she hadn't thought about for a long time. That God might want to do something good in her life. If she was willing to let go enough to allow him to be in charge.

"What do you want?" The question drifted out from inside the holding cell.

She could see the line of tension in Eric's body and how he cradled the bandaged arm against his front. "Just to talk. How are you doing?"

"How do you think?"

"Say the word, and I'll get you the best lawyer I can find. I'm not going to let you get railroaded by the system." Eric's voice stayed soft. "Have you been able to get ahold of anyone?"

"What's the point in trying?"

Nigel could have pushed his right to make a phone call. But if no one on the other end of the line picked up, then he was left here on his own.

"I have a question for you, if that's okay."

"As a cop," Nigel said, "or as my cousin?"

"I'm always going to be both of those things. No matter what happens, I'll be here regardless of whether anyone else is." Eric shifted, tension still in him. "That's why I'm the one here asking about Uncle Aaron."

There was a minute or so of silence, then Nigel said, "What do you want to know?"

"How many bombs did he plan on making?" Eric paused. "Do you know?"

"I only know that it was more than one."

"Any idea where he was doing it?"

That was a good question. Stella wondered if Nigel could tell them where to find the location the bombs were being constructed. That way they'd possibly be able to tell how many had been made.

Nigel said, "Somewhere up in the hills. He never took me there, but they always referred to it as 'the cave.'"

Eric nodded. He turned to her and walked stiffly.

Stella started to ask what that meant, but he shook his head and motioned to the hall. They stepped out and the door closed on the holding cells. "Did that mean something to you?"

"My dad used to take me to 'the cave' when I was little." His expression darkened. "It's a cabin but built into the mountainside above the camp. I might be able to find it on a satellite map."

"Do you think it's the same place, or is it possible they might have built a new one?"

"There was only one cave. It's possible." He shrugged. "But at this point I'll take all the leads we can get."

She nodded.

"I'm going to my desk to see if I can figure out where this place is."

Stella nodded. "I'll go check in on the interview with Salvatore. I want to know what was between him and your uncle Aaron."

Eric headed out first. She watched him go down the

hallway and then disappear around the corner. Then she made her way upstairs to the interview rooms.

If he wanted to keep his thoughts to himself and do the work on his own, she wouldn't begrudge him that time. Stella didn't want to be the kind of girlfriend who couldn't give a guy some space. If that's what she was to him. It felt like far more than just dating—even considering they'd never actually gone on a date. There was something between them deeper than what she'd had with anyone else.

Did he feel it, too?

Stella found the room where Addie was talking to Francisco Salvatore. He might have been arrested after the bombing, but they couldn't hold him much longer without filing charges.

Right now they didn't have much evidence other than an association with Aaron Hummet and a hunch he knew more than he was saying.

She entered the viewing room, her head full of thoughts about Eric when they were supposed to be centered on finishing this case. But so many people had lost their lives in the last twenty-four hours. Something about it made her want to jump on the things she wanted. The future she might be able to have, one that she'd never thought to dream about before.

Addie sat facing Salvatore.

The guy looked far less begrudging than he had the night before, probably because he was as exhausted as everyone else right now.

"So it's just business between you and Aaron?" she said.

"I've got no love for the guy."

"So you didn't know he was planning on setting off bombs? I guess your business deal is over now, considering he blew up Orlando's club."

He made a face.

"You don't care that he cost you? Or was it about handing him someone inside that club. Like the mayor's finance guy."

"You think I let him blow up my club?"

Addie shrugged. "Terrorist attack looks pretty good on the insurance claim. Can't really argue with that when you take the money and don't bother rebuilding."

Stella wondered if the guy had been in the back of the club with few employees and no bodyguards because he had known it was going to be attacked. Maybe he wanted nothing to do with Orlando's club and everybody on his payroll. Preferring to see it destroyed, and then let the business go.

His own way of cleaning house after his son's death? Consolidating his businesses back to the ones he wanted to run.

That would be an interesting tactic.

"Then again, I figure if you knew it was going to happen, you'd have been as far away as possible."

For Addie to put that together meant she was working on a comprehensive profile of the guy, a strength of hers. Stella wasn't super good at figuring out the why of the case. If she could prove what she believed was beyond reasonable doubt, she made the arrest and didn't think about it too much more.

People were dead. That was what would fill her mind at night, not the choices Salvatore and Aaron had made and why.

All she cared about was finding them.

And if she could do it with Eric? That would be so much better.

Her phone buzzed in her pocket. She slid it out and looked at the text.

. . .

I FOUND IT. MCCAULEY IS MOBILIZING THE TASKFORCE NOW.

27

"Smaller than I remember," Eric said.

One of the SWAT officers glanced over at him. "You've been here?"

Eric turned away on a shrug. He'd remembered the place after Nigel mentioned it, which made him wonder what else his mind had blocked out for the sake of his own sanity.

Or survival.

Some psychologists believed there were no hidden memories, buried in the mind. Only what a person remembered and what they didn't. So it was possible he had buried rather than forgotten what his mind didn't want to remember then, just like he didn't want to remember it now.

Stella was outside, talking to McCauley. Both were looking at the street—little more than a dirt path with some gravel. Probably a nightmare in bad weather, when the puddles hid deep ruts of mud that sucked tires down.

He was only interested in what was inside the house and anything that might tell them where Aaron and Ian were right now.

The SWAT sergeant strode past him. "Place is clear."

Eric shouldn't have come in so soon, but he wasn't about to wait outside. Not when he might have to talk them down like he'd done with Nigel. That hadn't gone well at the time, and neither his uncle or other cousin would be so amenable to standing down. But he had to believe he might be able to help save their lives if they were determined to go out in a blaze of glory. He could not give in to the despair and believe there was no hope.

So many lives had been lost, Eric needed to feel like he'd done everything he could to save anyone else from the same fate.

He walked through the cabin while the SWAT team milled around just in case. Waiting for the all-clear to move out.

The couch was threadbare and had seen better days. If anyone tried to clean it, the thing would probably disintegrate. It looked like something that might spontaneously combust. Same with the recliner. The wood burning stove had been in use, and the stack of split wood beside it was getting low. More had been laid outside, half a cord at this point.

The kitchen was about as clean as the living room floor. There was a single bedroom and a bathroom that had seen better days. The whole place looked like it'd been constructed a century or two ago and since been patched up over and over. The refrigerator was from the 1950s easily. He wondered how the inside smelled, but it was probably better not to know. Likely not much better than the bathroom.

He moved through the house, seeing the place through the eyes of the kid he'd been. He ran his thumb over the edge of the kitchen counter where the metal edging—better suited to joining two pieces of carpet—held two pieces of old countertop together. The matching scar was on his left temple, where he'd run into it and scratched up his skin on the screw.

Eric moved deeper into the cabin. The bedroom and bathroom were to the right, and the hall dead-ended in horizontal two-by-fours that didn't match the exterior.

He stopped and stared at it.

"This place is crazy." Stella's voice drifted into his thoughts. "Like it was literally carved out of the mountain."

Eric nodded. "It was an old homestead, I guess. Building it up against the mountainside keeps it from being exposed to the elements. Plus, they get protection from the back."

"But they're also boxed in. And it's freezing."

He glanced back and saw her shiver. "Keeps the milk cold."

"I prefer central heating," Stella said. "And in my apartment in Seattle, the refrigerator that beeps when I leave the door open too long."

He chuckled. "Fancy."

"CSU is on their way up to look at everything and see what evidence they can find." She waved a hand. "What's up with the wall?"

The reason why he hadn't told the SWAT guys he was good. Eric turned back. "Sergeant?"

The guy ambled over.

Eric said, "It's a two-handed job."

"Cover." The sergeant called back over his shoulder, and two of his guys headed to them.

Eric and Stella backed up to the wall on the left side. He remembered it opened from the right. "The seam comes away." He pointed over.

The sergeant pushed on the wall. "I don't see a handle." Something clicked. He eased his fingers in the seam between the wall and the joist where it met the hallway. The whole panel swung out, maybe a foot wide, but floor to ceiling in height.

"There's another room inside." Eric spoke aloud before he realized how obvious that was.

The sergeant motioned with hand signals. He stepped back, opening the door enough one of his guys could whip inside.

"Clear!"

The warrant covered the entire property and every part of it they found inside. A good thing, since they found long folding tables piled high with components.

"I've got the makings of several bombs." One of the SWAT officers scanned a table as he walked. "Military wrapper from C-4. The paper it was folded into."

"Copy that," the sergeant said. "I've got crates." He lifted a lid. "Empty. But my guess would be at one point they held the stuff that was stolen from the military." He tossed aside the lid, then uncovered two more. "CSU can go through all this, but I guess we found where they stashed it all."

"And made the bombs." Eric moved to the tables. The guy was right. Eric hadn't had much training in explosives or defusing devices, but he could spot the mechanics of the components necessary.

Stella turned to the sergeant. "Can you let the captain know we found this?"

"Yes, ma'am." He and his guys headed out, leaving Eric and Stella inside.

"I've been here," Eric said.

"Not for a long time."

Did she think he was still associating himself with them? It wasn't as though he'd been part of the bomb construction, or the murder of so many people. The death toll was nearly fifty already.

The whole thing made him sick just thinking about what he'd seen last night.

"Outside we found three sets of matching tire tracks." She nodded. "We have the van Nigel left on the street outside your grandmother's building, and the one that detonated in front of the club."

"That leaves one more." He glanced over and saw her. Still, he couldn't dislodge those images in his head. Broken and torn people who'd only been trying to spend the evening having fun or blowing off steam. With no idea they were about to be blown apart.

"We can pull in everyone from the camp. Interview them all."

"How will we round them all up? Everyone scattered after the first bomb went off." Eric hadn't been able to find his family, or any of their associates. None of the BOLOs had turned up anything. "It's not like they took roll call or had a database of members."

Wasn't it enough that he'd found this place? Eric got them the cabin where the bombs were made. Now she thought they should come up with even more. Like he had a hard line to fixing this.

Did she think somehow that he was responsible, even though she continued to espouse how he had nothing to do with his family's actions?

Maybe she believed her dad's conviction was somehow on her. So he should similarly be responsible for what his family had done.

She might even blame him for not getting more out of Nigel. Or for not seeing this whole thing coming. Like he should've known what they were planning.

"What about Nigel?" She spoke carefully. "Do you think he might be willing to give us some names, or descriptions?

He could help us figure out where we can find some of their known associates. That could lead us to Aaron and Ian."

If the camp residents even knew what his family was up to. Nigel hadn't. Why did she think the people who mooched off them, living at the camp, knew anything?

"You want me to flip him as an informant?" he said.

She flinched.

He heard that Addie had done so with a local guy, helping to take down a ring of flesh peddlers. Eric had been on the periphery of that. Now he was smack in the middle, getting a close up of how they operated.

"We need to run all this," he said. "Find out who it was that made the bombs, because if we don't have proof from fingerprints or DNA, then we have no way to be sure who set them off."

"Okay." Her tone had flattened, her expression blank.

"I need to get back to the office so I can write up a report. CSU can deal with all this. I don't want to be here longer than I have to."

"I'm sorry if it brings back bad memories."

He shook his head, trying to brush off what she said. His head pounded, and he found himself rubbing that spot where the scar was on his temple. The echo of his father's voice boomed through this cabin. Eric's breaths quickened.

"We could go outside," she offered.

"I'm fine." But he couldn't dismiss what this place did to him. Eric had to face the fact he was damaged, even though that was what he'd spent years trying to believe he wasn't. That God could make something out of him that was more than the sum of his parts.

"Kyle used to say—"

"I'm not Kyle." As soon as the words were out, he realized how loudly he'd barked them at her. And in a room cut out of the mountain, or naturally occurring, his voice echoed. "I'm sorry."

"Thank you for apologizing," she said. But with the same guarded expression on her face.

"Tell me about him."

She hesitated—and he figured she would brush him off—but finally spoke. "He would say he was fine. All the time, whether he was or not. In the end it became a code."

Hearing her story helped him focus on something other than where he was. "What did it mean?"

"Nothing was fine, but we were determined to power through."

"I'm sorry I bit your head off."

Stella's lips curled up. "That's quite the expression."

"Grams uses it. I'd get so freaked when she raised her voice, but she taught me how to say sorry and extend forgiveness so we could do that with each other when we needed to." He took a step closer to her. "Will you hang in there with me?"

"I know you're nothing like your father, and I never met the man, but I don't need to in order to believe that with all my heart."

Relief rolled through him.

"Will I withstand a lot for the sake of what I might get in return? Sure. We're all human, and we all make mistakes. We take the good with the bad." Stella spoke carefully. "But there is a point where I'd pull away because I have to protect myself. My heart. My sanity. Giving grace to someone shouldn't mean you let them bully you, right? But since I know you're not that kind of man I'm trusting what I see."

He wanted to tell her she could trust God but didn't feel like his advice had much credence right now. Mostly he figured whatever advice he would give her was what he should do himself first.

God, help me be the man she needs. "You can trust me. That's a promise I'm making to you."

Stella gave him a soft smile. They headed together out to the broken rail porch. He needed air, and seeing the sky provided him a peace that was missing inside the cabin.

The SWAT van had gone back to the precinct. A couple of the other cars were gone, including McCauley's.

She said, "How long will it take CSU to—"

Gunshots exploded across the clearing in front of the cabin.

Glass shattered. Stella slammed into him, and they hit the deck.

28

Stella sucked in a breath. One second all that was in her head was Eric's words. The way he'd snapped at her and how she was supposed to deal with it. Then there was nothing but one single word.

Gun.

She turned her head enough to see his face, inches from hers.

"Any other time, I'd think this was nice."

She glanced at the trees. "The shooting stopped."

Duh. Another single word. She took the risk and pushed off him but stayed low as she crept down the front steps of the porch. Gun out, safety off. She raced to the tree line in the direction of the source of the shots.

Only a coward would take potshots and then run. And this coward was someone she planned to hunt down and arrest.

Eric's boots pounded the dirt behind her as she raced through the trees.

Up ahead she spotted the figure she'd seen from the porch. "There."

He hopped on an ATV, the rifle he'd shot at them with was slung over his back. The engine revved. That throaty roar filled the whole area, and a couple of birds flew from the trees. Scared off by the sound.

She sped up, but the ATV started to pull away. Stella slowed enough she could change direction, angled slightly toward a tree, and slammed her shoulder into it. Without thinking much about that she lifted the gun and took aim.

Exhale. One. Two.

Squeeze.

The blast sent up a couple more birds. The guy on the ATV jerked. He cried out and fell from the vehicle. It continued on, until it hit a tree and toppled over.

The man didn't get up.

"Nice shot."

She didn't have time to glance back at Eric. Or talk to him more about what had happened inside the cabin. And what would she say to him anyway? He probably needed to see a psychologist. The same way she figured everyone in the world could use a listening ear. Someone to process their life and unpack it in a way that would help them deal. She could be that for him. But why put that in the bounds of a relationship? She wanted to support him, not wind up with some kind of terrible savior complex that she was the one who'd fixed his issues.

It wasn't her role here.

Not the one she wanted, at least.

Stella got within sight of the guy, who lay on his back. Teeth gritted. Clutching his arm and trying to reach around to get the rifle from underneath him. She held her gun trained on him. "Don't bother, Ian. You're going to get that arm looked at, and then you're going to jail."

While she covered him, Eric helped his cousin sit up. He quickly removed the rifle and slung it over his own back with the strap from one shoulder to his hip. Stella tossed him restraints from the back of her belt so he could cuff his cousin.

"It wasn't like I was trying to kill you guys," Ian muttered.

Eric hauled the guy to standing. "Just move."

Ian shook his head. "I wasn't!" This guy was different from the one who'd held a gun on them in the car, all his bravado gone. He'd acted tough then. Now he had no gun and was likely aware his family wouldn't back him up.

Stella couldn't believe he was pleading innocence, probably already trying to angle for lesser charges. "So you didn't try to kill us when you knocked us out and sent the car over the river?"

"You aren't dead, are you?" Ian yelled. "Like you aren't right now."

She figured that was some kind of defense, akin to *if I'd wanted you dead, you would be.* Too bad that didn't hold much weight in court. She would testify that firing a gun was intent to kill.

Eric grunted and walked his cousin back toward the house. "But you knew we'd be here. So you waited until we came out, when everyone else was gone, and you fired on us."

"You shot me!" Ian struggled against Eric's hold on his elbow and cried out. "I'm bleeding everywhere. This is police brutality!"

They emerged from the clearing, where the team of two CSU agents were gearing up in their overalls to go inside.

"Call in to dispatch," Stella told them. "Get some officers stationed here, for your own protection."

She didn't know the man's name, but he glanced at his associate and said, "Will do. You guys okay?"

"We're going to take him to the hospital."

She loaded Ian in the back of her car, and Eric got in the front passenger side. She pulled away from the cabin and passed a patrol car headed up the lane. Good.

Eric craned his neck. "Watson and Alvarez." He lifted his fingers and waved at them.

"They're solid?"

"I don't like that you have to ask, but yeah. They're good."

From the back seat, Ian snorted.

Stella pressed her lips together. There wasn't much she wanted to say to him. They were the arresting officers, and the victims of his attack. She shouldn't be doing the questioning anyway.

She kept quiet, as did Eric, all the way to the hospital. Eric glanced back every few minutes.

When she pulled into a law enforcement reserved spot in the hospital parking lot, she found Ian passed out in the back seat. "Poor guy is tuckered out."

Eric snorted. "He bled all over your seat."

Yeah, it was more likely the blood loss that did it. Still…

Stella woke the guy up, and he walked into the emergency department under his own steam. Her shot might have hit him, but it was only a deep graze. When the doctor declared it needed stitches, she and Eric were ordered out. She got a hospital security guard and called for an officer to sit on the door. Ian's good hand was cuffed to the bed, and they let the doctor get to work.

Out in the hall, she glanced at Eric. Stella didn't know what to say.

Adrenaline from being shot at lingered. It was clear he didn't know what to say either.

She bit her lip and leaned against the wall even though a security guard was inside the room and a uniformed officer on the way. She should ask him if he wanted to get a coffee or something to eat. There was time before Ian was ready to be questioned and she could email the taskforce and Addie while they waited for their food.

She looked at her phone and realized she had a missed call from her dad. In all the craziness she'd missed it, she had a voice mail she hadn't listened to.

"Hey, sweetie."

Stella looked up and realized Edith stood in front of her. She was talking to Eric, though, and pulled him down into a hug.

He smiled. "Grams."

"You don't look so good, honey. You should sit down."

He chuckled. "Yes, ma'am."

She came over to Stella and hugged her the same way. "Your friend Joseph is down the hall. He has to stay and be observed, because he knows better than to leave the hospital against medical advice."

She winced. "I try not to even land here."

Edith chuckled. "Yes, I know that."

Stella wondered if the two of them wanted a minute to talk. "I'm going to go see if he's okay." Joseph needed to make a statement, and she might be able to find out something about the bombing or the Hummets that had put him at the scene.

Edith nodded. Eric didn't say anything, and she didn't look at him on the way to Joseph's room. Whatever was going on, she planned to let him process. If he felt half as mixed up about her as she did about him, then he needed time.

And she needed to work.

Stella knocked on the door and heard, "Come in."

Joseph—or whatever his name was—lay in the bed with his head bandaged and the tattoos on his arms on display below the sleeves of his hospital gown.

"I heard you were down here." She smiled.

He smiled back. "I'm glad you came by. I'm getting sick of staring at the walls."

"Your accent is back to American." She stood at the end of the bed, remembering him at the bombing.

He winced. "What did I say? All I remember is being at the bar, and then a dark-haired woman. She was beautiful. Do you know who she was?"

"Helping everyone?"

He nodded.

"That's the medical examiner."

"Edith didn't know who she was. What's her name?"

He looked so hopeful it was hard to deny him. "Sarah Carlton." Before he could go off on a tangent, she said, "But that's not why I'm in here."

"Figures."

"How much can you remember about why you were at the club?"

"Is this an official taskforce interview?"

Stella shrugged. "Depends on your preference, but if it's going to be actionable, then I need official. It has to go in a report, even if I list you as an unnamed source—or a confidential informant."

Joseph nodded. "I can't remember much. I was there to surveil someone, a guy in a suit. Maxwell…something."

"Carl Maxwell. He's the mayor's finance guy," Stella said. "He died in the blast." She wandered to the chair and sat. This was much better than the strained atmosphere between her and Eric and trying to figure out what should happen next. Things were so up in the air, and people's lives were on the line. That had to be the focus.

"We think there are more bombs." Stella let out a long sigh.

"And the target is people who work for the mayor?"

Joseph looked relieved. "For a minute after it happened I thought it was directed at me."

"You?"

He shrugged. "I guess my cover held up."

The door swung open, and Russ strode in. "Hey..." He pulled up short. "Stella, everything okay?"

"Just discussing the bombing." Was Russ pulling double duty doing something else? If he was, and it connected to Joseph—which definitely wasn't his real name—then she wanted to know if it also related to Edith.

"Great. You're done?"

It wasn't a question. She stood. "Thanks for your help, *Joseph.*"

She left the room to the sound of his chuckle and saw Edith talking to Eric down the hall. Instead of interrupting, she listened to her dad's voice mail. He wanted her to call him, so she found a quiet spot.

"Davis."

Stella frowned. That was how she answered the phone. "Hey, Dad. It's me."

"Honey, hi." She heard his exhale against the phone and then a beep. "I can't work this new-fangled thing."

"You're doing fine. What did you want to tell me?"

"I spent all afternoon at the library looking at old newspapers, and I think I've got something for you."

She found a chair. "About what?"

"About five years ago Aaron Hummet wanted a piece of land close to Benson. It needed to be rezoned for mixed use. Who knows what he was planning on doing with it? But back then Mayor Wilton was the planning and zoning commissioner."

"You found that out?"

"I looked for both of their names in digitized copies of the local paper. Printed out what I needed. I didn't like computers before and I don't like them now." He huffed out another breath. "But I figured out the mayor denied the permit. Aaron didn't get the land. They had a big blow up on the steps of City Hall. Then there's an article about how Wilton was being targeted. His wife was mugged. His car was torched. All kinds of things."

Had things been getting progressively worse over the years?

Stella said, "I need to go talk to the mayor."

If the bomb had targeted the mayor's finance minister and not Wilton himself, maybe the mayor could tell her why.

And if he was the next target.

29

"We all have a long way to go." Grams reached over and patted his hand.

"Feels like too far sometimes." Eric still couldn't shake the fragments of memory from the cabin. The adrenaline of being shot at. Or the relief that they finally had Ian in custody. "And Ian needs to be questioned. There's work to do."

"Sort out your head first, kiddo."

Eric pressed his lips together and stared at the floor.

"It's okay sometimes if you feel like the mountain you have to climb is insurmountable. It is, by yourself. Let God walk you up there. He brought Stella into your life for a purpose, and things won't be perfect. But God is good, and He gives good things to His children."

"How do you say that, when your life has been…" He glanced at her.

"I didn't always to the right thing. Sometimes I did, and it's what everyone else would have called wrong even though God asked His people in the Bible to do the same when it was necessary. I saved lives." She paused. "We're all given a measure of faith, and some have more than others. I don't know why this was supposed to be my life. I've been living in hiding for years, because leaving Benson means I'd be taken out."

He frowned. "Like a hit?"

She nodded, a tiny movement. For years, he'd had a clue that his grandmother had been some kind of secret agent in her former life, though he never figured out how to ask about it. How was he supposed to start that conversation? They all knew she had serious skills. He'd seen her work firsthand when his dad had been about to kill him, but only remembered it through the eyes of a terrified child.

In the end she'd been his heroine. The one who saved him from the monsters.

The idea her life was under constant threat didn't sound good. Surely she could have avoided that, or it was long enough the threat was done by now. What had she been into?

Eric said, "You've been here for thirty years."

"The people who are hunting me won't ever stop. But they will also never find me."

It made sense why she had no social media, when so many her age took advantage of the ability to connect with people. Eric said, "Are you sure?"

She nodded again. "There are safeguards in place."

"Who is that 'Joseph' guy? I heard him use a British accent."

Edith's brows rose. "He isn't a threat to anyone in Benson."

"He can't leave, either?"

"Nope."

"Okay." Eric blew out a breath. He spotted Stella at the end of the hall and lifted two fingers in a wave. She walked toward him with that gorgeous, athletic stride of hers. He wanted to ask if she ever thought about growing out her hair and tell her he loved it short. Talk about where she liked to go on vacation and what kind of place she'd buy if she settled permanently in Benson. All that normal, everyday stuff people talked about if they were dating. A little of that between them, rather than criminal family members and running for their lives, would be great.

Stella tipped her head to the side and smiled as she reached him. Eric had already pushed out of his seat, drawn to her like she was a homing beacon.

She certainly was a gift he hadn't been expecting. He prayed he wouldn't ever take her for granted.

Eric tugged her to him in a hug. She lifted her face, and he touched his lips to hers. Grams had said that things weren't guaranteed to be perfect, but the truth was it felt pretty perfect with her body up against his while their lips danced together.

Grams cleared her throat. "Don't mind me."

Stella tipped her head back and laughed. She peered around him at Grams and said, "Sorry."

"I'm not." Eric wasn't going to lie. Things between him and Stella had a tendency to ignite like a wildfire, something they were going to have to be careful with. But the truth was he couldn't think how he'd rather it be than electrifying. She was everything he'd been looking for, and dreamed of, while at the same time he'd convinced himself he could wait for God to bring him the right woman.

Grams said, "I'll call the pastor about premarital counseling."

Stella's eyes widened.

Eric panicked. "Uh..."

Grams said, "For, you know, *whenever*." She chuckled to herself, got up, and headed away from them toward Joseph's room. Still laughing.

"She thinks she's hilarious." Eric tried to figure out how to do damage control. Had Grams just scared off Stella? "Don't worry about what she said. I'm sure she just—"

"It's fine, Eric." Stella squeezed his middle. "I don't mind."

His mind blanked as he stared at her. They were on the same page about where this was going?

"She *is* pretty funny."

So she thought it was just a joke? He wasn't sure what…

She lifted up and kissed his cheek. "We'll get there."

"Huh?"

"One step at a time." She lowered back down. "That okay with you?"

"Like, we go out for coffee?"

"I was thinking more like dinner, but coffee is fine."

Ack. Why was it so hard for him to remember she didn't drink much coffee? He was sure coffee could be special, especially since that was how she drank it. As a one off, an occasion. He drank the stuff like it was gasoline for his body, which it pretty much was.

He pulled himself together. "Dinner sounds good."

Eric wanted to dress nice, pick her up, and take her somewhere classy.

"To start with."

He smiled at her words and saw both interest and excitement flare in her eyes. Something he wanted to see a whole lot more.

It didn't take long for an officer to show up to take custody of Ian. Stella stood. "We should get back to work."

He made a face and she laughed.

"Agreed. But we still have to go."

"Yeah, we do," Eric said. "What's the latest?" She'd talked to Joseph, so maybe she had something. And Ian was going to be a while before he was released to be interviewed—which wouldn't be by them.

"Actually I talked to my dad, and we're going to the mayor's office right now to ask about the longtime beef he's apparently had with your uncle." Stella headed for the elevator, her arm through his good elbow. "I'll tell you all about it on the way. I already called his office and he's expecting us."

Fifteen minutes later they checked in through security at City Hall and were directed to put on their visitor's badges and told where to go through the maze of hallways to Wilton's office.

His perky assistant hopped up from her desk. "Special Agent Davis and Officer Hummet?" When they nodded, she said, "Right this way."

"Thank you." Stella smiled at the young woman.

The assistant opened the doors and pushed them wide. "Sir, your appointment is here."

"Thank you, Lindsay."

She shut the doors behind them, and Stella strode to the desk while the mayor scanned both of them. He had a squat glass of amber liquid in one hand. It was a power move, and he stood behind that mammoth cherry wood desk. Indicating to them that he was the one in charge and they were guests at best.

Eric had actually voted for the guy. Now he wasn't so sure, even if he didn't object too much as far as policy and decisions the guy had made. He just didn't like Wilton personally.

Maybe the mayor felt the need to distance himself from the people he served. Could just be a protective measure. Self-preservation.

His mind wanted to do the same thing to prevent distress every time he was presented with the reality of his past. Or the uncertainty of his future, and what might be with Stella.

He needed peace—and he knew it could be a reality even in the middle of what was going on.

"Mr. Mayor, I know you're a busy man," Stella said. "so I'll get to the point."

He set the glass on the desk.

"Are you aware of a man named Aaron Hummet?"

Wilton glanced at Eric, then back at Stella. "And if I am…?"

"We believe you and he may very well be the reason why your finance manager is dead."

Eric took half a step forward and leaned his good hand on the back of a fancy chair. "You know he's my uncle. You might not know that we just arrested his son Ian—my cousin."

"You did?"

Eric nodded. "He's tried multiple times to kill us."

"Did he set the bomb?"

"If he did," Stella said. "I'm certain it was under orders from his father."

Eric figured that was true. Not that Ian had been coerced to do whatever his dad wanted, but that he wanted to cause as much chaos as possible. He'd probably agreed the whole time. The guy thrived on destruction—the way Aaron and Eric's dad also had. They'd made Ian in their image and the guy had no choice. Nigel hadn't been wired the same way, and Eric wanted to give him the chance to make a new life. It wasn't exactly the rescue operation Grams had performed, but Eric would do what he could to help his younger cousin.

"Why do they want to hit back at you?" Eric said.

The mayor slumped into his chair. "They've had it in for me for years."

Stella shifted her stance. "Because you wouldn't give them that land."

Wilton nodded. "They had nothing but dirty money.

Wanted me to take half in cash, and they never intended to pay the full price."

Eric frowned. "You owned it? I thought you were the planning and zoning guy back then."

"I'm part of a group that buys property around Benson. Places that are falling down, we rejuvenate the area. It's about gentrification."

"And they wanted property you owned?"

"We bought it fair and square at auction, over the asking price. We weren't going to rip off the owner." Wilton sipped from his glass. "Aaron Hummet tried to buy the block for a compound in the center of town." He shook his head. "No one wanted that."

"And he just gave up, but came after you?"

"He didn't make another camp in town. Just kept the one you guys have now."

Eric shook his head. "I have nothing to do with that place."

"Well, anyway, he decided to get vindictive. Every time I do something, he's right there trying to thwart me just for kicks. Because he wants to play his sick game. Like running my wife off the road the week of the mayoral election."

Stella blinked. "And you didn't think to report it to the police?"

"Of course we did! My wife had to have her hip replaced because of that man." Wilton slammed the glass down on the desk. "But there was never any evidence it was anything other than an accident."

"Why would he target you now?" Eric asked. "Is he escalating because he's bored, or is there some reason he's doubling down and setting bombs?"

Wilton frowned. "Neither device was aimed to hit back at me, at least I don't think so."

"We agree with that. With the exception of your finance

manager. We think the three were trial runs. The first two were messages aimed at someone else," Stella said. "But the club explosion could well have been aimed at you."

"And Francisco Salvatore." Eric figured the fact it was his club was deliberate. "Whether it was about doing him a favor or costing him money and bad press. But he also killed a man who works for you. Why might that be?"

A muscle ticked in Wilton's cheek.

"Tell us," Stella said.

Wilton stared at the blinds over the window for a while. Finally, he said, "I'm getting ready to announce a run at the governor's office."

"Officially?" Stella asked. "When?"

"Tomorrow at the Pavilion Hotel."

30

"With all due respect, Mr. Mayor, you cannot hold a public event until we have Aaron Hummet in custody." Stella was dead serious.

The mayor's gaze scanned her face. He'd see plain as day that she meant exactly what she'd said. Then his expression shifted. Wilton sat back in his chair. "You expect me to change my plans out of fear?"

"We're talking about people's lives." Stella put her palms on the desk and leaned forward. "Eighteen people are already dead because of these guys. You can help us prevent even more deaths."

Was he really going to be selfish, just for the sake of his own agenda? She could understand not wanting to cave to a bully, especially considering how long Aaron had been targeting him. Wilton probably felt the need to take a stand —the way he had been doing for years.

"We're not telling you to cancel," she said. "We're asking you to wait. Can you just sit on the announcement until he's caught?"

Wilton stared at them, calculating the odds. Or working

out how to get his own way and not come off looking like he cared nothing for innocent people.

Eric moved to stand beside her, two cops in solidarity. "Mr. Mayor, we need your help on this. We need you to do the right thing for the people of Benson, Washington."

Wilton said, "You think I'm going to come off as putting people in danger?"

"This isn't about your image." Stella shrugged. "But I'm guessing it won't look good when your constituents and donors find out their lives are in danger by throwing in with you. Especially when you're trying to convince them to vote for you."

Wilton made a face.

Eric said, "As soon as Aaron is in custody, you can spin this however you want."

"Can you even find him?" Wilton said. "He's gunning for me, trying to take me out. You don't think I need protection from him?"

"The taskforce will provide officers to ensure your safety." Stella could provide concessions if he was willing to cooperate. "Provided you take our advice and let us work this. If you're causing problems for the taskforce, that's time and resources diverted to keeping you and people safe instead of putting everything we have toward running down Aaron Hummet."

She pushed off the desk and straightened, which put her shoulder beside Eric's. Exactly where she wanted it to be. Standing side by side. Together with the man she loved.

Stella sucked in a breath. In the next second she wondered why that was such a revolutionary thought. There was no question she wanted a relationship with him, and whatever the future held she was contemplating loosening some of her control on what happened. Thinking about trusting God, and what that might look like.

She had no idea how it worked, but so many people in her life had that relationship with the Creator that her mom had held onto in the beginning. That her grandmother had continually led her toward.

If she was going to honor what they'd given her, she needed to take another look. Go to church with Eric.

Wilton said, "Tell Captain McCauley to call me."

Stella nodded. It was as good as a dismissal, so she headed for the door. If she stuck around, she'd end up saying something that got them thrown out with no cooperation from Wilton.

"I voted for that guy."

She glanced at Eric, then shoved open the fire door that led to the stairs. No elevator. She needed to pound down a concrete stairwell and get rid of some of this restless energy.

Stella rounded the first floor, headed down. Eight to go. "Do you think he'll hold off until we find your uncle?"

"I think he doesn't want to wait, but if he jumps, he puts people at risk, and he doesn't want the bad press that comes with it." Eric followed close behind her. "That won't look good for him."

"I'm counting on that. But we'll have to see what McCauley can persuade him to do."

They headed over to the police department and clocked in at the taskforce office for the meeting. Stella grabbed a smoothie from the FBI office refrigerator on the way. Eric was talking to McCauley in his office, so she got on her computer and looked up the progress of the tech working through Ian's phone.

They had his call and text history. She wondered if Eric could figure out which number belonged to his uncle.

Stella grabbed the nearest notepad and wrote down a series of ideas of how they could find Aaron. Even when the ideas got crazy, she didn't stop. It was part of her process to list anything and everything she could think of.

She felt someone move up behind her, and when the hand touched her shoulder, she realized it was Eric and let go of some of the stiffness she'd been holding.

"That one is a good idea." He pointed midway down the list. "Not sure about some of the others."

"You've got to list all the bad ideas with the good to get your creative juices flowing."

Eric chuckled. "Maybe that's just an FBI thing."

"It's a quality policing thing."

"Mmm."

She glanced over her shoulder and eyed him.

"Agree to disagree?"

She wasn't going to get into it with him about the FBI versus local cops. Working together was worth more than that rivalry, but she was more than happy to joke around about it when they weren't facing down another possible terrorist attack.

Stella glanced over at the board covered with photos of everyone who had perished in the club bombing. She let out a long breath.

Eric squeezed her shoulder and shifted to sit beside her. "I know. It's so terrible seeing them all, those photos taken at a time when they had no idea how their lives would end." He sighed. "We have to find him."

Stella nodded. "And we need to use Nigel and Ian to do it."

Eric said, "They're bringing Ian over from the hospital. If you get Nigel in the interview room, I'll get him to the right spot. Make it look like we got our wires crossed."

"You really think they won't realize it's a setup?"

Eric shrugged. "What do we have to lose?"

Ten minutes later Stella walked Nigel into an interview room. "The officer will be along shortly. Please wait here."

Treating him like a danger to her and others was the reality of the situation, but she did feel bad for the kid. He'd been raised by monsters who willingly hurt others. He also could have walked away at any time or made different choices.

Some people had no choice, but Nigel Hummet wasn't one of them. He'd had an example in Eric. However bad things were, he had come to Eric for help—he just hadn't stuck around. He'd let fear get the better of him.

The way she'd let her grief do the same thing, and Bridget ended up dead.

Then again, if she hadn't pursued the case, would they have known the Hummets were up to something? She wasn't entirely sure. If God was in control, then He might have led the people who trusted Him so that fewer people were killed. So many had lost their lives, but it might've been so much worse.

Stella wanted to be someone who was led and directed by a being who knew everything. That could only help her do her job better, right? If she listened to Him, she might save even more people.

Nigel looked like he wanted to say something to her.

She shut the door in his face, hoping he'd be out of sight when Eric walked Ian down the hall.

She slipped into the viewing room right as she got the text.

A uniformed officer opened the door. "Wait in here."

Ian stumbled in, glancing back over his shoulder.

Eric slipped into the viewing room with her. "Did it work?"

Stella said, "See for yourself."

The door in the interview room closed. Nigel pushed off

the wall. "Ian, what are you doing here? What did they do to you?"

They both looked a little banged up, but considering Ian had stitches from where she'd winged him, he was the more injured of the two. Nigel tried to hug his brother even though he had cuffed hands. Ian didn't seem that amenable to it.

"What did you tell them?"

Nigel flinched. "Nothing."

Eric crossed to stand beside her, going all the way around so she wasn't beside his bandaged arm. He slung his good arm around her shoulders. "It's hard to believe they're any family of mine."

"Family isn't just blood. Sometimes that has nothing to do with it." Stella had found family in Kyle after she lost her mom and grandma. Now Kyle was gone and she had her dad in her life. She had what could be with Eric, and how that would mean he had more family. "Staying here in Benson, putting down roots and making a life? That means I'd have family I never had before."

Eric looked down at her. "We're supposed to be listening to them."

She grinned. "The feed is recording everything. We're good as long as they don't kill each other."

"That could go either way."

He was probably right about that. She watched through the window at the heated conversation taking place. Stella wasn't sure they'd say where Aaron was currently hiding, but it was worth the chance to get a lead.

They had nothing, and she figured that was by design. If Aaron planned to set off a bomb at the mayor's announcement tomorrow then the guy was probably laying low, staying off the radar, making sure no one found him. He'd want to do everything possible to make sure it all went to plan.

Her phone rang in her pocket, but she ignored it in favor of listening. And saying, "I want to live here." She glanced up at Eric. "Permanently."

He smiled down at her. "I'm glad."

Eric gave her a quick kiss, and she was glad he did it. Just as she was glad he kept it short. They were working. The pull to make this about them was powerful. It should be about saving people's lives.

Ian shoved Nigel away from him. "Who cares? Just keep your mouth shut. Dad's gonna do what he has to."

"And we go to jail?" Nigel's face scrunched up, probably fighting a breakdown. "I don't want to go to jail. You should've told me a bomb was in that van when you tried to blow up Grams. For all I know you wanted me dead, too."

Ian made a face and glanced at the door. To check there was no one listening? "I can't believe Eric didn't even leave the building." He huffed out a breath. "He could've had the decency to do his job and check it out. I had to blow it when he was standing at the window. At least I got to see him fly through the air." He chuckled.

Beside her, Eric stiffened.

Her phone rang again. She reached for it. Eric moved behind her, to the door. The halfway house number flashed on her screen. "This is Special Agent Davis."

"Yes, I'm the manager here. Your father never came home tonight. I was wondering if everything is okay."

The door to the interrogation room whipped open, Eric stood there, asking, "Where is your father?"

Ian shifted to stand in front of Nigel. Not as a protective gesture, but more likely to cut him off from saying anything. "We don't know where he is. It's part of the plan."

"He's going to kill people," Eric said. "Help me save their lives and I can get the charges against you reduced."

Ian shrugged. "What do I care? I'm still going to jail, and Nigel knows nothing."

"Hello? Are you there?"

Stella realized the halfway house manager was still talking to her. "Right. I'll find him."

She hung up.

31

Eric stood face-to-face with his cousin, not about to back down.

"You won't be satisfied until we're all in prison." Ian called him a foul name.

"You killed eighteen people. I'm supposed to let you walk free?" Eric shook his head. "You and I aren't family."

He would help Nigel as much as he could. Ian was beyond help. He couldn't be saved.

"Officer Hummet."

Eric spun to find his shift supervisor scowling in the doorway. The sergeant said, "In the hall. Now."

Ian snickered and shoved him.

Eric stumbled two steps. The sergeant's expression hardened, and Eric figured the guy had an idea what he wanted to do in response to his cousin. Instead, Eric strode to the door where the sarge held it open.

There were things he'd have said if it were only him and Nigel. With Ian in there as well, it would only escalate.

The sarge waved a hand. "Nigel, if you'd come with me."

Eric's younger cousin exited.

The sarge called out, "Officers!"

Two cops at the end of the hall turned, both in uniform. Eric figured they'd clocked out already since they looked like it was the end of a long shift—but hadn't changed yet.

The sergeant got one to take Nigel and the other to escort Ian. "Both of them go in holding, separate ends. No contact."

"Yes, Sarge." The off-duty officer glanced at Eric.

He probably looked a sad sight, considering one arm was bandaged he'd been through a lot in the last few days and he needed a change of clothes. He'd always felt more reassured wearing his uniform. However, the drive to make detective meant he'd trade that in for street clothes and a job he was thinking he'd like a lot.

"Care to explain what that was?"

Eric blew out a breath and ran his good hand through his hair then down his face.

"I'm guessing I can figure it out." The sarge frowned. "You sure this taskforce was a good idea?"

Eric winced. "If I felt like I was contributing more than just having a personal relationship with the prime suspect. As it is, we've got no idea where my uncle is."

"You caught your cousins, though."

"Doesn't matter if Aaron sets off that bomb tomorrow. People could get hurt. More could die."

The sergeant nodded. "That's always a risk in this job."

"So how do you not take the responsibility on yourself?"

"You do what you can and let God pick up the responsibility."

Eric walked to the wall and leaned against it. He'd been the judge and jury—Edith filled the third role in a way he didn't want to think about and wouldn't if no one ever found his dad's body. He'd pronounced a sentence on Ian already.

Eternal damnation.

What else did it mean that Ian was beyond saving? It meant he didn't deserve redemption. But Eric wasn't the one who could make that call. Even if he'd spent years working to be worthy of the life he'd been given, the relationship he had with Grams and how great it had been to be raised by her. He'd earned everything he had as a cop and wanted the police department to be as good as it could be—with him in the middle of it all.

Good enough to be called one of the good guys. Worth the things he gained, the way he wanted to earn a detective position.

He'd divided everyone he ever met into two categories. Worthy or unworthy. His family most of all.

Eric had to get past this, or he would work himself to death earning trying to prove he was good enough. "The department has a shrink, right?"

The sergeant nodded. "He's full time now. Not just for after an incident, he'll talk to you anytime."

"Okay."

"Let me know if you need anything else." The sergeant glanced down the hall. "You know where to find me."

"Thanks."

Stella came out of the viewing room, her face pale.

He went to meet her. "Did something happen?"

Surely they were due for a break sometime soon. Things had to calm down sooner or later, didn't they? God could give them some peace so they could go on that dinner date they'd talked about.

To his surprise, she walked all the way to him and wound her arms around his waist, keeping to his side where his arm wasn't against his front in the sling.

"What is it?"

She spoke against his shirt. "My dad never came home

tonight. The manager of the halfway house can't find him or contact him." She shivered.

He knew what he would do, but that didn't necessarily hold true for her. "What's your first move?"

"I need to track his phone." She gave him a quick squeeze and pulled away almost as fast as she came over to hug him. "Let's go."

They headed downstairs to the FBI office. She slid her ID card through the reader, and he did the same with his police ID. Inside the small FBI office, barely bigger than the mayor's office except for their tiny kitchen and bathroom a group huddled by Addie's desk.

Russ, Addie, and McCauley talked together, and it didn't look good.

Addie broke off their conversation and turned. "Stella, what is it?"

"I need to find my dad. He's missing."

It almost sounded like she was asking permission to leave for the day and search on her own time.

Stella said, "The halfway house manager said he didn't come home. He was supposed to be at the library, and talking to the pastor about a Bible study for guys on parole. I want to track his phone."

Eric wanted to tug her to his side. Hug her again as they had upstairs, but not in front of his captain, Stella's supervising agent, and the police commissioner.

Russ pointed to a computer. "Addie, can I?"

"Yeah, Russ. What are you going to do? We don't have a warrant to intrude on his privacy."

"You might not, but he's on parole and I'm the police commissioner."

Addie frowned. "Maybe you should use your own log in."

Russ just grinned and settled himself in the desk chair.

"Give me a second, Stella. I'll see if I can tell you where he is."

Stella nodded. "Thanks, Russ. Uh…sir."

Russ chuckled. "We're all getting used to that."

Eric wasn't sure what he was supposed to do. McCauley was on his phone, the expression on his face not a good one. "Captain? Everything okay?"

McCauley said, "Addie, you have a screen I can cast this to?"

Addie turned on the TV. He tapped the screen of his phone and the TV flickered. It changed to looking like a phone, the vertical column of an image banded by two black vertical bars that filled the rest of the widescreen.

McCauley's captain of the Benson PD social media account had a lot of notifications he hadn't looked at yet. He was looking at a post from Mayor Wilton's personal account, not his official profile. The image filled the screen as the TV caught up with what it was displaying.

Addie turned up the volume on whatever Wilton was saying.

"…light of recent events. Out of respect for those who lost their lives it doesn't seem right to celebrate, so I'll be canceling tomorrow's gala and plan to reschedule soon. There will be a time for partying and congratulations, but it will come in due time."

Eric frowned at the guy's expression. "Anyone else buying this as sincere."

"Doesn't matter how he feels, only what people take from it. What they decide to believe." Stella made a face and he gathered that she didn't much care for the side of politics where genuine intention was overshadowed by what people chose to think. At the bottom of the video, comments popped up, one after the other in rapid succession.

The mayor continued, "Tomorrow I had planned to

announce the next step of my career. As I'm unable to do so at the event, I've chosen to make it public now. I'll be running for governor in the upcoming election, and I hope you'll carefully consider who you would like to lead this great state of ours."

He went on, but Eric tuned it out and started reading the comments. What if Aaron was watching? He might know his plan to bomb the official announcement had been foiled.

"He's goading my uncle." Eric made a mental list. "We should have officers head to his kids' schools or wherever they are, have uniforms watch over wherever his wife is. And his office. They need to be safeguarded just in case Aaron tries to hit back when he realizes his plan has been foiled."

McCauley said, "Already dialing," and lifted his phone to his ear. He headed for the door.

"You need to go with him?" Addie said.

Eric glanced between the captain, now out in the hallway headed for the PD side of the office building, then back to the commissioner and the two FBI agents. "I can't be on shift, in uniform, with this injury." Plus he would rather be here if needed, running down leads and helping out—finding Aaron or Stella's father. "Anything on the phone, Commissioner?"

Russ said, "It's switched on and unmoving. The phone company gave me access to his GPS."

"Where is he?" Stella moved around the desk to look over Russ's shoulder.

"Behind Halloran Street, between Fourth and Third."

Eric said, "That's a strip mall. Rundown though, most of the units are empty because the businesses caved." A few years ago it had been a bustling retail district, with clothing and bookstores. Now it had a tiny branch of the library, a couple of independent clothing stores, and a smoothie place that was always open but rarely had customers.

"Show me?" Stella grabbed a set of car keys from a hook by the door.

Eric nodded.

"Addie?"

She said, "Keep me apprised."

Fifteen minutes later they pulled onto the street and Stella drove slowly through the lot. "I don't see his car."

Eric checked his texts. "Addie says the phone hasn't moved. The GPS still shows it here, but you know it's not super accurate."

"He could be in any of these buildings, or even a street over." She worried the edge of her lip.

"You think something happened to him?"

"I don't think he lost track of time and is enjoying a latte."

Eric said, "But you don't know him all that well, right?" Her dad might have seemed interested in the investigation at dinner but he had also just been released from prison.

"So you're going to assume the worst?"

"I'm going to move forward based on the evidence and keep an open mind." At best he figured this was a distraction when they should be finding Aaron. But he wasn't going to say that. Her dad was important, and he was important to her. Still, one could save many lives and the other was concerned with only one.

"If he isn't here, I'm going back to work. But I have to look." She turned at the end of the aisle.

"You said a silver Volvo, right?"

"You see it?"

Eric pointed. "The driver's door is open." He also thought he spotted a cell phone on the ground.

She parked close by, and they headed over. "I see blood on the steering wheel."

"And on the door." Eric frowned. The phone on the

ground was shattered. "Something definitely happened." He glanced around, looking for surveillance cameras.

"Where is he?" There was so much fear in her voice.

Eric said, "We're going to find out."

Even if that meant leaving his uncle to the rest of the taskforce.

Lord, help us.

32

Stella shook her head. Then she caught herself and reached for Eric, who held onto her hand for as long as she stood there trying to figure out what had happened. Her dad. Gone.

"I only just got him back."

Eric tugged her close.

"I didn't even get to know him."

"We don't know that he's dead. He could have been hurt and got in someone's car, and they're right now driving him to the hospital."

She tried to be reassured by his words, but the fear of losing another family member made it so she could barely think, let alone breathe. "I only just got him back. He's all the family I have."

Eric pulled her close and kissed her forehead. "Let's go check the cameras. We need to know what happened." He'd already called it in, and a patrol car was on the way.

The first store they tried had nothing to do with the cameras. Stella didn't hear half the conversation between Eric and the clerk, who had paused vacuuming to speak with them. After a couple of minutes, he led her out and they found an office around the corner, where a seating area filled the space between buildings. One of the lights was out, so half the picnic benches and the fenced dog area were cast in a darkness that made her shiver.

Who knew what hid in the corners?

Aaron might be behind this, but were any of the other camp residents involved?

The security guard opened the door with a bleary blink, like they'd woken him from a nap. Stella erupted with hot anger. She dug out her badge and put it in the guy's face. "Show us your camera feeds. Then you can explain why an incident happened in your parking lot and you haven't called the police, because you *didn't even notice.*"

He backed up and got on the computer. Stella stood back while Eric took the lead again. *Find my father.* She had to get him back. No way could she go through losing the last of her family. All she would have left was whatever family she made for herself, and she *wanted* blood relations.

Certainly some people didn't get that in their life. Through neglect or loss, they had no family. Her heart broke for those people, knowing she could so easily be one of them. Even while she raged at God the way she always did when things didn't go her way.

Tears gathered in her eyes.

She'd been angry with God for every loss in her life. The idea that He was good and wanted good things for her was the opposite of the reality she lived with every day. It was hard to reconcile except when she looked at Eric.

He was a gift. A good thing in her life, and he would attribute their meeting to God's work in their lives. She could believe it when he said it. When her heart tried to take it in? All she felt was hardness. Stone.

"Whoa." The security guard rubbed his face and peered

closer at the computer monitor. "We need to call the police!" His head whipped around. "Oh, right. You are police."

"There are officers on the way," Eric said. "They'll need a copy of that footage."

Stella said, "Back it up and show me again."

She moved so she could see the screen while he played it. She couldn't make out much, but there was someone in the driver's seat of her dad's car. With the blurriness she wasn't sure it would be admissible unless at some point they got a clear view of his face.

Someone crept up to the car. She watched the video as Aaron Hummet whipped the car door open and hit her dad with something. "Stun gun?"

"Looks like it," Eric said. "But there was blood in the car."

"Now what is he doing?" Aaron was bent down by her dad's feet, out of sight under the door.

Her dad moved. It looked like a struggle broke out. Aaron grabbed her dad by the back of his neck and slammed his face into the steering wheel. "The blood."

He popped back up to the window and stood to haul her dad out of the car.

Eric frowned. "Was he down there moving your dad's feet?"

"But he drags him out of the car." What had Aaron crouched to do before he put her dad over his shoulder and hauled him away? "Can we get the plate on that van he's driving?"

The security guard said, "I'll check the other feeds and see if I can get another angle."

"Good. You do that." Stella headed for the door.

Eric kept pace with her. "What are we doing?"

"Checking something," she said. "And as soon as we get all the available information on that van, we need a BOLO."

He nodded. "And the taskforce can check available cameras in the local area, see which way he went from here. Try to track him that way."

"Good idea." Stella crouched in the open driver's door. Aaron had been doing something down there, and with the help of her phone flashlight she discovered the folded paper under the seat. "I'm guessing he put this here."

"Planted it?" Eric took the paper with a pinch of two fingers, keeping as much of his prints from it. She couldn't recall if Aaron had been wearing gloves. Evidence was key here.

She needed to alert McCauley if he wasn't already aware of what had happened and how it related to the taskforce investigation.

This was personal now. It was also the most recent sighting of Aaron Hummet that anyone had.

A lead.

Eric unfolded the paper on the hood of her dad's car. The patrol vehicle headed into the parking lot. She waved them over, then looked. "A map?"

"Of Benson." Eric frowned, lighting the paper with his own flashlight. "It's old, though. Some of the newer road construction isn't on here." He ran a finger down the east side of town where she knew a new subdivision had been built. Stella and Kyle had mountain biked those trails.

"What's that?" She pointed to a red circle in the bottom left fold.

"The hospital."

"Where we were?"

He nodded.

"This is calculated. It's not scrambling because the mayor jumped the gun and already announced his run for governor." Stella took a breath. "He's going to frame my father for the third bombing, make it look like my dad is the one. And the hospital is the target?"

"That doesn't sound good."

She turned and spotted McCauley walking toward her. The captain turned to the two officers and said, "I want an all-points bulletin in the next five minutes with everything you can get me on the van Aaron Hummet is driving."

"Yes, sir." The officers jogged to the office.

McCauley turned back to them. "Thoughts?"

"He's pivoted," Eric said. "Or the hospital was the plan all along, and not the mayor's event."

Stella crossed her arms and tapped her finger on her elbow. "But my dad asking questions has to have drawn Aaron's attention. He's diverted at least with that, if not also with the location. Or he had plans on plans on plans, all figured out, and he's just picking and choosing like from a menu."

Eric winced. "That actually sounds like Aaron."

Stella reached over and squeezed his shoulder.

McCauley said, "Your dad was asking questions?"

Stella figured the captain may as well know her father's good side, considering he might be top of the suspect list soon enough. "He seemed interested in the case, helping us think it through? I advised him not to poke around asking questions, since he's on parole and he starts his new job soon."

She hated the idea that he'd stick his neck out to help her or get her to see that side of him. Or for some nostalgic need to feel like he was doing police work.

Whatever it was, he'd been alone. He'd gotten in over his head without backup and paid the price.

Don't be dead.

She realized that instead of just thinking it, she could pray. *Please protect him. I know You can. You know where he is, and*

You can save him. She needed to trust God, the way she hadn't in a long time. At the same time, she planned to do everything she could.

Years ago, when she was little her faith had been like a tiny bud, not even a flower yet. Life had stomped on it, and Stella had hardened her heart.

She could do this. She could trust God, let Him take that stone and make it beat again. The way Eric had done with her feelings, bringing them back to life. God could do that with her heart.

"Captain!" One of the officers jogged over. "We have the van in the hospital parking lot!"

Stella headed for her car at a dead run.

McCauley called out, "No one approaches before the bomb squad gets there."

Eric got in before she hit the gas and tore out of the parking lot. He turned to look out the back window. "He's following."

"Good." The more people there the better everyone would see that Aaron was setting up her dad for another bombing. A disaster.

"They set the other bombs off remotely."

She said, "They drove the van into the club."

"Because Ian got out and rigged it to accelerate into the building."

And her dad was already in the hospital parking lot? "We need to know if he's parked like the first bomb, or moving like the second."

Eric nodded. "We'll be there in a couple of minutes. In the meantime, let's pray."

She would rather pester everyone she knew and demand to know what was happening until the second she saw with her own eyes. "That's a good idea."

"You think so? I wasn't sure."

"Go ahead. I don't really know how to, and it's been a long time." Stella gripped the steering wheel. "I want to."

Eric spoke aloud, praying the entire drive to the hospital for God's will. Not exactly what she'd have done, but maybe better than making demands and pleading. Or offering God concessions if they could come through this the way she thought it should happen.

Your will, God.

"I want to go to church."

Eric glanced over. "Amen."

"Sorry. Amen." She was already doing it wrong. "When we get a Sunday off, I'd like to go to church with you."

He nodded. "Okay." And took her hand, giving it a squeeze before she pulled into the parking lot.

Both of them switched to work mode, something that was getting easier the more she did it. Stella liked working with him. She wanted to keep doing it, even while they grew closer in their relationship.

Right now she couldn't imagine him not being here.

Kind of like she couldn't imagine having to say goodbye to her father.

Stella whipped into the underground lot, and a space reserved for law enforcement. A van at the far end of the parking lot was surrounded by black-and-white vehicles, lights flashing. Officers with their weapons up stood around the van.

She left the keys in the ignition and raced over. "Stand down! Everyone stand down!"

The light down in the basement was so shadowed she could barely make out her dad's face. But she could plainly see the terror there.

He knew there was a bomb in the back of the van.

"Everyone *stand down*," Stella ordered. "Where's the bomb squad?"

"On their way," McCauley said. "Everyone back up. You heard the fed."

Her dad's gaze pleaded with her.

Stella moved.

Eric called out to her, but she ignored it and moved around the van.

She pulled the passenger door open and got in.

"Whatever happens to you, happens to me."

33

Eric stared at her.

One of the officers shoved him back a step. "Get behind us, Hummet."

He didn't even look to see who it was. Nor did he bother being offended—as if that was the point here. Eric deserved it, getting in the way of uniformed cops on duty trying to do their jobs and prevent a tragedy at the hospital.

This was so much bigger than Eric and how he felt about the choice Stella had just made.

"Hummet!"

He found McCauley and saw the captain wave him over. Eric figured he didn't have a choice right now but to comply, and he needed to walk away from the van. He was about to explode, but he took a minute to pray Stella and her father didn't.

"She just got in the van?"

All Eric could do was nod.

McCauley hissed out a breath through clenched teeth.

"I agree, Captain."

"I'll bet you do."

Eric winced. What was happening between them wasn't a secret, and there was no point believing they'd fooled anyone. "I can't believe she did that."

"Women often make choices we don't understand."

And yet, had she ever made one without having a good reason? Eric didn't think so. "Right."

She'd just gotten in the van with her dad.

"She's going to get herself killed."

"Is her dad the kind of guy who deserves having her give her life for his?" McCauley glanced over.

"I barely know the guy." His gut was to take what he knew about her dad's mistakes and write him off. To say no. He wasn't the kind of person who deserved someone good like Stella giving her life so that he wasn't alone.

McCauley checked his phone.

"We need this bomb disarmed. It could go off at any moment."

"Bomb squad is seconds away."

Eric gritted his teeth. "She needs to get out of there." He realized he had shouted the words.

"She knows what she's doing. She made her choice." McCauley got in his face. "Is that what you want me to tell you, Officer? Tough luck. Your girl didn't choose you."

Eric's body flexed.

"Careful."

He took two steps back while his arm pulsed with pain. Once in a while he could forget he had a hurt arm, even with the bandage and the sling. Except when he moved wrong.

"Figure out who you're mad at. And stay out of the way while I do my job and try to save people rather than just being butt hurt about a girl." McCauley paused. "Then again, that's probably why she divorced me."

Eric paced away and ran his hand through his hair. He couldn't even look at Stella, knowing at any moment he could be watching while the bomb in the back of the van went off. He'd see the whole thing tear apart. Her and the vehicle, and her dad.

She'd chosen her dad.

It wasn't betrayal, though. It was pure fear.

God, help me.

He didn't know how to do this. He didn't know how to feel this much fear as an adult and not a child who hid and waited for rescue that never came. Until Grams kicked the door in and shot his father.

Eric blinked.

He'd sat beside his mother's bed in the hospital for two days, until she coded right in front of him. He was shoved out of the room. He'd fallen over and no one stopped. They all just ran in his mom's room and tried to save her.

But she died anyway.

The best person he knew, and she was gone. Eric had tried to be that good. Even knowing he would meet the same end didn't stop him from trying to be the best he could be. Save people. Follow God's rules. Make all the conditions perfect for a good life.

And now in one second it could all blow to pieces.

Is her dad the kind of guy who deserves having her give her life for his? Eric wanted to be that good, but he wasn't no matter how hard he tried. And a dirty cop just out of prison on parole was.

It made no sense. It was just sacrificial love, and no one deserved it any more or less than anyone else.

The bomb squad van circled the entrance ramp and sped onto this floor of the parking lot.

Eric couldn't even watch. He wanted to call Stella and ask her why she did it, even though he knew. He wanted to tell her he loved her like that. The way she wanted to be loved by her dad. The way God loved her.

He paced away knowing he could do nothing, praying and not getting in the way of the on-duty cops.

Across the lot, over by the elevator to the hospital lobby, Edith walked with a dark-haired man toward her car. The guy who'd spoken with a British accent outside the club, after it was blown up. He was being released?

McCauley called out, "Hummet!"

Eric spun around, and the world kept going while he stilled. He half expected the van to blow up. "Captain?"

"We got word from two units at your uncle's house. He's been spotted going inside."

Eric could get out of here. He wouldn't have to watch Stella and her dad get blown up.

"Sit tight," McCauley said. "This is almost over."

He knew the guy was doing him a favor. The captain understood how hard this whole thing had been, and he wanted to reassure Eric this was *almost* over. Which meant it wasn't over yet. And these last few seconds felt like a year of his life.

If that van exploded…

Eric couldn't even stomach the idea of it. Why had she gotten inside? He couldn't stay and watch.

Instead of responding to McCauley's statement, he jogged to where Edith was about to get in the front seat of her car. "I'll drive."

Her penciled-on brows rose. "And where are we going?"

"Away from the bomb, for one." Eric got her in the back and shut the door. He slid in the driver's seat beside her friend, who looked a little sick. At least it wasn't a stick shift. "Aaron was spotted at his house."

Stella had chosen to be part of this scene. He wanted to make sure Aaron was arrested—which meant he was making the choice to see for himself that this was finally over.

He kept his foot heavy on the gas, bandaged arm in his

lap as he found the alternative parking lot exit and sped over to Aaron's.

"What's going on?" The guy sounded like he was in considerable pain.

"What did you say your name was?" Eric couldn't study the guy and drive at the same time, so he decided to trust Edith's obvious attachment to the guy.

"Joseph, I think." He twisted in the seat to look at her in the back. "That is right, yeah?"

Grams said, "I always thought Casper was a bit ridiculous."

Joseph snorted.

"O-kay." Eric hurtled around a corner. "I have no idea what you guys are talking about, but Aaron was spotted entering his house."

"The cops had someone sitting on it?" Grams asked.

"Of course. And now they're going to arrest him." Something Eric needed to see with his own eyes.

"They should be careful."

"They will be," Eric said. "They'll follow procedure."

He had the same training, and everyone knew this was a serious situation. That only made him want to drive faster, and he got there as fast as possible. Eric pulled over down the street and shoved the gear lever into park. He used the same hand to reach across and pull the door handle. He nearly stumbled getting out with nothing to steady himself with. Falling wasn't going to feel good.

He needed his arm in a cast. Then again, he needed it not to have been broken in the first place.

He pulled his gun and held it angled down as he headed past empty police cars to the front walk. Aaron's house looked like any other in this neighborhood. Eric wondered how long ago he'd moved here from the compound. Maybe that whole camp thing was nothing but a smoke screen. A way to look like he played the game of antisocial, even while he lived like any other middle-class suburbanite.

The whole thing was bizarre. He couldn't puzzle it out, except that clearly Aaron needed something before he ran. He must've rushed home to get it after leaving the van with Stella's dad in it outside the hospital. Maybe all his money, or a fake passport so he could make a run for it.

Yelling echoed out from inside.

A dark figure filled the doorway, running fast. He slammed into Eric just as the house shuddered with a *boom*. The walls ripped apart in a ball of fire that whipped outward with a sound like a sonic blast. The figure slammed into him, leaving him flat on his back on the grass.

Everything went black.

Then it was like things flashed back into focus for a second before going black again. The night sky. Smoke and flames. The sound of screaming.

Nothing.

He heard a crack, like a firework. Or a gunshot.

Eric tried to move. Pain rolled through his head and arm. He blinked, and the world swam like he was underwater. He fought to stay awake.

Stella.

"No, that one."

He frowned. He knew that voice. She always saved him, not because he had earned it but because she loved him.

"Quickly."

Warm metal pressed into his hand, and his fingers clenched. His gun.

"Go!"

Heat rolled over him. Eric tried to hang on to those flashes of clarity. The brief wisps of consciousness.

"Hummet." Someone shook his shoulder.

Eric braced, and the world flashed back as consciousness hit him like a train.

"Easy. Take it easy." The hand on his shoulder held him down.

Eric blinked and looked around at the ocean of people. Flashing red and blue lights. Someone was crying. The face in front of him swam around and he had to latch onto it. "What happened?"

"A bomb went off."

"Stella." He tried to get up.

"No, not the van. Here. But you shot your uncle."

Eric frowned, which hurt his head a lot. "What?"

"Your uncle." The officer waved beside them.

Eric looked over and saw Aaron lying on the grass, a bullet hole in his forehead.

"Nice shot, dude." The cop slapped him on the shoulder. "You took him down. Not before the bomb went off, but you stopped him from getting away and killing anyone else. You're a hero."

Eric looked at the house. He managed to sit up. "The cops. Inside…"

"Alvarez is critical. They took him in. The other three were spread out. Omara got blown out the window, twisted his ankle when he landed, and Jesse hit her head. They're gonna be fine. We've just gotta pray for Alvarez." He squeezed Eric's shoulder. "No one could've predicted it would go down like this. Not with Aaron in the house at the time. Do you think he tried to kill himself?"

"Unlikely." Eric looked at the guy's body and winced. Had he done that?

The more he stared at the hole in his uncle's forehead, the more he…wasn't sure what had happened.

"What's going on with the van?"

"Bomb squad are working. We're all praying."

Eric nodded.

"You need a hand?"

Eric shook his head. He looked where he'd left the car, with Edith and Casper in it. Or was his name Joseph? It was gone now. Whoever that guy was.

He needed to get up. "Can I get a ride to the hospital?"

The cop chuckled. "Let's get you a seat on the ambulance. They're rerouting to West Memorial."

"No, I need to be at Benson General. Stella is there."

The cop frowned.

"I need to be there."

"Okay. I'll get you a ride."

34

Stella gripped the sides of the seat. At any moment she could be blown to bits, along with the whole parking lot, unless the bomb squad finished their work and defused the device. From here, the shockwave would blow out. The pressure would take the easiest route out. Toward the hospital building, the elevator and on the other sides to the earth around them. Concrete supports.

Could it bring the hospital down on them?

It seemed all her mind wanted to dwell on was the fact Eric had left.

"He's mad at me," she muttered.

Her dad quirked an eyebrow. "Ya think?"

She twisted in her chair. "Is that helpful?"

His lips twitched. They'd chatted a little bit, mostly him asking her why on earth she got in the car and telling her to get out. As if she was going to let him die alone.

He didn't seem to think that was a good choice for her to make. Which she'd countered by saying that he had nothing to do with her choices. He hadn't liked that much.

Stella sighed. "I can't believe he didn't stay."

"Maybe something happened. A lot of the cops here cleared out. It looked like something was going down."

She bit her lip. "He had better be okay."

"You think maybe that's why he was mad that you got in the van? Because he was worried and didn't want you to meet the same fate as me?"

Stella didn't want to talk about that. She'd done what she'd done and that was it. "I know Aaron kidnapped you, but what else can you tell me about what happened?" She needed the distraction.

"All his friends from that camp deserted him."

"He told you that?"

Her dad shook his head. "I talked to a few of them at the camp. He had plans, but none of them cared about getting back at the mayor."

And yet, the mayor wasn't here. "Why the hospital?"

"It was the mayor's baby, getting the second one built. Half his family's fortune was tied up in this facility." Her dad waved at the building. "They were about to put his name on the side of the building."

"So not a threat to his life, just his intentions."

He nodded. "Now he's flying solo, reacting. Makes a guy like Aaron Hummet dangerous."

"Maybe that's why everyone left. Because they found him." At least, she hoped that was the case. Eric had to have a good reason for not sticking around. Then again, would she want to watch him explode if the situation were reversed?

Maybe not.

She winced.

Lord, I messed up, didn't I?

"Do you think he'll forgive me?" she asked.

"You love him?"

"Yes. I do."

"He'll forgive you."

"How do you know?" Stella paused. "Did mom ever…"

"Your mom was different, honey. She didn't think the way you and I do."

Stella frowned. "What do you mean?"

"She was gentle. She needed protecting, and I was a strong presence. A cop. She took a chance on me that maybe she shouldn't have, but I did everything I could to shield her from the pain in the world. Until I destroyed it."

"Do you know where we went after the trial, and how she died?"

He nodded. "Your grandma wrote to me."

"Oh."

"I thank God every day that you're stronger than she was. You've weathered more than she could have, and now you have a man in your life who cares about you. Someone strong enough to hold you up."

"I really do." Stella swiped a tear from her cheek.

Someone moved up beside her window—a bomb tech in full gear. He knocked on the window, then removed his head gear. "You're clear. You can both get out."

Stella reached over and squeezed her dad's hand. "Let's get out of here."

Relief washed through her in a rush as she shoved the door open and stumbled out. A few cops gathered around, probably to get a look at the device. One held out a hand.

Stella clasped it and gave the woman a nod. "Thanks. My legs are unsteady." Then she looked through the cab to where her dad got out on the other side. "You good, Dad?"

He called back over the roof of the van. "I'm good."

Stella strode to the back of the vehicle. She wanted to look at the device that had nearly killed her and destroyed the parking lot. The one Aaron Hummet planned to blame on her father.

He met her at the back, one arm raised. She hugged his side and looked at the bomb. "Whoa."

"Yeah, that's big."

She chuckled. "You could say that." Stella glanced at the closest bomb tech. "We're good?"

"All good." He nodded, sweat on his hairline, and pulled off his suit. "That thing would've cracked the supports in this parking lot. Who knows how much of the hospital would have collapsed into the hole?"

"Here's the scary part…," one of the cops said. The guy had sergeant stripes on his shoulders, and his nameplate said *Jackson*, but she didn't know him.

Stella frowned.

He continued, "There's a natural gas pipeline going to the hospital right under here. Over there is the standby generator and natural gas main." He waved. "Destroying that would have a knock-on effect of cutting power and the backup for the hospital. Life support systems would go down. The destruction he could have caused would've been catastrophic with loss of life and the cost to repair the hospital."

"What about the mayor? Have we confirmed he's all right?"

The cop nodded. "The detail put on him reports he's at home with his family. Thankfully they agreed to stay in tonight."

Stella nodded. "Good."

She spotted McCauley headed toward them. He came straight for her dad and said, "Mr. Davis? We need you to accompany us to the precinct, unless you need medical attention first. I'd like to take a full statement from you."

She was about to launch into an explanation of why that was necessary, but her dad just nodded. "Sounds good. I've got a headache, but I feel fine otherwise."

McCauley nodded. "Special Agent Davis?"

"Yes, Captain?"

Her dad shot her a look of pride she wasn't sure how to process. Maybe he'd never heard her referred to like that before, and it was his first time hearing it aloud. She wasn't sure, but he squeezed her shoulder and she figured she was on the right track at least.

McCauley said, "I need to fill you in on everything else."

"Great," she said. "I'm assuming something happened that caused Officer Hummet and half the police here to leave suddenly."

They wandered away from the van, and a paramedic over by the elevator intercepted her dad. One tried to get her attention, but she waved the guy off. She wasn't any more injured than she had been the last time she received medical attention.

She wanted to hear everything from McCauley.

"The cops on Aaron's house saw him enter. Four officers breached the house and Hummet wasn't far behind them, but it was rigged to blow."

Stella gasped.

"No one died, but we've got officers receiving medical treatment and one is headed for intensive care. I'll update you when I know more, but Eric was thrown through the air." McCauley paused. "It's what happened afterward that's curious."

"What do you mean?"

"Dazed from the explosion, Officer Hummet managed to take out the suspect. His uncle Aaron Hummet has a bullet hole in the middle of his forehead. An expert marksman killed him."

She knew Eric was a good shot, but when a house was blown up? She wanted to talk to him herself about what had happened and find out what he'd been through. It couldn't have been easy for him to kill his uncle even under the best circumstances. The guy had been a terrorist, but he was still Aaron's family—for good or ill.

"The gun was his, in his hand. It was a good shoot, but I'm trying to ascertain what happened as there were no witnesses." McCauley scratched at his chin.

"You think he's lying?"

"Officer Hummet hasn't said anything yet. I'm going to take his statement before I take your father's. The police department in Benson can't afford any whiff of impropriety or scandal." McCauley paused. "But if Eric took out his uncle, a terrorist, we can let everyone know that we care more about justice than our personal feelings."

Stella wasn't sure emotion should be completely divorced from policing, at least not the way she did it. She'd solved cases before simply because her heart wouldn't let the victim continue knowing there was no justice.

Heart, like empathy, could be a serious asset.

Stella caught on something he'd said, "That's why you let him work the case? Because the target was his uncle? I'd think that would be a detriment, not an asset."

"Eric had intel no one else did. And he's been on leave for his injury this whole time. But I'll have to figure out him being back tonight." McCauley worked his mouth back and forth. "It'll be an interesting report."

"We have a journalist I work with sometimes who will write the story we need put out in exchange for an exclusive. I just need to give her as much of the truth as possible."

She nodded. "So Eric is okay and no one died except a man determined to destroy a hospital and kill who knows how many people."

"Right. That's good." He tapped the screen of his phone and wrote a bunch of stuff, probably noting what she'd said.

"Where is Special Agent Franklin?" She'd left her phone

in Eric's car, and it was still here so that was good. How had he gotten to Aaron's house?

"With Officer Hummet. She's the one bringing him to the precinct."

"Good," Stella said. "Your officers will bring my father?"

At that, her dad turned to her. Stella didn't really want to leave him, but her emotions were creeping close to the surface.

McCauley said, "We will."

Stella walked over to her dad and kissed his cheek. Neither of them said anything other than that. She was so relieved to still get the chance to know him. To have a family again. She gave him a squeeze and headed for Eric's car.

Stella called Addie on the way. As soon as her friend and colleague picked up, Stella said, "What is going on?"

"It's done," Addie said. "Eric is with me in the car. He's okay, but he got shaken up pretty well."

"I'm fine."

The sound of his voice, even with that disgruntled tone, warmed her. "I'm glad."

I love you. She wanted the chance to tell him face-to-face, not in the car while she was on a call with someone else.

She cleared her throat. "Back to the office?"

"Yep. See you there?"

"Yes."

Addie hung up.

Stella felt the shaking come over her. She pulled into a pharmacy parking lot and parked straddling two spaces. She managed to get the car parked before the tears came, so much relief that they were all alive. All that pent-up stress she hadn't been able to show in the car rushed through her until she cried aloud and shook her hands, trying to get rid of it.

She grabbed the wheel and touched her forehead to her

hands. Crying big sobs she didn't like at all, but getting them out was far better than keeping it in.

They're all right, it's over. It's done. No one died today except Aaron. It took a second for her to realize she was praying. *You keep us all safe, and I still get to have my dad in my life. And Eric, if he will forgive me for taking that risk. You did that. You can do this, too.*

In that moment, Stella surrendered everything she had to God and what He wanted to do in her life. She found some napkins in the glove box and mopped up her face, laughing and still crying at the freedom she found there in submitting. In letting God be in control.

Whatever happened with Eric, she would still have that.

And no one could take it from her.

35

"Your gun was used to kill your uncle." The sergeant sat across from him in a conference room.

Eric was surprised they hadn't just led him to an interrogation room. He sipped the coffee they'd given him.

The sergeant tapped his forehead. "Right here."

"If you say so." Eric set the cup back down on the table, determined not to let his hands shake. It would only let on how out of it he felt. Probably he should wait a couple of days to do this, considering he'd nearly been blown up. Calling for his union rep was also a good idea, since this could easily turn into an inquiry.

Too bad he could barely remember anything other than a few abstract sensations in the middle of a mass of total blur. They'd insisted he get checked out at the hospital because he'd lost consciousness, but considering the number of cops currently waiting in the halls he figured one more might be too many. And he knew they would keep him overnight, so he'd go after this.

After he saw Stella.

Eric had been afraid to ask, but he wanted to know what

had happened to her. Turned out everything was fine there. They'd prevented a tragic disaster, but he was the one who had shot Aaron. Supposedly.

Except that Eric wasn't so sure something else hadn't happened.

His brain was having serious trouble assimilating the truth.

"You don't remember?"

Eric considered straight up lying. For about a second. That wasn't the man, or cop, he wanted to be. "I lost consciousness. Honestly, I'm not at all sure what happened."

"It might come back to you."

"I don't like thinking I did something and don't remember it."

The sergeant tipped his head to the side in a nod. "I can imagine. You've been through a lot, and I'm guessing you haven't had time to talk to someone."

Eric had so many things on the topic list for that, he was running out of mental space keeping a tally. "How about body cam footage?"

The sergeant was already shaking his head.

"A witness who recorded it all on their phone?"

He shook his head some more.

Eric let out a sigh and leaned back in the rolling chair. He felt like he'd been hit by a truck. "All I remember is that house exploded with the cops inside and it hit me."

"Not Aaron?"

Eric shook his head.

The sergeant said, "CSU already went over the house. They think the charges were placed so it looked good from the outside, but Aaron could assure himself a getaway. So we'd think it was bigger than it really was."

"So the explosion was just a show?"

The sergeant shrugged. "You thought for a second that you were dead, right?"

Eric nodded, even though he didn't want to.

"Then it worked. Aaron was able to get away unhurt, which meant none of the cops inside died. There was a blast, enough to knock everyone down and cause damage, but the structure of the house was undamaged."

"Wow." His uncle had used a smoke screen to try to get away. Until someone had intercepted him. Edith and her friend—whatever his name was.

They'd both been there.

Eric tried to think what'd happened, but his head pounded so hard he couldn't come up with any thoughts.

"I'll give you a minute." The sergeant got up. "Anyone you want me to call for you?"

It was on the tip of his tongue to say, *Stella*, but something held him back. Then he saw her in the hall. She came in before the sergeant left. Waited until the door closed behind him. Then she rushed over.

But she didn't touch him.

Instead she sat in a chair, so they were almost knee to knee when he turned to her. "Are you okay?" she asked.

Eric looked at the door, unsure if anyone could hear them. He didn't want to voice his deepest fears aloud if someone was listening.

She scanned his face with that dark gaze of hers. "Tell me."

I love you. Eric gritted his teeth. "I thought you were going to die."

Stella winced. "I couldn't let him go through that alone."

"Is he okay?"

She nodded.

"And you?"

"Please tell me if *you're* okay," she said.

Eric shut his eyes for a moment. He went back to those moments just after the blast. "Aaron ran out of the house. That was right before it exploded." He winced and opened his eyes. "We were both hit by the blast."

"They're saying you shot him."

Eric shrugged his good shoulder, though it wasn't much less abused than the other. His whole body was sore. "I heard voices. I think it was Grams and that guy she's been hanging around with. Working with." He didn't know which it was, but in his mind he recalled the press of the gun into his fingers.

A shot to the forehead, when he'd been nearly blown up?

"Surely no one believes I actually did this, right?"

Stella shrugged as he'd done. "Do you want to just go with it? You could take the win, follow the narrative. Seems like there's a lot of that going around right now."

He frowned.

She waved off the beginning of his question. "Just something McCauley said. What you do next is up to you."

"I need your help." *I love you.* "I don't even know what to think right now."

"Then don't make an official statement until you do."

"Okay. That's a good idea," Eric said. "Do you want to tell me what happened?"

"I love you."

He blinked. It wasn't him that'd said that? He'd sure thought it several times since she got here. "You make it sound like a bad thing."

To hear it from her lips was a blessed thing, despite the sour look on her face. She didn't like how she felt? Apparently she didn't care that he might've essentially executed his uncle and had no memory of it. Like it wasn't big enough he should remember it every day for the rest of his life.

"I guess we'll see."

He wanted to find this funny, but none of it was. Eric also wanted to pull her close, but his entire body was a mass of aches and pains. He wasn't sure how he would walk out of here. Maybe they would carry him out on a stretcher.

He could be a super cop, a hero, and a victim all in one go.

It wasn't like his life would ever be less complicated than that. And now Grams had gone and done it all over again. Eric needed to go talk to her. But what was he supposed to say?

Stella frowned, and he looked away. Maybe she could see the turmoil on his face and knew he was in the mental crisis of his life.

He hadn't been able to be the cop, or the man, he wanted to be. Now or in that moment. All these years of striving to be who he wanted to be, it was as though God had swept down with His hand and said, *You don't need to do the work*. It had been taken care of, through no effort of his. Things resolved themselves with two situations, and Eric hadn't had to do much of anything.

God had taken care of him, of the other cops, of Stella and her dad. And Eric was getting the recognition. He'd done nothing.

It didn't feel like grace, but it definitely was His handiwork. Until he considered Edith and her friend. What they did certainly wasn't God's work. No one would argue that point, even if He had done something in Eric's heart and life that didn't mean the cause was His business—just that He had known it would happen.

Kind of like how what God had said was in him didn't always fit with what he felt. It didn't make sense.

Eric let out a sigh, because trying to figure it out made his head hurt.

Stella shifted back in her chair. It took her farther from him. She eased the chair back a couple of inches and stood.

"Stella—"

"It's fine." She lifted a hand. "Don't worry."

He caught her hand and stood, tugged her toward him, and pressed his lips to hers. "Where are you going?"

Stella's eyes flared.

"I love you, okay? I just have a lot going on right—"

She lifted up and pressed her lips to his. Slid her arms behind his neck and held on gently. Before things got going, she pulled back. "You should be in the hospital. But I'm glad you can get up without passing out."

"Me, too." He grinned, his arms around her waist—not just to hold her. Only a little bit to hold himself upright.

"Good. Then we're agreed you're going to the hospital." She tugged on his arm and got him to the doorway.

Two cops raced past them in the hallway.

"What's going on?" Stella called down to their retreating forms.

One glanced over his shoulder. "We got rerouted to the front desk since there's practically a riot out there."

Stella glanced at him. He wasn't sure what she saw, but since she said, "Let's go out the back," he figured he didn't look so hot.

They took the elevator down to the motor pool, the back exit to the precinct where the cars were parked. A van due to take several prisoners to the jail sat parked just outside the gate.

He glanced back over his shoulder. Cameras high on the wall beside the elevator showed the front entrance. An ocean of people outside, picketing who knew what. He tried to make out faces, but that was virtually impossible with the grainy picture.

"Let's go." The sergeant led a trail of guys, all in cuffs, to the van.

Stella held his hand and leaned close against him. She'd told him that she loved him, and he knew in his heart that she was the woman for him. He wanted to make detective, ask her to marry him. Eric hadn't done anything to earn the gift she was. She didn't love him because he'd proven he was worthy of it, or because of the things that he did.

She was a strong and capable woman who didn't need his help most of the time. And yet, she chose to have him by her side. Right where he wanted to be.

The officer standing guard on the guys being loaded into the van glanced at them and lifted his chin.

Eric raised his in reply.

A scuffle drew his attention back to the line of suspects who had been arrested. Four of them. In the line were Nigel and Ian. He could see his cousin Ian now up by the van, hands cuffed in front of him given the angle of his arms. His cousin looked over, and Eric saw the dead stare in his gaze. There was no life there, just the intent to end it.

Ian broke out of the line.

Someone shouted.

Eric made a beeline for the group. Ian grabbed the gun from the officer's holster, swung around, and fired at Nigel.

His younger cousin cried out and fell with a thud. Dead before he hit the ground.

Eric cried out. "Ian!"

His cousin swung the gun again and fired. Stella shoved Eric out of the way.

Someone else fired. Ian hit the ground. Eric stumbled two steps and fell to his knees. He slammed his good hand on the ground to brace himself. He cried out as pain sliced through him and turned.

Stella fell back, her legs gave out.

Blood blossomed on her chest.

36

Eric scrambled toward Stella. He caught her limp body as she fell, then laid her gently on the ground. "Get help!"

The officer across the bay blinked at him right as a prisoner broke from the line and raced for the street.

"Go," the sergeant ordered.

The officer snapped to attention and raced after the prisoner while the sergeant grabbed his radio. "This is Sergeant Jackson in the motor pool. I have an officer down, and I need backup and an ambulance."

Eric's thoughts swam. He looked down, his hand on Stella's sternum. Blood seeped through his fingers. She blinked at him. Her mouth moved, but no sound emerged.

Eric shook his head. "Don't try to talk. Just hang on."

Her mouth moved again.

He leaned down and listened.

"Love you."

Eric lifted back up, tears spilling from his eyes. "Don't do that. *Hang on.*"

Sergeant Jackson corralled all the inmates in the van and

shut the door. He raced over as two officers came out, ordering, "Guard the van!" He slammed to his knees beside Eric. "We need something to staunch the bleeding."

Jackson ran for the storage shelves and pulled out several bags, then a storage bin. He came back with a new cloth, the kind used to wash a car. "Here."

Jackson pressed the cloth to Eric's hand. He got his hand on the fabric, over the bullet wound in Stella's chest. "You do it. I only have one hand."

Jackson shook his head. "You're doing fine. Just keep pressure on. The ambulance will be here in a second."

Eric didn't want to look at the fear on her face. Not when it was likely mirrored on his. The last thing he wanted was for Stella to be gone from his life, seemingly as quickly as she'd shown up. Her dad would never be able to get to know her. Eric wouldn't get to ask her to marry him, or watch her belly grow round with his child—his ring on her finger.

"We have a date." He choked the words out. "You promised."

Determination flashed in her eyes, and she mouthed, *I know.*

She wasn't going anywhere. She couldn't. *God, help her. Don't make me do this without her. I need her, and You gave her to me.* He was rambling, but God knew his heart.

"Watch out."

Eric didn't move. He spotted the EMTs coming and held on to the towel as they realized who was on the ground.

Freya dumped her bag beside Stella's hip. "You two have been through it the last couple of weeks."

"She needs to survive this."

Freya nodded. "Let me see."

Eric had to force his elbow to bend and let go of the cloth. Freya looked at the wound, seeping blood with each pump of Stella's heart. Eric reached two bloody fingers and felt her pulse while she blinked at him and struggled against the pain.

They rolled her and looked at her back. "No exit wound." Trey crouched. "Let's get her out of here."

Eric didn't like the urgency in his voice.

Freya said, "She needs to be in surgery ASAP," and they got her loaded on a backboard.

Sergeant Jackson helped him to his feet. "Go with them. I'll work things out here."

Eric looked at the two men on the ground, dead.

Ian had shot Nigel and Stella, then he'd been hit by Jackson, who looked calm and cool as anything. One was his family, and the other were criminals. Everyone who wore a blue uniform, who carried a police shield, *they* were his family. Not a group of men who would murder. Blow buildings. Threaten lives. Destroy.

He had nothing to do with them.

He avoided looking at the bodies again. Seeing Nigel like that would be too hard.

Eric shed a couple of tears at the thought he'd never get to help his young cousin make something good out of his life, then he climbed in the ambulance.

The doors shut. He sat where he wouldn't be in the way of Freya's work, but where he could hold on to Stella's hand. Feel the pulse in her wrist.

His phone rang, but he ignored it. "You're going to be okay," he told her.

Freya glanced over.

Eric ignored that as well, praying harder than he ever had in his life that she would live. For her, and for the rest of them. He knew now how she'd felt losing Kyle. Knowing she would never hang out with her friend or work a case together. There was so much promise wrapped up in the future, and so much finality in knowing it would never be.

She'd grieved that loss. Been determined to take down everyone responsible.

Instead of discovering stolen weapons, they'd done that and so much more. She was responsible for uncovering a bigger plot. Aaron might not have done what they'd expected, but it was over now.

All three of them were dead.

The ambulance stopped. He got out of the way while they rushed her out and into the hospital. Eric climbed out of the ambulance, feeling far heavier than he was. His limbs were weighty with fatigue.

Addie rushed over, along with Russ. He wasn't sure if the older man was here in the capacity of police commissioner or friend—or both, more likely. Addie hugged him quickly and gently. "She's headed for surgery?"

Eric nodded. He didn't know what to say.

"Come on." Russ waved for him to move. "Let's find somewhere to sit and wait. Unless you need to be seen by a doctor?"

Eric took a step, and his legs collapsed. The two of them caught him.

Russ said, "Let's find someone to check you out."

"Okay." Eric didn't care about anything but finding out what was happening with Stella. "We need to call her dad."

"I'll do that," Addie said. "Don't worry."

Eric frowned. "What happened at the precinct?"

"The riot?" When he nodded, Addie continued, "I think it was related to Ian, but you don't need to worry about that. Whatever they were planning didn't work."

STELLA BLINKED AWAKE and immediately groaned.

Someone moved beside her, and a warm hand slipped into hers. She clung to it but without much strength.

"Hey." His voice was soft. Warm.

The way she felt, but for that nag of pain at the edge of everything. Her mouth was fuzzy. She could taste metal on her tongue.

Stella found him standing over her.

"Hey. There you are." Eric's face softened. "I've been waiting to see your eyes for a couple of days now."

"What...h-happened?" she asked, her voice cracking.

"Ian shot you." Eric frowned.

If she was alive, surely that was a good thing.

He continued, "You shoved me out of the way and took a bullet for me. You could've died."

"Okay."

He let out an exasperated breath. "We need to talk about *that* when you're more awake. When you feel better. Not right now when I'm mad enough to wring your neck because you did that. Why did you do that? You nearly died." Eric's eyes filled with tears.

Stella couldn't put much together. But she knew one thing for certain. "Love you."

Eric dipped his head and touched his forehead to hers. She felt him let out a long breath that broke in the middle. "I love you, too." He kissed her forehead. "I need to tell your dad that you're awake. He's been waiting to see you."

Stella tried to squeeze his hand. There was barely any strength in it, but he knew.

Eric lifted her hand to his mouth and kissed the back. "I'm going to go tell the doctor you're awake, and let your dad know. I'll be back, okay?"

She closed her eyes, then opened them. A semblance of a nod.

She drifted, half awake. In her mind Stella saw the

muzzle flash. Even before that she'd read the intent in Ian's eyes. Her thoughts coalesced into one idea. Protect Eric at all costs. He was her partner and the man she loved. He had better not be mad at her for doing that, and she had the feeling he was—or he had been.

Why did you do that? His voice echoed in her head.

"Honey?"

She blinked again, and her dad's face swam in front of her.

"Oh, it's good to see you." He smiled. An old man she didn't know. Until the cop ingrained in him from years of service shone through. *That* man she knew. Or at least she understood him. "Doing okay, Stell'?"

"Yeah." The word was low and breathy, but she got it out.

"I just wanted to see your face before the doctor came in. After he checks you over, you'll probably be real tired. I'll be back later, okay?"

She managed a real nod.

He squeezed her hand. "Everyone is praying for you. Even me."

"Good." She smiled.

Stella's doctor came in. He checked everything out, but considering she had no desire to look at her wound, she closed her eyes for most of it. He asked a few questions, and she managed to answer.

The doctor said, "Just rest. Everything looks good, but you'll be healing for a while."

He said some more things, but Stella didn't retain much. She blinked again, and he was gone. She tried to figure out the scope of what happened. She remembered what she'd seen, but there was more to it.

What she did know?

God had brought her through all of this. He'd protected

her, watched over her, and given her the ability to do what she needed to. A lot of people had died in the club, but they'd saved even more lives. Aaron and Ian were dead. Nigel's death was just sad.

So much of this had been sad, but something good bloomed. A field of dead shrubs and in the center one flower —the love she had for Eric, which he felt for her. Strong enough she'd been willing to die to save his life.

The door opened again. She expected Eric, but it was Addie who came in.

"Hey, girl." Addie came over and pulled up a chair. "How are you feeling?"

"Hey." Stella made a face that should say enough.

She figured it had when Addie chuckled. "Did anyone tell you about the riot?"

Stella frowned.

"I'll fill you in now, since I'll be in and out. But just know I'm holding down the fort, and you don't need to worry about anything." When Stella nodded, Addie continued, "Out front of the police precinct we had about thirty guys. At first, it looked like a protest, but it turned into more of a riot. After we arrested everyone, we got some answers. Ian had called them all there as a distraction. When he made his bid for freedom—which you know didn't work—they were supposed to draw the bulk of the police force to the front of the building to control the crowd."

Stella felt her brows lift.

"Right?! It was crazy. Most of them were arrested, and a couple of cops now have black eyes. I don't think there was much drive in them, but they showed up to help Ian. Probably threatened into it because I'm guessing he played it off like he's the big boss now." Addie shook her head. "In the end only Ian and Nigel died. The guy who tried to run was caught before he reached the street. The rioters who were arrested? They even admitted where the rest of the stash of weapons were. When they found out Ian was dead, they all rolled. Said he strong-armed them into it."

"Wow."

"Anyway, you don't need to worry, but I figured you might want to know the whole story."

"I did." Stella smiled at her friend. "I was thinking it didn't totally make sense."

Addie hopped up. "I'll let you get some rest."

"Thanks."

"I'm sure Eric will be back in here soon. I saw him talking to Edith."

37

"What am I supposed to do with this knowledge?" Eric stared at Edith, both of them sat in the hospital waiting room.

He'd only come out to tell them all that Stella was awake.

"I need to get back in there."

She said, "I'd like to resolve this first, Eric."

He stared at the woman who had raised him. He'd always been scared of her, but speaking aloud the things she'd done wasn't even something he did with his cousins. Even when they'd been on speaking terms.

"You put my job in jeopardy." He couldn't say it more plainly than that. "I could get in trouble if too many people question how I could possibly have made that shot when I was half conscious."

Eric could've done it at the range. He wasn't certain about how it would've come out in a high-stress situation. Staring down the barrel at his uncle. The point was whether anyone would actually believe it.

Had Edith even thought that far ahead?

"You've always seen the world as black and white," Edith

said. "You saw it as a good thing to be that clear cut about yourself and how you viewed other people. It played into your role as a cop. Seeing the police as good guys and the criminals as bad guys. Because the moment you start to sympathize with them, or see yourself in them, you'd lose some of that purity of heart that I love about you. The thing that keeps cops noble."

"Until we believe we're above the law."

"With how you saw yourself?" She shook her head. "I knew that would never happen to you."

He wanted to comment on the fact she seemed so sure. Instead, he said, "Who was that guy?"

"It's safer for everyone if you don't ask that question."

Her friend, whoever he was, was likely the one who had taken that shot. Edith could've done it years ago. He would never consider her anything but deadly, even these days when she seemed to be slowing down. Her mind was sharper than ever.

He still wasn't sure he would ever measure up.

"Stella is okay. So are you." She frowned. "A lot of lives were lost at the club, but life will go on. Francisco Salvatore will be convicted for his part in all this."

"Why bring him up now?"

She shrugged one shoulder.

"Grams, what do you know about his part in this?"

She sighed. "Fine. I guess it doesn't matter that you find out. It's over anyway. He's in jail."

Eric waited.

"He bartered for the RPG that killed Special Agent Kyle Averson. Got it from Ian and gave it to his son."

"Because he wanted the men the FBI had in custody dead, or the FBI agents, or both?"

"Both. Either," she said. "The dead can't implicate him in anything. His son is dead now, and the hassle that Orlando was isn't part of his life anymore. Now the club is destroyed. I doubt he'll rebuild. Mostly I figure he'll sell and let someone else have it.?

"But he was arrested. It's not like he's going to run the business anymore."

"I doubt he's worried, with that team of lawyers he pays a pretty penny for."

"So all's well that ends well?" Eric asked. "Is that what you're saying?"

He had so many things to contend with he didn't know where to start. McCauley had come by and given him two weeks off. Eric planned to study for the detective exam while he helped out Stella—whether that was in the hospital or at home. If they were married, she'd be able to recuperate at his house. Did she want to get better in a motel room?

Probably it was too early to ask. Though he'd admit he wanted to.

Edith said, "The Lord works in mysterious ways?"

He shook his head. "Try again."

"We don't always know the answer to our questions. Or why one person's path looks so different. Why one is burdened so much greater than another. All we can do is trust what He has already done."

"Better." Eric didn't know if he would ever be able to reconcile what Edith felt as though she had to do. But it wasn't his path to walk. All he could do was go the way God put in front of him. And yes, trust what He had already done.

He lifted up, his broken arm now in a cast. The way it would be for six weeks. He kissed Grams on the cheek.

She patted his.

"One day you might find yourself in need of help. You know I'll always be there for you." He just prayed it was help he could give. Not the kind that would put his oath, or his integrity in jeopardy.

"As will I, for you."

"Sometimes too much."

He walked away, listening to her gentle laughter. He wouldn't wish his Grams on any unsuspecting person. She was far too formidable, and even with his experience he could barely handle her. He loved her. God had given her to Eric, so she could raise him. A woman who had killed her own son. Maybe even both of them, though he had no evidence. It wasn't like he could turn her into the police with only a hunch.

Life had brought her to being the kind of person who could—or would—do that. He couldn't even imagine what she'd gone through. Though, Eric had seen the scars she carried. The ones in her mind, and the ones on her body. He wouldn't wish that on his worst enemy. Not even the man who'd nearly killed him and had killed his mother.

God had used Edith to save his life. More than once.

Thank You.

The way Stella had saved his life by taking a bullet for him. Eric stopped outside Stella's hospital room. What was it that inspired the women who loved him to want to save his life, when that was what he always tried to do for them?

All we can do is trust what He has already done.

38

Three weeks later

"This is the place?"

Stella turned her head only, something she'd discovered worked far better than twisting her torso. At least for now. Her chest was a mess of scars. They'd cut her open to get the bullet out—and saved her life in the process.

She eyed Eric, in the driver's seat of his car. "What do you mean, is this the place?" Not exactly what he'd said, but he got the point. "What's wrong with it?"

Eric stared out the front windshield, his expression all judgy. "It's…"

"A rental house." She'd seen in it the potential to do what he'd done with his place, fixing it up into a cute little home. However, she didn't plan to be here that long. In fact, she'd been meaning to mention that part. "It's only a six-month lease."

"Why?" He frowned at her. "Where are you going after that?"

She kind of figured he'd have an answer to that. But

could she say it aloud? Tell him that she'd thought maybe she would be at least making wedding plans by then.

Way too awkward. Even with the fact he'd outright asked the pastor about premarital counseling and how that worked. Right in front of her.

They'd met with the pastor a few times over the last two weeks—since she'd been released from the hospital. Talking about the Bible, and how having a relationship with God worked. She'd made the choice to give her life to Jesus. Gone to church. Talked to a lady about attending a Bible study about a guy named John, or a book he wrote in the Bible. Something like that. She was eager to dig in and learn more.

"Come on." Eric shoved his door open. "Might as well get this over with."

She wasn't going to point out that she'd already signed the lease even though she hadn't been inside. Addie, who Stella had been living with since she got out of the hospital—along with Russ, and Addie's half-sister Mona—was the one who'd toured the house and taken pictures for her.

Addie had told her to jump on it. Though, she'd also offered Stella an apartment in Addie's fiancé's building. She wasn't going to take a handout though. She was going to make her own way in the world.

In fact, she planned on starting a scholarship for a criminal justice college student out of the money Kyle had left her. It wasn't much, but it could help change someone's life. The way her life was changed by a foundation who had paid her tuition.

Stella got her legs out of the car first, turned her whole body to face the way she wanted to go, and Eric helped her stand. She was getting better at doing it herself. Eric had gone back to work, though only on desk duty. Stella was supposed to start with the same in a couple of weeks.

In fact, Addie had already started sending her emails about a rash of murders in the local area.

They planned to dive in and solve them as soon as she was ready.

Eric held her hand as they ascended the front steps. He put the key in the lock. "Six months?"

She shrugged one shoulder. "Keeping my options open."

Sure, she was baiting him. Getting him to give her a commitment. He'd been hedging since she got out of the hospital, sending her longing looks when he thought she wasn't looking.

Eric shoved the door open on a huff. When he stepped back, Stella headed in first.

And stopped.

Christmas lights had been strung from the ceiling, and there had to be a thousand woven in and out of each other.

Rose petals laid a trail through the hall. She followed them to the kitchen, where a small round dining table had been set with flowers and candles.

"Why does it smell like something is in the oven?" She turned.

Eric was in front of her, on one knee and holding up a ring box. The diamond winked at her. Nestled there with it was a pink silicone ring.

"One is your actual ring. The other is if you don't want to wear the fancy one at work or working out." The nervous look on his face was adorable. "Stella Davis, will you marry me?"

He'd thought of it all.

Stella felt the tears roll down her face and didn't bother to wipe them away. She nodded. "Yes."

He stood to slide the diamond ring on her finger, and then kissed her the way she'd wanted to be kissed since she found out what weddings were. Still, he held her gently in deference to her injuries. He still had a cast on his arm. Neither of them would ever forget what had happened, but their relationship had begun in that fire. Stella for one didn't want to waste another moment.

It was time for forever to begin.

The front and back doors opened, and it seemed like everyone she knew invaded her tiny house. Until her brows lifted at the sight of all these people.

"I've already signed the lease."

Eric grinned. "How does a six-month engagement sound?"

Getting married over the holidays? "Amazing."

The noise level in the house shook the walls as the place erupted with cheers. Someone called out, "The table is set for two, so we all need to leave."

Stella laughed. "Russ is right."

Addie kissed her cheek. A half-dozen people squeezed her elbow, or shoulder. Eric got a lot of thumping back slaps. He was supposed to be Addie's fiancé's best man in a couple of months. She figured he'd ask Jacob to return the favor.

Stella wasn't sure what she would do with Edith as her children's great-grandmother, but God had that in His hands.

Just like He'd held her, all this time.

And He always would.

I hope you enjoyed reading *Hollow Point*, would you please consider leaving a review? It really does help others find their next read, and is greatly appreciated by me!

Turn the page to find out more about the final story in the Downrange Series…

Last Chance Downrange wraps up in *Terminal Velocity*, releasing late June 2022

A last resort.
One final chance for the future they want.

Joseph is the name they've given him. Before that, he was Casper—a trained killer. Now he's been sidelined to a summer camp retreat center, and if he doesn't make this work he'll get kicked out of the Accountant's Office program for good. The only problem is this retreat center is a hotbed of decades old mystery and murder—and missing treasure.

Medical Examiner Sarah Carlton wants to make chief. When the boss orders her to take a "vacation" volunteering at the retreat center she's not exactly jazzed. But she'll use the down time to work on the drug overdose deaths she's been puzzled by lately. Until the nightmare from her past shows up in her cabin, and everything crashes in on her.

With Sarah the target of a deadly group, Joseph is the only one with the skills to keep her safe. But how can it possibly all be connected? Is this about a new drug about to hit the market…or decades old missing treasure?
Together they're going to find out. No matter if it costs them everything.

This stand-alone story is part of the accountant's office series, Last Chance Downrange.
An all-new setting. An all-new set of characters.

*Christian Romantic Suspense.

ALSO BY LISA PHILLIPS

The whole Last Chance Downrange series:

Point of Impact

Hard Target

Hollow Point

Terminal Velocity

Find more stories based in Last Chance County at:

www.lastchancecounty.com

Find out about Lisa's other series and stand-alone books at her website:

authorlisaphillips.com

Other series by Lisa:

Chevalier Protection Specialists

Last Chance County

Northwest Counter-Terrorism Taskforce

Double Down

WITSEC Town (Sanctuary)

Numerous "Love Inspired Suspense" titles

ABOUT THE AUTHOR

Find out more about Lisa Phillips, and other books she has written, by visiting her website: https://authorlisaphillips.com

Would you also share about the book on Social Media, leave a review on Lisa's page and share about your experience? Your review will help others find great clean fiction and decide what to read next!

Visit https://authorlisaphillips.com/subscribe where you can sign up for my NEWSLETTER and get free books!

www.ingramcontent.com/pod-product-compliance
Lightning Source LLC
LaVergne TN
LVHW040733250326
834688LV00031B/278